MURDER
AT THE
TEA SHOP

BOOKS BY ALICE CASTLE

MURDER
AT THE
TEA SHOP

ALICE CASTLE

bookouture

Published by Bookouture in 2024

An imprint of Storyfire Ltd.
Carmelite House
50 Victoria Embankment
London EC4Y 0DZ

www.bookouture.com

Storyfire Ltd's authorised representative in the EEA is Hachette Ireland
8 Castlecourt Centre
Castleknock Road
Castleknock
Dublin 15 D15 YF6A
Ireland

ISBN: 978-1-83525-347-2
eBook ISBN: 978-1-83525-346-5

To Ella and Connie, with love

ONE

Sarah Vane squinted, her cap of silvery blonde hair falling into her eyes. She was scrawling away on a piece of paper, just as she used to do as a busy GP in London. But this time she wasn't writing prescriptions to cure her patients' ills. Instead, she was doing her best to capture the essence of the fruit bowl in front of her, as part of her new hobby – art.

'Ugh,' she said, looking at her work in disgust.

'Come on, Sarah, it's not as bad as all that,' said her best friend Daphne Roux. Daphne's own sheet was covered with wild swirls that were almost as colourful as her outfit; today she was in a green leopard-print top teamed with zingy orange linen trousers. She looked at Sarah's rather small and grey drawing. 'Look, you've got the bowl nicely,' she added encouragingly.

'That's not the bowl, it's a banana,' said Sarah, putting the pencil down with a sigh. 'I much prefer art class when we have Mr Williams as a model.'

'Gosh, really?' Daphne wrinkled her nose, causing her elaborately tied headscarf to wobble. 'Those big flapping ears – not to mention all the wrinkles!'

'Ah, but it reminds me of my anatomy classes, years ago,' Sarah said with a smile. 'I wonder where he is today?'

Daphne looked around the crowded Willow Pattern Tea Shop, as though Mr Williams was going to pop up from behind one of the other ladies' tables. The pretty room was draped in bunting and had shelves lining its walls, displaying the antique blue and white china that gave the place its name. There were six budding artists working away today. Over in the corner was old Pat Buchanan, a lady with a bent back and fearsome cackle, who was a fellow member of the book group held in the local pub, the Jolly Roger. Elegant, hollow-cheeked Mavis Trussock was also wielding a paintbrush with some vigour. In her mid-forties, she was the leader of ScaleScanners, Merstairs' premier weight-loss club. Daphne had been a little shamefaced when introducing Sarah to Mavis, giving her friend the distinct impression this was yet another group she'd joined for a moment and then thought better of. Sarah could also see Belinda Jones from the pharmacy, who must be on a much-needed break from her work keeping the ageing population of this pretty little seaside town in such fine fettle. And there was dark-haired, smiley Penny Booth, on a half-day from her job at the busy Merstairs post office.

Everyone was concentrating on capturing the nuances of the fruit in front of them – and enjoying delicious, light as air cupcakes and mugs of tea while they did it. It was a warm sunny day in June, so all the windows were open. There was also a fan whirring away discreetly in the corner to keep the ladies cool.

'I think Mr Williams must just be away or something,' said Daphne vaguely. 'He's usually so keen. But forget about him. Look, here's Arabella, she'll give you some pointers about getting that banana straight.'

'Whoever heard of a straight banana?' Sarah muttered. She wasn't keen to attract the attention of Arabella Findlay. For one thing, Sarah felt she was a little too free with her artistic opinions, often making her rub out the bits of her drawings she was proudest of. And it also felt a little too close to home. Arabella was the daughter of Charles Diggory, second-hand clothes salesman, antiques expert – and owner of arguably the bluest pair of eyes in Merstairs. Although she was recently widowed, Sarah had to admit she was in danger of becoming rather fond of Charles. And, despite his fearsome soon-to-be-ex-wife Francesca, the mayor of Merstairs, Charles seemed pretty keen on Sarah, too.

Rather to Sarah's initial surprise, Arabella was a nice, level-headed woman in her thirties. She was making some pin money after her divorce by holding the art classes, and planning to return to her career in finance when her twins, Max and Calista, were older. She had her father's eyes, but had seemingly inherited little from her overbearing mother apart from glossy chestnut hair. That didn't mean Sarah wanted her leaning over her sketch and offering sincere but annoying advice on perspective, however.

'I think it's time I called it a day,' said Sarah more loudly, putting down her board and removing the unsuccessful drawing, which now looked like a very hard day in the produce aisle at their local supermarket, Seastore.

'Oh, are you sure, Sarah?' Daphne was clearly disappointed. 'If you just added a dash of yellow... maybe some bright green?'

'No, I must be off.' Sarah stood up and swung her bag onto her shoulder. 'Apart from anything else, Hamish could really do with a walk.'

As Hamish, her little black Scottie, was currently asleep under her chair and had just let out a little doggy snore, Sarah didn't quite know who she was fooling.

'Oh, all right then,' said Daphne. 'I'll see you later, shall I? At the book group.'

Sarah groaned inwardly. She'd been trying to up her quota of activities, to keep herself busy. Since arriving in Merstairs two months ago, she'd successfully sorted out her own cottage so that it was as neat as a new pin. She'd tried to do the same with Daphne's own shop, Tarot and Tealeaves, with very limited success. Oh, and she'd solved a few murders.

While some parts of her sleuthing activities had been great fun, Sarah was the first to admit that things had got a bit out of hand last time, on the cliffs high above Merstairs. Finding herself – and her dog – being threatened with sudden death, when she'd unmasked the murderer of beloved local teacher Abi Moffat, was not part of the retirement package she'd envisaged. To keep mentally stimulated, yet safe from harm, she'd resolved to take up some less potentially fatal hobbies. Hence this drawing of a banana suffering from what looked like rickets. And now, thanks to Daphne's reminder, she realised she hadn't even opened the book they were due to discuss that evening at their scheduled gathering in the Jolly Roger pub.

There was nothing for it but to get home and get stuck in, Sarah decided, saying goodbye to her fellow artists and taking a more circumspect leave of Arabella Findlay, who gave her a slightly formal smile in return.

As usual, Sarah felt miles better the moment she was striding along the seafront, with Hamish frisking at her heels. It really was a glorious day in this very special resort. Merstairs was sandwiched between chi-chi Whitstable and historic Reculver. Sarah relished its sleepy charm and was head over heels in love with the view. Miles and miles of sea stretched as far as anyone could possibly wish, in an infinite variety of shades of azure. The air was full of the tang of salt and, although the sun was beating down strongly now they were entering high season, the breeze kept things fresh. As they walked along, a few people smiled at Sarah and even more at little Hamish; they were becoming fixtures. They lingered a few minutes longer on the beach, Sarah drinking in the view and

Hamish taking his honorary position of seaweed inspector very seriously indeed on the tideline.

As Sarah finally tempted the little dog away from a promising clump of kelp, she looked up to see Mavis Trussock rushing along the esplanade. She must have finished her picture just after Sarah left. As she watched, Mavis turned up the side street that led to the pharmacy and disappeared out of sight. At the same time, Hannah Betts, the wonderful chef-cum-proprietor at the Beach Café, one of Sarah's favourite eateries, bustled the other way, no doubt going back to her kitchens to cook up more delights for her adoring clientele.

Sarah loved the fact that she knew so many people by sight already. She really felt part of the community, perhaps even more than she had as a GP in London. Then, she'd had a professional involvement, an obligation even to those she met. Now she could just enjoy people's company without worrying about when they'd last had a tetanus jab. Nevertheless, she decided to just nip in and see if Mr Williams was OK before she went home to start her speed-reading. It was the kind of small thing people did for each other round here. Last week, he had been complaining of a cough. She really ought to check it hadn't got worse. He was a nice old man, with that twinkly look about him. He was also pretty good at staying still when being drawn, which was very useful for someone of Sarah's limited artistic skills.

She knew he lived in one of the little crooked cottages on West Street, leading off the main esplanade. He'd once hailed her as he'd been on his way out, when she and Hamish had been going for a ramble around the town. His front door was an unusual shade of deep magenta, she remembered, so she was fairly sure she could track him down.

Sure enough, she soon came upon the darkly painted door, in a row of very similar little homes. These had once belonged to the fishermen who plied the seas off the Merstairs coast, but now they were mostly gussied up to the nines for the Airbnb market. A lot had arty wooden seabird sculptures in their windows, or whimsical signs saying 'Life's a Beach'. Mr Williams's, though, was still in 'before' condition, with peeling paint, rather draughty-looking old-fashioned panes of glass, and a total absence of coastal décor anywhere on display. She looked for a doorbell, but found only a heavy iron knocker, so she banged twice. Then she and Hamish waited.

And waited. A grey-haired lady came past wheeling a trolley bag full of shopping. 'Excuse me... do you know Mr Williams, by any chance?' Sarah asked politely.

The woman shot her an alarmed look. 'Certainly not,' she replied, and pushed her trolley faster and faster until she was out of sight, one wheel squeaking as she went. Sarah shrugged and took the knocker in her hand once again, ready to let it fall. But then she noticed that the door moved slightly as she pulled it, as though it wasn't properly shut. Well, that was very odd. She looked at Hamish, who peered up at her, head at an angle, his little pink tongue hanging out. Then he whined slightly. It was as if he was urging her to go ahead and open the door.

Sarah knew the most sensible course of action would have been a call to Daphne, to ask if anyone at the art group had a contact number for Mr Williams. Or she could even have rung Daphne's daughter, Mariella, who was Merstairs' most newly appointed police detective, after her starring role in untangling the recent bloodcurdling crimes that had beset the area. But Sarah had spent over sixty-five years being pretty sensible. For once in her life, she was going to listen to a small dog and her own insatiable curiosity.

A few seconds later, she rather wished she hadn't. The door to the cottage swung open straight onto Mr Williams's living room, the name of which was rather ironic – considering he was dead.

For a moment, Sarah was transfixed in shock. This just

couldn't be happening. Could it? She really wasn't sure she could face any more bodies. But then her many years of training prevailed. This was the situation she found herself in and, as ever, she wanted to help if she could. First of all, she had to make sure that her initial impression was right. She rushed forward. Was there any possibility that life was not extinct?

But Mr Williams was sitting fixedly in his chair, his jaw slack, his eyes open but curiously devoid of that spark of consciousness. Worse still, if her nose didn't deceive her, the poor man had been sick before passing away. Luckily he had managed to reach the wastepaper bin just in time. Had he inhaled anything? This could sometimes be a cause of death. But it seemed unlikely in this case, given that he was in an upright position. Such things usually occurred when victims were on their backs, most often when alcohol or drugs were in play. There was no sign of anything of that kind here. There was also something else about the odour in the room that sharpened her senses.

Hamish was now barking in distress, and she hurriedly tied his lead to the bannisters to keep him as far out of the way as possible. She stepped closer carefully. Mr Williams was staring sightlessly right at the front door, which was a little odd as his comfortable chair was angled towards a big TV, which was still on. The sound was turned down but the flickering pictures cast strange shadows over the old man's face and large ears, adding an eerie touch to the scene. A small rustic table was pushed up to the chair. It bore traces of the man's last meal – a cup of very cold-looking tea, gone an uninspiring dun colour, and a slice of Victoria sponge cake, oozing with thick red jam, sliced strawberries and a cushiony layer of cream, its top lavishly dusted with icing sugar. There was a very large bite taken out of it.

Next to the cake was a scrap of paper. It had been crumpled up, and then smoothed out again. Sarah couldn't resist peering at it. It seemed to be from the betting shop in the high street,

BetStairs, and was for a horserace the next day. There was something scrawled at the bottom of it. She didn't want to get too close to the body, but she craned in a tiny bit. There were two letters written in a very shaky hand, an H or an M, or was that even a P, and then a B or a T. And the number thirteen. 'Unlucky for some,' Sarah murmured under her breath, moving her gaze back to the cake.

Almost against her will, she now registered that she was actually very hungry, and that sponge looked delicious. But nothing on earth would have induced her to taste it, tempting though it undeniably seemed. Because, if she wasn't very much mistaken, this was the source of all Mr Williams's woes. The strong whiff of bitter almonds coming from the bin, and from either the tea or the cake on its faded Pyrex plate, suggested the man had met his maker thanks to a rather retro murder method. It couldn't be, could it? But Sarah was almost sure she was right. This was cyanide poisoning.

TWO

Though Sarah had seen more sudden deaths during her long career than she cared to remember, and definitely more than she'd been expecting post-retirement, she would never get used to the pathos of witnessing a fellow human at their most vulnerable and helpless. Poor Mr Williams was a sorry sight.

With a trembling hand, she found her phone, thanking the heavens that she knew exactly who to get in touch with. She quickly dialled Mariella's number, and explained the situation, glad to note her voice didn't waver too much. If anything, Mariella sounded more shocked than she did.

It wasn't many minutes until the policewoman turned up, but for Sarah it seemed like an eternity. Hanging onto an overexcited Scottie in the middle of a street with nothing to occupy either of them wasn't much fun. She hadn't wanted to stay inside, however. The day was growing increasingly hot, the smell in the tiny house seemed to be getting stronger, and Sarah didn't want her dog to inhale any fumes. She felt very sorry for Mr Williams, yes, but she really didn't wish to spend a moment longer staring at him.

She was thrilled to see Mariella clambering out of the

unmarked police car, her plume of red hair worn today in a thick plait. Mariella, however, was not nearly as pleased to see her. Newly liberated from her uniform thanks to her promotion, the young woman looked smart in a stylish pale grey suit, but was undeniably rattled.

'For goodness' sake, Aunty Sarah, can't you go more than a day without finding a dead body?' She slammed the door of her car with what seemed like unnecessary vigour.

'I mean, it's been, um, quite a while,' Sarah started – then realised barely a month had passed since she'd stumbled on dying teacher Abi on the doorstep of Daphne's shop. 'Anyway, it's hardly my fault...' she finished lamely, but Mariella was clearly in no mood to listen. She put on thin latex gloves with a snap of disapproval, and pushed the front door open.

'I take it you've been inside.' She turned to Sarah again.

'Well, yes, otherwise I wouldn't have known he was dead... It wasn't latched. And once I got in there, I wanted to make sure there was nothing I could do,' Sarah said. 'It seemed obvious the poor man was deceased, but of course I did need to check.'

Mariella shook her head. From a handbag that was almost as capacious as her mother's, she extracted a pair of blue shoe covers and slipped them on, steadying herself with a hand on Sarah's shoulder. 'Don't know why I'm bothering with these,' she muttered. 'Seeing as you've already contaminated the scene.'

'I didn't touch anything,' Sarah protested.

Mariella only grunted. She stepped forward, the bootees rustling slightly, and picked up a leaflet Sarah hadn't noticed on the doormat. 'ScaleScanners', it said. 'Guaranteed success on your weight-loss journey. Say goodbye to your appetite with our new app!' She raised her eyebrows, and put it in her pocket. Sarah hovered on the threshold after her telling-off. But then Mariella beckoned her inside.

'Oh. Is it OK if I come in with my shoes?' Sarah hesitated.

'It won't make any difference as you've already traipsed everywhere,' said Mariella. 'Anyway. Come and tell me what you think.'

Sarah stepped forward, tying Hamish to the bannisters again and doing her best to ignore his 'Are you serious?' look. She and Mariella stared down at the mortal remains of Mr Williams. He really wasn't a pretty sight. Both studied him with a curious mixture of detachment and compassion.

'What do you think?' Mariella finally asked, all trace of her earlier pettishness now gone, leaving only a keen air of professionalism. This is what Sarah liked so much about Daphne's daughter; she was serious about her work. All the chiding was, surely, just the girl going through the motions, ticking boxes to appease her superiors, while underneath she was intent only on getting to the truth. Sarah heartily approved of that.

'I don't think there can be much doubt, can there? It's poison, and almost certainly cyanide, judging by the smell.'

Sarah and Mariella looked at each other, the young woman's eyes stretching wide with dawning consternation.

'I know what you're thinking,' said Sarah. 'And I can't believe it either.'

'It's so awful,' said Mariella.

'Yes, poor Mr Williams. Who'd have thought he'd meet such a terrible fate.'

'Murder. Again,' said Mariella, suddenly looking far older than her years. 'And you're absolutely sure? There's no doubt in your mind?'

'Well,' said Sarah cautiously. 'Of course I'm not a pathologist. Your Dr Strutton will be able to tell you a lot more,' she said, remembering the calm and competent woman who'd helped out on previous cases. 'But the only alternative I can envisage is suicide. And it's a very odd way to do it – in the middle of eating cake, while watching television. There's nothing to suggest Mr Williams was feeling suicidal, either – he was very chipper, actually, when I last saw him.'

Mariella turned to the older woman with suddenly narrowed eyes. 'When was that, exactly?'

All at once, Sarah felt how formidable Mariella could be if she was on your tail. Luckily, Sarah had a clear conscience. 'He was at the art group, posing. This was last Monday. He's our regular model. But he didn't turn up today and we had to make do with a banana instead.'

'I see,' said Mariella, raising her eyebrows. 'Well, a lot can happen in a week. Maybe he had a terrible few days.'

'Maybe,' Sarah conceded. 'It's not impossible. But it would still be a very odd way to kill yourself. I suppose putting poison in a treat you like might be a possibility, but usually, if you've got to the stage where you know you want to kill yourself, you just get on with it. You don't pretend it's something it's not. And then the television is still on, too.'

'Have you seen a lot of suicides?' Mariella asked.

'Not a lot,' Sarah conceded. 'But a few. It happens, people get to such a low ebb that they can't see a way of turning things round. They don't always leave notes, but many do. And they usually prepare in some way. For instance, they may have paid up all their bills. Or the fridge will be empty. There are signs that the person is checking out, so to speak. I haven't looked in Mr Williams's fridge, and there doesn't seem to be a note, unless you count that betting slip with the scribbles on it. But would someone put money on a horse and then kill themselves before the race? No, I'm just not convinced this is a suicide.'

'Hmm,' said Mariella noncommittally. 'What about the choice of cyanide? It's not exactly something you can buy over the counter, is it?'

'It's not used domestically any more, that's true, though people once got rid of wasps' nests with it and it was in pesticides as well. But you can actually make it out of various household substances, and even these days you can still get it online.'

'What, from Amazon, you mean?' Mariella looked as sceptical as she sounded.

'Well, no. But I had a sad case in London not so long ago. A young boy. He was very troubled, problems at school and some mental health issues. He ended up ordering cyanide on the dark web.'

'That's awful,' said Mariella thoughtfully. 'You're not suggesting old Mr Williams might have done that, though? Would he even know there's a hidden part of the internet that you can only access with a special browser?'

'I think it's really unlikely, don't you? He must have been in his late seventies or eighties, and didn't strike me as very tech-savvy. I don't see any signs of a laptop and I'm not sure he even had a smartphone.'

'OK. We'll look into the dark web angle. Lots of older people are fine with technology,' Mariella said doubtfully.

'That's true. It's just an impression I got about him. I didn't know him that well. He seemed to have a full life, though.'

Mariella suddenly swung round to face her. 'What do you mean by that?'

Sarah was a little surprised. 'Oh well, modelling for the art group. He really seemed to like posing for the ladies. And I'm sure he had lots of other activities as well. I used to see him around the place and he always had a smile on his face.'

'Did he, now?' Mariella said slowly.

Sarah, who had the feeling that she was missing a vital nuance, just shrugged. She decided to turn her attention to the interior of the little cottage. It wasn't exactly bare, but was utilitarian in that way that suggested the distinct lack of a woman's touch. Everything was a bit drab, with a colour palette heavy on murky browns. There were no cushions on the chairs, and no photographs on display. But a lack of design sense was no reason to dislike someone, or get a shiver down your spine, Sarah told herself.

Just as she was wondering where on earth Mariella's colleagues might have got to, and whether she could ask without seeming overly critical of the Merstairs police, there was a loud rap at the door. Then it was thrown open so hard that it ricocheted back and almost slammed shut again. Finally, it was wrestled open properly and Sarah wasn't altogether surprised to see the rather vacant faces of local constables Dumbarton and Deeside peering round it. Mariella had nicknamed them Tweedledum and Tweedledee with good reason. They shambled into the room and looked around, mouths slightly agape as they spotted the corpse. They hadn't been exactly welcoming towards Mariella when she'd been a trainee, but now that she'd leapfrogged them and gone into plain clothes, Sarah noted extra hostility in their curt greeting.

'Oho, got another one, have you, love? The DI will be thinking you're knocking them off yourself, just to get the glory,' said Dumbarton waspishly. Then he caught sight of Sarah – not difficult in the tiny confines of the cottage – and belatedly ground to a halt. It was Deeside who actually recognised her.

'You're that doctor lady, aren't you?' he said, screwing up his face at this tremendous feat of memory.

'That's right,' said Sarah, in gently encouraging tones. 'Unfortunately, as you've noticed, we have another body on our hands,' she added.

'There's no "we" about it, Aunty Sa— I mean, Dr Vane,' said Mariella.

The policemen nudged each other and smiles spread over their faces. Immediately Sarah was furious on Mariella's behalf. The least little slip, and these two were cock-a-hoop. Meanwhile, they had shown barely any interest in the dead body, which was surely the main issue.

Sarah was itching to ask whether the pathologist was on her

way, and what her estimated time of arrival might be, but she knew better than to say a word in front of the constables. It was a shame, though, because there were few things more time-sensitive than crime scenes. Even a soufflé can survive a minute too long in the oven, but evidence decayed in a body at an alarming rate. If they wanted to have any chance of identifying the type of cyanide used, they needed to conduct the post-mortem as quickly as possible.

That thought reminded Sarah of how stifling the little cottage was becoming. Hamish was already suspiciously quiet; she hoped he wasn't feeling peaky. She sidled over to Mariella. 'I know the crime scene should be sealed, but I really think we need to keep the cottage door open. There are a lot of us breathing not very much air, and depending on the levels of poison here, it could potentially be dangerous,' she whispered urgently.

Mariella gave her a sharp look, as if assessing whether or not Sarah was trying something on. After a moment, she gave a brief nod, which Sarah took as permission to go over to the door and reopen it. On the way, she stooped to untie Hamish – and immediately, the naughty little scamp streaked off up the stairs, as though the hounds of hell were on his tail.

'Hamish! Not up there, you bad boy,' Sarah shouted, and started running after him.

'Aunty Sarah! You shouldn't be going up there,' Mariella remonstrated, pushing past the bulky forms of the two police-men. 'But also – stop him destroying any evidence!'

Sarah, who'd paused on the stairs, horrified that she was compromising even more DNA traces, shrugged and started up again. Hamish had a head start on her now and was just disap-pearing off to the right when she puffed up to the top of the flight. The cottage was as tiny upstairs as it was down. There was a bathroom to the left and doors to what she guessed were two bedrooms on the other side.

The décor up here was even more minimalist than it was on the ground floor. All the walls were painted in a drab green, while the carpet running up the stairs and into both rooms was a faded treacle shade. Mr Williams certainly wouldn't be winning any posthumous interior design prizes. But far worse was to come, when Sarah made it round the corner and peered into the first bedroom.

THREE

First of all, there was the dispiriting sight of Hamish, tail wagging, on top of Mr Williams's grungy-looking unmade bed. Sarah knew it was probably irrational but she immediately wanted to give the Scottie a good bath – not to mention an epic telling-off. The second, even more worrying thing, was that the room seemed to be draped in women's underwear.

Sarah wheeled round, trying to understand what she was seeing. There were pink panties dangling from Mr Williams's bedhead, there was a row of dainty lace underthings hanging on his radiator, there was a large bra slung over the dusty mirror on the dressing table. Did Mr Williams... like to wear women's undergarments? Sarah didn't ever want to be the kind of person to judge others' lifestyle choices, but this was a surprise to say the least.

Sarah left Hamish where he was, despite the insanitary-looking sheets, and thought for a second. There was nothing about Mr Williams that had given the slightest indication he might have had any interests of this type. He'd seemed a typical blokeish elderly gent, often to be found propping up the bar in the Jolly Roger giving his views on the latest football debacles or, even more frequently, smiling at the ladies. Sarah realised this meant nothing, and even the most outwardly conventional people could have enthusiasms you wouldn't expect. Human nature was complicated. And this was not her business, anyway. But she was pretty sure that this wasn't Mr Williams's stuff. For one thing, all these bits of underwear were in different sizes – and very few of them looked as though they'd fit the dead man downstairs.

With a frown on her face, Sarah tiptoed into the room next door. This was a tiny boxroom, which might once have been used as a nursery for a small baby. Now it had a different purpose. It was full of yet more underwear. There were pants strewn across an old camp bed, lying in lacy clumps on a chest of drawers, even spilling onto the dirty floor. Then she saw something that really made her blood run cold.

'Mariella?' she called, her voice wavering. 'Mariella, I think you need to get up here – right away.'

* * *

It was a relief when they were outside on the pavement once again, with Hamish looking none the worse for his romp in the dead man's bed. Sarah, however, still felt a little trembly. She was rather more shocked now than she had been even when she'd found the body, in fact. The sight of a pair of her own knickers in the pile had been like a blow to her stomach. She recognised them immediately as she had bought them only a week or so before in the town's leading ladieswear shop, Merstairs Modes. She wasn't quite sure what had got into her, she thought with a hot blush, but she'd decided to treat herself. Seeing the pretty lace lying on Mr Williams's horrible old carpet was mortifying.

'Well, that was a bit of a turn-up,' Mariella said, patting Sarah's shoulder in consolation. 'Don't worry, Sarah, you're not the only one by a long way, as you saw. I wonder who knew about this habit of Mr Williams's, though?'

Sarah looked at Mariella quickly. 'You mean... it could be a motive?'

But before the younger woman could open her mouth, there came a cry both were familiar with.

'Coo-ee!' Suddenly Daphne was bearing down upon them. 'Art class has just finished, so I came to see if Mr Williams was OK. You got me worried, Sarah. Then I bumped into Tweedledum round the corner waiting for reinforcements and he gave me the news,' she said, her face long. 'Poor old thing. That cough must have been worse than anyone thought.'

'Well, not really,' said Mariella a little evasively. 'But listen, Aunty Sarah's had a bit of a shock.'

'Of course, poor you, Sarah. I'm sure it was awful finding him. I bet it took you right back to your London days, the big city must have been full of all sorts of ghastliness,' Daphne said with a shake of her purple earrings.

There'd been a fair bit of it recently in Merstairs too, thought Sarah, but Daphne probably didn't need any reminders.

'It wasn't so much that... though it was awful,' said Sarah, her cheeks cooling down now somewhat. 'But there's something else. Something really... odd.'

'You're not going to tell me it's another *suspicious death*,' said Daphne, mouthing the last two words in a way that made them seem much louder than the rest of her sentence.

'Well, yes. And I'm afraid there's more.'

'You're joking, aren't you?' Daphne shied away like a nervous horse. 'What could be worse than that? Who would have done anything to poor old Mr Williams? Honestly, it'll be a wonder if I can get any Tarot readings done this afternoon, with all the disturbance to the Beyond this is going to cause,' she said, shaking her head. She'd always been firmly of the belief that she had clairvoyant powers. Neither her best friend nor her daughter was quite as convinced. They exchanged a quick glance.

'It's a bit delicate,' Sarah now started, wondering how she was going to convey the disturbing news to her friend. 'Mr Williams... had been stealing women's underwear.'

'What?' said Daphne. 'Pinching pants? Nice Mr Williams? Is this true, Mariella?'

Mariella nodded. 'It's like an M&S lingerie department up there. But don't say a word to anyone about it. Listen, I've got to get back to the investigation. I'll talk to you later.'

'Of course, love,' said Daphne automatically. 'I can't believe this, Sarah. Are you sure there's no mistake?'

'None at all,' said Sarah. 'I was stunned when I went into his bedroom.'

'What were you doing in there?' Daphne said.

'Oh, Hamish dashed up and I had to go and fetch him. The whole place was just festooned in pants! And as for the spare room...'

'I wonder where on earth he got them all from?' Daphne said.

'That's what gave me such a turn. You won't believe it, but he actually had a pair of, well, my knickers too! It was so awful seeing them there.'

'The naughty old blighter!' Daphne was thunderstruck. 'And you were always so nice to him, going to see if he was OK today for instance. Do you think he broke into your house?'

'No, I don't think he was a burglar,' Sarah said slowly, thinking things through. 'The truth is, I did put some underwear out on the line the other day. The weather was so good,' she said, shamefaced. But why shouldn't she dry her own clothes in the privacy of her garden?

Well, the reason was now very clear. Because men like Mr Williams might take advantage.

'A pair was missing when I brought everything in. I thought they might have been blown away by a gust of wind. But he must have sneaked into the garden somehow and stolen them. Honestly, how *disgraceful*.' Sarah shook herself.

Then she heard a funny noise. She looked over at Daphne in surprise. She was either stifling tears... or trying to control some totally inappropriate giggles. Sarah glared at her.

'Come on, Sarah, you have to see the funny side,' Daphne said, now puce in the face and with her shoulders shaking. 'I know it's terrible, but of all the pairs of pants to pinch!'

Sarah gave her old friend a very frosty look. Theft was theft, and no laughing matter. As for the things Mr Williams had stolen, well, that made the whole thing even less funny, in Sarah's book.

FOUR

In the Jolly Roger pub that evening, Sarah nursed a tonic water as the ladies from the book group gossiped around her. She need not have worried about her failure to read this week's novel – finding a corpse was the perfect let-out on that front. No one had the slightest interest in literature, they were too busy pressing her for details about her grim discovery.

'I can't believe old Williams has died, I thought he'd go on forever,' said Penny Booth from the post office. 'And there was *something funny* about his death, that's what I've heard,' she added, her eyes fixed on Sarah's face. 'What did you see?' she asked.

Sarah blushed faintly and bowed her head to sip at her tonic again, hoping the difficult moment would pass. Not for the first time, she cursed Merstairs' hyperactive gossip grapevine.

Then Pat, sitting two down from her, chipped in. 'I heard he had a pair of the mayor's big-girl pants on his head when he died,' she said with her distinctive smoker's rasp. 'Is that true?'

Sarah looked up, now painfully red, then tucked her head down again quickly. How on earth had Pat got hold of details about Mr Williams's unpleasant habit so quickly? She hoped

Mariella wouldn't think she'd leaked anything about such a sensitive ongoing investigation. And she really didn't want to have to admit Mr Williams had kept her own pants in his horrible collection.

Luckily, no one seemed to follow up on Pat's comment, perhaps because she was prone to making rather odd statements. Sarah breathed a sigh of relief. She wondered if the two constables had been indiscreet. Honestly, they needed to be taken in hand.

Just then, Mavis of ScaleScanners wafted past, looking enviably slim in a bias-cut skirt and pretty top.

'Heard the news about the killing, Mavis?' Penny called out.

Then Pat waved to her. 'All right, Mavis?' she rasped. 'You look ready to run a marathon, I'd say,' she added with a huge wink. Mavis gave Pat a furious glare and made for the door. Before Sarah could wonder what on earth Pat had meant this time, Daphne waded in, addressing the whole table.

'Now you mustn't ask Sarah anything else, she can't say a word, she's working with my Mari on this and it's really important that it doesn't get out about the poisoning... whoops!'

At this, Sarah put her head in her hands for a second. It wasn't just frustration at Daphne letting the remaining cat out of the bag, though. She didn't know whether it was imaginary or not, but she'd had a gathering headache since her grim discovery and she really hoped it was nothing to do with those cyanide fumes. She cast a quick glance at Hamish under the table, to make sure he wasn't suffering any ill-effects. As Daphne kept slipping him crisps, some intentionally, some via her way of waving them around then dropping them when making a point, he was in his element and showed no signs of sharing his mistress's desire to escape. Sarah squinted at her watch. She was just wondering if she could make her excuses and leave, when the door swung open and Charles Diggory sauntered in.

He spotted Sarah immediately, and held his hand up to

mime a drink. Sarah pointed to her glass, signalling she already had one – then realised the rest of the table had fallen silent and were watching the pantomime between the pair with an interest that almost rivalled their thirst for details of Mr Williams's demise.

Sarah shrugged. 'Listen, everyone, I haven't read the book as you know, and I do need to have a word with Charles, so...' Saying this, she slid to the end of the bench and extracted herself from the gathering, perfectly well aware of the nudges and significant glances travelling around the table like a Mexican wave. It seemed a relationship between consenting adults of a certain age was as much of a hot topic as the latest murder.

Sarah was all the more perplexed as she didn't really know if she could quantify what lay between her and Charles as a relationship at all. There had been a gratifying moment, a while back, when he had seized her hand under one of the tables in this very pub, and given it a reassuring squeeze. It had been rather lovely and comforting, particularly as the gesture came just after someone had been trying to hurl her off a cliff. There had also been talk of a dinner. But the squeeze had not been repeated, and the meal remained unbooked. Even worse, Charles had not really been able to meet her eyes since then. But Sarah didn't mind admitting she felt just as shy. She still felt a huge pull of loyalty to her late husband, Peter, and an equal amount of guilt at the fact that she'd even looked at another man. The situation was more complicated yet for Charles, as his soon-to-be-ex-wife was very much alive, and prone to popping up all over Merstairs at the worst possible moments.

So she wasn't at all sure she should be sitting down with Charles in full view of all the biggest gossips in town. But on the other hand, she'd had quite enough of fending off questions about Mr Williams, and didn't want to listen to a half-baked discussion of a book she hadn't read either, if they ever got onto that. She slid into the banquette seat next to Charles with some misgivings, but mostly a feeling of relief.

'Hello, Hamish,' Charles said, greeting the dog affectionately. 'I heard the news, Sarah. Poor old Mr Williams,' he added, shaking his head. 'That must have been awful.'

'It was pretty ghastly,' said Sarah, taking a sip of her tonic and wishing it contained a slug of gin.

'Terrible, that you were the one to find him,' said Charles with an arch of his brows.

'Oh no, not you as well,' said Sarah with a sigh.

'What do you mean?' Charles furrowed his brow.

'It's just that everyone keeps commenting on the way it always seems to be me that finds, erm, things,' said Sarah, feeling flustered. She knew it was only coincidence at work, but she certainly didn't want to get a reputation.

'Don't give it a thought,' said Charles, patting her hand where it lay on the table. 'You know how people around here have a tendency to chatter.'

Sarah certainly did. Charles's little gesture might as well be occurring under a microscope. She was aware of eyes trained on them from the book group table, and that was without counting any other interested spectators in the small pub.

'What do you say we get out of here and maybe get a bite to eat?' Sarah suggested a little desperately. She wasn't sure what, if anything, she wanted to happen with Charles – but she did know she'd rather not have an audience for it.

'Oh. Well, there's an idea,' said Charles, seeming a little stunned.

Immediately, Sarah kicked herself. She was being pushy, and that would never do. It was something men hated, it always put them off. But then, did she want to put him *on*? Drat, everything was so confusing. She tried to remember what had happened when she'd met Peter, long ago. Dear Peter. So handsome, so kindly. A little absent-minded, certainly, but always devoted to her. She missed him so much. Everything had been so easy. They'd met on day one at university and got along famously. It had all seemed natural and inevitable. Or maybe she just couldn't remember the awkward bits.

While she was mulling, Charles finished off his drink and put the glass down. 'Well, lead on then, dear lady,' he said, getting up and signalling for her to go first.

'Oh! Oh, right then,' said Sarah, realising some sort of decision had been made. She took a last sip of her tonic and left it on the table. As she turned, she caught sight of Daphne, grinning at her and making a jaunty double thumbs-up sign which she did her level best to pretend she hadn't seen. As the pub door swung shut behind them, she could have sworn she heard Pat and the rest of the book group cackling with laughter.

* * *

Outside again, and with the sea murmuring gently to their left as they wandered along the esplanade, Sarah and Charles were silent, seemingly absorbed in thoughts full of complications. Luckily Hamish, trotting along in front of them with his little Scottie tail very erect, turned at that moment to give them an encouraging woof. They both laughed, the tension broken. Sarah felt her heart lift. Happiness wasn't a given in this life. One look at Mr Williams's miserable house, and particularly his, erm, hobby, had told her that. It felt almost a duty to take whatever chance at fun one was given. She smiled up at Charles, and his hand automatically reached out for hers and squeezed it gently.

Perhaps it was inevitable that, at exactly this satisfying moment, there was a squawk from the other side of the road, and then a cacophony of shrill little barks. Before Sarah realised quite what was happening, she was being assailed by a tiny dog, snapping frantically at her ankles.

'Good grief! Down, Tinkerbell, down,' said Charles ineffectually as the Chihuahua darted about. Hamish, growling and looking on in doggy consternation, was clearly tempted to dive in and protect his mistress, but his loyalties were torn – he'd had a not-very-secret crush on the dreadful little dog that Charles co-owned with his estranged wife since he'd first set eyes on her.

Just then, there was a loud command of, 'Tinkerbell! *Sit,*' from over the road, and the dog immediately desisted and plonked its minuscule rear down on the pavement, its bulging eyes fixed in a malevolent stare directed squarely at Sarah's flushed face.

'I might have known it would be *you,*' came Francesca's patrician tones, glaring at Sarah almost as fiercely as her dog as she strode over to pick up the pooch. 'She's a very sensitive creature, she doesn't respond well to riffraff,' she added with a frown. 'And as for you,' she said, addressing Charles. 'You honestly should know better.'

Whether Francesca was referring to Charles being out on the town with Sarah, or to his less-than-commanding ways with the dog was not clear. But as usual Charles seemed much diminished by the woman's presence, and Sarah found herself wondering why she ever found him attractive.

'Anyway, Charles, I need to speak to you. Let's go,' Francesca said, walking off.

Charles looked at Sarah with a pleading expression in his eyes. She just shrugged. She wasn't going to give the man permission to abandon their plans at the whim of his ex, if that was what he was after.

'Erm, what's this about, Frankie?' Charles called to her retreating form, playing for time.

'I'd have thought that would be obvious,' Francesca snapped

over her shoulder, but she did slow her pace, so that she wasn't having to broadcast their business to everyone on the street. 'It's about Arabella.'

'Bella? What's she up to now?' Charles asked, relaxing a little and giving Sarah a more confident smile.

'Oh, *nothing*,' snapped Francesca, retracing her steps until she was confronting Charles and Sarah. 'She's just rung me in tears. If you insist on discussing it in front of strangers then I will,' she hissed, giving Sarah plenty of side-eye. 'She's been a victim... of an absolutely horrible crime,' she hissed, covering her mouth with a crumpled tissue, and looking genuinely woebegone. 'Our own little girl, picked on by a dreadful old...'

Sarah suddenly realised what this was all about. Mr Williams must have had some of Arabella Findlay's items in his furtive collection. She had every sympathy with the young woman – and her mother. As he had been recruited by Arabella as a model, and had chatted with her respectfully every week before and after the art classes, it seemed doubly wrong that he had her stolen underwear in his possession.

'I'd have thought you'd want to help protect your only daughter from a pervert like that,' Francesca continued.

'What? What's all this?' It was clear Charles didn't quite understand what Francesca meant – but he was already in full-on protective father mode. His fists were bunched, he was holding himself stiffly – and then he strode forward to join his former spouse without a backward glance at Sarah. They marched off together, quite literally into the sunset.

Sarah shook her head, and then stared at the wide skies over the beach, streaking the sea with reflected shades of pink and orange. She could understand the Diggorys' fury at developments. She had felt completely revolted herself when she had discovered her own smalls in Mr Williams's fetid room. But that was no excuse for Charles leaving her cold. For once the view gave her no pleasure at all.

'OK then, boy, looks like it's just you and me again,' said Sarah, looking down at her dog. Hamish stared up at her, bottomless love in his brown eyes. He licked her hand briefly. Part of him wondered where his lady-friend was off to, but he knew better than to turn and watch the Chihuahua as she high-stepped away with her humans. His mistress needed him now.

FIVE

The next morning, Sarah woke up in a tangle of sheets, feeling uncomfortably hot. How annoying, she'd thought the days of hot flushes were far behind her. Then she realised what the problem was. Next to her on the pillow, with an expression of mingled guilt and triumph, was the whiskery little face of Hamish.

'You're a very naughty pickle, yes you are,' said Sarah, ruffling his fur and trying to maintain a grumpy voice, even as she remembered the undeniable comfort of the dog's warm body snuggling up to her in the night. She'd been much too sleepy to kick him off, she told herself, and he'd taken advantage. Nevertheless, she gave him a big hug before putting him down decisively on the floor. 'That's not happening again, just so you know,' she added.

Hamish wagged his tail happily and trotted off down the stairs. He was glad his mistress had seen sense about their sleeping arrangements at last.

Downstairs, and with the kettle boiling away merrily, Sarah opened the back door so that Hamish could potter into the garden. He liked to do a daily check to make sure all his boundaries were secure and that there was no sign of that ginger marauder, Daphne's cat Mephisto, lurking anywhere.

Despite Hamish's best efforts, Sarah's flowers were really coming on. The pink rose bush she had only just put in was beginning to bloom. The irises were over, but she was glad to see the lupins and peonies were still going strong. She decided to take her breakfast outside and was soon sitting in a warm patch of sunlight, sipping her tea and munching at a piece of golden toast, slathered with delicious apricot jam. Mm, that sharp, tangy sweetness really was divine.

A moment later, the tranquillity of the garden was shattered. 'Coo-ee,' came a call over the fence, and then Daphne popped up, scarf flapping. 'I thought I could hear you munching.'

'Oh, was I that loud?' Sarah mumbled, a little shamefaced. But Daphne had her beady eyes locked on her toast.

'That's the apricot jam from the Beach Café, isn't it?'

'Well spotted. Come over. I'll put another slice of bread in the toaster.'

'Hold that thought,' said Daphne, disappearing as rapidly as she'd appeared.

Sarah retreated into the house, opened the front door and cut a fresh slice of lovely sourdough bread from the Seagull Bakery. A couple of minutes later, there was a jangling of bracelets as the whirlwind that was Daphne made its way down the narrow cottage passageway and erupted into the kitchen.

'There you are,' she announced loudly, as though Sarah had been hiding in her own home.

Sarah, feeling a little nonplussed that Daphne was actually dressed while she was still in her gown and slippers, submitted to her friend's usual enthusiastic hug.

'Where's Hamish?' Daphne asked.

'Patrolling the fences, making sure your cat doesn't get over.'

Sarah raised an eyebrow as she spread Daphne's toast lavishly with the silky apricot jam.

'My, that does look good,' said Daphne, unabashedly sticking a finger into the jar and licking it. Sarah frowned and whisked it back into the fridge before she could try that again. Honestly.

'Right, there's a mug of tea for you. Let's take this out, shall we?' said Sarah, sliding Daphne's plate onto a tray.

'What a treat! Thanks, Sarah. I was up early because I had an urgent appointment at Tarot and Tealeaves, quite an important reading. But they cancelled.'

'Oh, I'm sorry to hear that, Daph. How annoying for you,' Sarah commiserated. Luckily, Daphne was not financially dependent on her clairvoyant activities – otherwise she'd be starving in a gutter by now. But that didn't dent her passion for the Beyond.

Daphne settled into Sarah's garden chair in the sun. 'It's not annoying, as such,' she said, as clearly as she could through a mouthful of toast. 'I try not to harbour negative emotions,' she added, giving Sarah a reproving glance which stung less as she had a large blob of jam on her cheek and Sarah couldn't take her seriously at all. 'It's just that I feel sorry for the lady. She's in a quandary and of course she can't really make a logical decision without my input.'

Sarah thought it was best not to offer her own views on logic and the occult, and merely nodded as understandingly as she could while she sipped her tea. Just then there was a creak from inside the house. She looked up in alarm, only to see Charles emerging into the garden, Tinkerbell clamped under his arm.

'Daphne, why on earth didn't you shut the front door?' she said sharply. Then, realising that hardly sounded welcoming, she stood up and offered Charles her seat. 'This is a nice surprise,' she added.

Charles looked a little disconcerted at seeing Daphne

tucking into what was probably her second breakfast. 'Oh, erm, hope I'm not disturbing?'

'Not at all,' said Daphne expansively – *very* expansively, Sarah thought, considering it wasn't actually her house. 'Sarah, I don't know why you're so paranoid about doors. You're perfectly safe here in Merstairs.'

At this, Sarah disappeared into the kitchen for a second to grind her teeth. A place where a man had just been poisoned wasn't perhaps *that* safe. Once she'd composed herself, she called through the kitchen window, 'Tea and apricot jam on toast, Charles?'

'Oh, er, how lovely,' he said.

'Good grief, what is Tinks wearing today?' asked Daphne, gazing at the tiny T-shirt. It was a screaming pink (the sort of colour Sarah rather thought Daphne would approve of) with lettering in shiny foil spelling out 'Gold'. As Tinkerbell writhed in Charles's arms, enjoying the attention, Sarah caught sight of 'Digger' written on the back of the little garment. She sniffed. Francesca could never resist the temptation to score a point.

By the time Sarah came back out into the garden, though, with Charles's tea and toast, the T-shirt had been removed and left at the foot of Charles's chair.

'I really don't know where Francesca gets these things from,' said Daphne, furrowing her brow over it. 'But I thought the poor doggy would get a bit hot. It's going to be a lovely day today.'

Hamish was sitting at Charles's feet, a look of ineffable longing on his small fluffy face. Tinkerbell, naturally, had her back to him.

'Thanks for getting her out of that, Daphne. She nearly took my hand off when I tried to undress her earlier,' Charles confessed. 'Anyway, Sarah, I thought I'd just pop round and say, er, hello, before things get busy at my shop, you know. I didn't mean to take your seat.'

'Oh, I've got another here,' said Sarah, unfolding a spare metal chair. She wasn't sure there was ever going to be a rush of customers at Charles's antiques emporium, unless a coachload of tourists arrived straight from 1820, desperate to replenish their stocks of warming pans, bellows and candlesticks. But she smiled kindly and poured the tea.

'And, well, erm, I had to rush off last night.'

'Oh yes?' said Daphne, immediately sniffing a story. 'You two were going to get some dinner, weren't you? Shame really, you missed an epic row in the book group,' she said to Sarah. 'Honestly, some of those girls didn't seem to get what the author was on about at all.' Daphne tutted.

Sarah, who knew Daphne hadn't got past page sixteen of the book, wondered whether the ending was crucial to understanding the story. 'When I left, everyone seemed more interested in talking about Mr Williams.'

'Yes,' said Daphne, looking pained. 'Well, you know how I feel about things like that.'

'Did, erm, Pat say anything else? And you didn't mention the, er, pants, situation yourself, did you?' Sarah asked. She wanted to know whether the whole of Merstairs now knew about Mr Williams's little hobby.

'I didn't breathe a word, Sarah. Mariella would kill me, and she'd never speak to me again either. Pat left just after you, actually. Said she had to get her beauty sleep.'

Sarah immediately suppressed the thought that Pat had her work cut out there, and passed Charles his mug. 'Sugar?' she asked.

'Surely you know by now Charles doesn't take sugar in his tea?' said Daphne a little coyly. Sarah didn't quite know where to look, and Charles bent over Tinkerbell and adjusted a collar that was patently fine already. Sarah put the mug down on the table. Sometimes Daphne seemed to assume things had gone much further with Charles than they actually had. You really couldn't tell whether someone liked sugar after holding hands with them once. Or even twice.

'Erm, lovely tea,' said Charles, and a short silence fell. Then he said, 'And, er, lovely toast.'

Sarah, who rather thought the poor man had suffered enough at this point, turned to him. 'So, was Arabella all right last night?'

'Ah. Yes. Poor girl. Well, she was thoroughly disconcerted. As anyone would be. I gather you know about Mr Williams's unfortunate predilection, Daphne?' Charles said, an expression of disdain on his face.

'I saw Daphne right after making the discovery,' Sarah explained.

'I see,' said Charles. 'Well, unfortunately Arabella's, ahem, underthings were also in that ghastly man's house.'

'Oh,' replied Daphne, who again seemed to be suppressing a smile. 'I saw Francesca storming down the esplanade through the pub window, I wondered if she'd catch up with you. I take it she did.'

'Honestly, Daphne, it's not a bit funny. It's really sordid. He was pawing things in such close contact with people's bodies,' Sarah said crossly.

'Well, when you put it like that,' Daphne said more thoughtfully. 'But he probably meant no harm.'

'If he meant no harm, he could have stolen men's clothes,' said Charles flatly. 'I didn't like the chap, I have to say. And I hate to think of him with his hands on my daughter's... well, anyway. Good job he's dead.'

'Charles! I'm surprised at you. His soul may still be hovering near us as we speak,' said Daphne, with a faraway look in her eye.

'I doubt it. His body will soon be six feet under and his soul is already a lot lower than that, I'll be bound,' said Charles firmly.

'Apart from anything else,' said Sarah, before Daphne could get a word in. 'It's humiliating for anyone whose, um, intimate apparel is now being examined by those policemen,' she added.

'Hmm. I'm not a fan of Mariella's constables,' Daphne conceded.

'I think they've been quite indiscreet. You heard Pat last night. It's already out that he had some kind of shameful secret,' Sarah said disapprovingly. 'Mariella wouldn't have said a word, and nor would the pathologist.'

'Of course not. It's bound to be those idiots. And they've started to play pranks on my Mariella,' Daphne said.

'Gosh, have they?' Sarah frowned. 'She could report that sort of thing to someone, couldn't she?'

'Who to? DI Brice is just as bad as them. He just laughs when they put salt in her coffee and hide all her biros. Only yesterday she arrived to find a phone message from a Mr P Freely on her desk, and they all cracked up when she said it out loud. Honestly, it's like being back in the playground.'

'I'm beginning to wonder if she might be better off working up in London, you know. At least she'd have a few more resources and the people would be more professional,' Sarah mused.

'Oh, don't say that! It's wonderful having her here, and you know how I dote on little Leila and Louis. And I'm not sure John could transfer his job.'

'He's an accountant, though, isn't he?' said Sarah. Mariella's husband was a kind, dependable man. He was a good foil to a woman whose restless spirit at last seemed to have found its niche in policing. 'I'm sure he could move to one of the big firms.'

'Isn't there a simpler way to get that undynamic duo out of her hair?' said Charles in amused tones. 'We seem to have been landed with another mystery. Let's do our best to help Mariella solve it again. Then hey presto, she'll surely be looking at another promotion. We could even mention that details got out about the crime scene that only a very few people know. Those idiots would just be dots in her rear-view mirror after that.'

'You're right, cracking the case is a great idea,' said Sarah enthusiastically. 'Let's try not to get those constables involved, though. We don't want to sink to their level.' Although she wasn't sure that Mariella had enjoyed a totally central position in solving either of their previous cases, she was more than happy to let her take all the credit. And, judging by the way Mariella had allowed Sarah to give her thoughts on Mr Williams's body yesterday, she was becoming a little more relaxed about accepting assistance when it was offered. That was all to the good. Sarah raised her mug in salute, and after a second, Daphne followed suit, then laughed.

'We're just like the Three Musketeers, aren't we? One for all, and all who sail in her,' she said, holding her cup aloft and spilling tea on Tinkerbell, who whimpered theatrically even though it was stone cold.

Sarah looked round at the smiling faces of her friends and for a moment felt only warmth and comradeship. Then she thought about what they were actually toasting – a quest to find a murderer, something that was potentially so dangerous she'd taken up life drawing to get away from it. Oh well, she reasoned. At least she'd now have a great excuse for dropping out of the art club – and maybe even the book group too.

SIX

By the next morning, Sarah had come to the realisation that she probably needed to join more clubs, rather than leave any. Where, otherwise, was she going to get her information from? Mr Williams had been killed, that much was clear – but there was no indication who might be in the frame as the murderer, although the more she thought about it, the odder it seemed that Pat was so well-informed about the man's horrible habit. The old lady didn't strike Sarah as the kind of person who'd hang out with Tweedledum and Tweedledee. So how, exactly, did she know?

Something else that niggled was the fact that there was very little apricot jam left for her toast. Apart from eating nearly two whole jars of the stuff, and then moving swiftly on to a long lunch, she wasn't sure Daphne and Charles had really helped her make much progress at all yesterday.

Well, this would never do. Sarah needed to concentrate and give the matter some proper thought. Mr Williams's character must be the key to the whole business. This wasn't a random murder; this had involved forethought, planning – and hatred.

Someone had gone along to the old man's house with the express intention of leaving him dead.

Until she'd discovered the cache of underwear upstairs in his house, Sarah would have assumed Mr Williams didn't have an enemy in the world. He'd seemed a benign old thing, doddery, smiley and apparently well-meaning. Now, in the context of the vast array of stolen ladies' pants, Sarah couldn't help re-evaluating him. There was a tendency to desex older people, to assume they had never known the fires of youth and certainly had no yearnings while collecting their pensions. People probably looked at her, a lady of a certain age, and imagined she had put romantic thoughts to one side. And to an extent she had, she told herself, with a slight blush at the thought of Charles Diggory.

That underwear collection was very disturbing... wasn't it a distinct possibility that someone else had found it revolting enough to kill him over? All right, Daphne had sniggered over it, as though the man's habit was an innocent bit of fun. But what if her good-natured friend was wrong not to take it seriously? What if one of the women whose garments were in Mr Williams's trophy collection knew what he was up to, and was so angry that they'd decided to get revenge on him?

And what about those initials he'd scribbled on that betting slip? P, H or M, and a B or T? What a shame he had such awful writing, though she couldn't talk as her own scrawl was terrible. There was that number thirteen, too. Could it all somehow refer to a woman whose underwear he was targeting? What if that person had got wind of his plans, and decided to do away with him? Or maybe an enraged husband, boyfriend or father had taken the law into their own hands. Look how cross Charles had been, and he was the epitome of a civilised man, every gesture the product of centuries of good breeding. All that had been stripped away when he'd realised his precious daughter's underwear had been nabbed by Williams.

There was nothing for it, she was going to have to think hard about people who might fit the bill. And she'd also need to check Charles's own alibi. Though she really couldn't believe for a second he was capable of such evil, and he hadn't seemed to know about the underwear until told by Francesca, she still needed to ask the question. He could have been hiding prior knowledge, after all. But first of all she had to sort out the time of death, to tie down when the poisoning must have taken place. If she just pictured the scene again and analysed the medical evidence carefully, she might be able to narrow it down.

Sarah got herself another cup of tea, and made sure Hamish was happy rooting around at the base of a shrub Mephisto might, or might not, have once touched, at the far end of the garden. Then she settled her comfy garden chair in a patch of sunlight, and thought as hard as she could. What had happened on Monday? She'd opened that magenta door, she'd stepped inside and immediately seen the body. There'd been a brief period of shock, when her mind had almost shut down. But then, when she'd been able to take in what had happened – what had she seen next?

What about the cake by Williams's lifeless body? Surely she could get a bit further with that. It had looked pretty fresh. The weather had been lovely all weekend, and it had been nice and warm on Monday, yet the cream in that Victoria sponge had looked perfect – neither dried up, nor runny from the heat. The strawberries, too, had looked recently cut. Old berries tended to shrivel a little around the edges, soften and lose their colour, but these had been deliciously red and bright. If she hadn't been so keen to avoid the cyanide fumes, she could have sniffed them to see if they still had their alluring smell. The tea, however, had looked distinctly tepid, if not outright cold. In hot weather, it would cool less rapidly. She really didn't want to think about the contents of Williams's bin, but that had not been fully dried up.

Although she was now feeling considerable revulsion, imagining herself back at the scene of the crime so efficiently that she could almost smell the noxious odours, the exercise had been very effective. She was now pretty sure the man had been killed, at the most, two hours before she had arrived. That was enough time for his tea to cool, but not for the cake cream to curdle or the cut strawberries to perish. If she had been able to touch the body, she might have been even more certain, but she was happy with her estimate for now, until she had more information.

Was there anything she could glean from the cake itself, perhaps? There were plenty of ladies in Merstairs with a Victoria sponge in their baking repertoire. Sarah could pull one off herself, if she needed to – weighing out all the ingredients meticulously was quite therapeutic, and although oven temperatures and the freshness of the raising agent added a little peril to the proceedings, she'd created a fair few she'd been proud of. Dear Peter had always been so complimentary about her baking, she remembered with a fond smile – perhaps to encourage her to do more of it. Having said that, there was no doubt that the Beach Café sponges were far better than hers.

Had Mr Williams been eating a slice from there? Or was the sponge purchased from one of the other cafés in the town? Sarah put a hand to her forehead, and concentrated. Back, back, to the whiff of bitter almonds, the flickering TV, the overheated room, the betting slip, the old-fashioned Pyrex plate with its floral rim, worn out by use... there had been no cake knife, but there had been something else on the plate. What had it been? Something which had made her discount the idea that it was an amateur cake, as it were. It had been shop-bought, she was sure. But why? What had given her that impression?

Just as Sarah was driving herself mad, there was a call from over the fence. 'Coo-ee!'

She opened her eyes to the sight of Daphne, resplendent in

an acid yellow scarf. The combination of this with her auburn hair had Sarah reaching automatically for her sunglasses. In her neighbour's arms was Mephisto, cradled like a huge marmalade baby. He turned baleful green eyes on her and, she could have sworn, almost winked at her. Just then, Hamish bounced along, barking up a storm, braced on his haunches as though he was going to leap right over the fence and get the cat by the scruff of the neck. Mephisto gave him a look as though to say, 'In your dreams, buster,' and wriggled out of Daphne's embrace. Sarah couldn't see him hit the ground on his side of the fence, but she certainly heard the thud, followed by the rattle of the cat flap as he pranced back inside, leaving her poor dog in a state of impotent rage.

'Come here, Hamish, good boy,' she called. After struggling with himself for a moment, Hamish trotted over, and then did his best to explain to her that only the fence had separated him from a slap-up lunch of annoying cat. 'I know, boy. Next time,' she whispered into his tufty ears, mindful that Daphne wouldn't be nearly as understanding about the dog's futile ambition to tear Mephisto limb from furry limb.

'Thought you'd like to know,' said Daphne, oblivious to the pet wars raging in the vicinity. 'Mariella is popping round for coffee. To discuss the kids' new teacher, weekend plans, all that stuff. Just in case you fancied a cup. But I can see you've already got some—'

Sarah immediately threw the rest of her tea into the nearest flowerbed. 'Give me five minutes, I'll be over,' she said, bustling Hamish into the house.

SEVEN

In the middle of gathering up her handbag and keys, Sarah wondered whether or not to leave Hamish at home. He'd be pretty disgruntled, and he was still at an age when she didn't like to leave him long, but it might be more relaxing. In the end, though, as she put her hand on the front door, she saw that Hamish had somehow inserted himself between her and the mat, so she would have had to step over a vocal Scottie to get away without him.

'OK, you win,' she said, taking down his lead and shutting the door behind them. 'But if there are any fisticuffs with Mephisto, there'll be no walkies for you,' she said, as sternly as she could manage.

Hamish looked up approvingly at his mistress. She'd not only got down his lead (big tick) but was using the magic 'W' word (even bigger tick). He gave her an encouraging bouquet of licks. Training was so important and, whatever anyone might say, he still thought she was young enough to learn.

'Really, Hamish,' Sarah remonstrated, wiping her face hastily with a tissue as they walked up the gnome-strewn path to Daphne's cottage. 'I hope you'll be on your best behaviour now,' she added. Daphne's door was swinging open in the breeze. She went in and shut it carefully behind them.

'Daph, please do listen to me about locking up,' Sarah began, striding down the passage which was an exact mirror of hers next door. 'There's a killer on the loose, you know.'

'Honestly, you know how I feel about that kind of talk.' Daphne turned from the sink, where she was filling the kettle. 'And Mari will be here in a minute. We'll have a real-life police-woman on the premises! What could be safer?' She shook her head at her neighbour's overcautious ways, stopping for a moment to fish her earring out of the washing-up bowl.

'Well, she's not here yet.' Sarah shrugged.

Daphne only tutted, then said, 'Now, where's my favourite tray?' She looked around the cluttered surfaces, as though it was going to jump out at her any second.

'This?' Sarah said, pulling an old-fashioned 'Guinness Is Good for You' tin tray from under a pile of old newspapers. 'Or that?' she pointed at a large melamine tray which looked as though it would be right at home in a school canteen.

'No, no,' said Daphne vaguely. 'That's the trouble when everything gets put away,' she added a mite crossly. 'I can never find anything.'

Sarah looked round the room and wondered which centimetre had been tidied. The place could easily have been the 'before' ad for a TV show about hoarders. Hamish panted at her and then, sensing the coast was clear, took himself off to curl up in Mephisto's cosy fleece bed.

'Um, where is your cat?' said Sarah, who lived in terror of a replay of a recent incident when the creature had definitely got the better of her poor pooch.

Daphne took a quick look at the clock on the wall, which seemed to have stopped at a quarter past three. 'Oh, he'll be off down to Tarot and Tealeaves now, he likes to settle in there just before his lunch.'

Sarah, who knew the portly cat's meal was probably composed of ill-advised mice who'd set up home in Daphne's paperwork in her Tarot shop, tried to banish the picture of Mephisto crunching on small bones.

'Um, OK then, where did you last see your tray?' she asked helpfully.

'Well, under my teapot, of course,' said Daphne, as though her friend had taken leave of her senses. 'Oh! It's probably outside.' She flung the back door open and, sure enough, there was a tray balanced on a pile of magazines on a three-legged table that was listing badly to one side. 'Just as I thought. Bit of method, that's all you need, Sarah,' she said, striding out to get it.

Sarah blinked, then heard the doorbell shrilling. 'I'll get that, shall I?'

She trooped back along the corridor and greeted Mariella on the step.

'Lovely to see you, Aunty Sarah. And before you even ask, I can't tell you a thing about the investigation,' Mariella said, pushing her sunglasses up onto her glorious hair as she stepped inside the dim hallway. 'It's nice and cool in here. I was getting quite puffed in the heat,' the girl said.

'I think your mum is making some coffee,' said Sarah optimistically as they walked to the kitchen. She'd seen the kettle go on, but the trays had been a diversion, and who knew what stage they were now at? As Daphne was still in the garden pottering around, she took the opportunity to spoon some ground coffee into the large cafetiere she found behind a stack of cat food tins, and soon found a jug to fill with milk. Once she'd assembled all that on the Guinness tray, and added three mugs for good measure, she took the whole lot outside. 'Nicer to sit out on a day like this, I think?' she said over her shoulder.

'I quite agree. Sitting in one place is perfect, toiling up the esplanade not so much,' said Mariella. She plonked herself down gratefully, and then fished a hardback library book out from under her seat cushion.

'Oh, really, Sarah, you know that's not the right tray,' said Daphne, watching Sarah fill the mugs with the delicious-smelling coffee. She was standing in a flowerbed, and had both hands full of straggling blooms. 'And you've forgotten the biscuits. But never mind, I suppose it doesn't matter,' she added, in tones which rather suggested that it did. She went inside, returning with the flowers bursting forth from a jam jar, which she put on the table by the side of the tray, together with a crumpled packet of custard creams. 'There,' she said, sounding as though she'd just restored order to the universe. 'Now, then, Mari, what can you tell us about poor old Mr Williams?'

Immediately Mariella frowned and Sarah silently cursed her friend. That was not the way to get the detective to open up. But luckily Mariella, much like her mother, never stayed cross for long. She helped herself to a biscuit, and then mumbled, 'Honestly, Mother, you know the drill by now. Of course I'm not going to tell you a sausage.'

'Sausage? We're not interested in sausages, ladies like us,' Daphne said, her whole body shaking with laughter. 'Or I'm not, anyway,' she said, slanting a glance at Sarah. 'It's just that, well, we do need something to say to the art group, don't we, Sarah?'

Sarah nodded her head. 'You know what people are like, Mariella. They can be so curious.'

'Yes, I do know that,' said the young policewoman, and now it was her turn to bestow a steely glance on Sarah. Then she sighed. 'Well, I suppose it wouldn't hurt to go over what's already in the public domain, as you're both so keen. After all, that's common knowledge, isn't it?'

'Exactly, of course,' said Daphne heartily, taking a swig of coffee. 'Um, what is, exactly?'

'Oh, you know, all the stuff about it probably being someone

Mr Williams knew, as there was no sign of a disturbance, no other fingerprints in the place – apart from yours, Sarah,' Mariella said with a lift of her eyebrows.

'Sorry about that,' said Sarah, eyes downcast. Then she thought for a moment. 'Wait a minute, does that mean he never had any visitors? Not at all?'

'Not since the last time he cleaned,' Mariella confirmed. 'And that looks like an age ago. I can't say it surprises me particularly, knowing what we now do about his, erm, habit.'

'And no one in town knew about that? It's just that, last night—'

'Another biscuit?' Daphne leant across her, shaking the packet at her daughter. 'You're looking a bit peaky, darling, you need building up.'

'Honestly, Mum, I'm not twelve any more,' said Mariella, but she obediently fished a custard cream out of the wrapping. While she was nibbling at it, she said absently, 'Dr Strutton did say Williams hadn't been dead long. But you knew that anyway, Aunty Sarah.'

'Yes. I thought maybe a couple of hours?' Sarah said tentatively, hoping to get either a yea or a nay.

'She thought maybe less, given the ambient temperature of the room and so on... It was quite a hot day.'

'Agreed. The cream hadn't turned at all,' Sarah said slowly.

'Goodness, you really peered at that sponge, didn't you?' Daphne said a little disapprovingly.

'Well, it's a shame you weren't there with me. You'd have probably been able to tell me who'd baked it.' Sarah smiled.

'The main point is that the poison was in the cake, not in the tea or an injection or anything,' said Mariella absently, crunching the last of her biscuit.

Sarah didn't want to pounce too obviously on this tasty – or not – morsel of information. But, on the other hand, if she didn't ask, she wouldn't get anywhere, would she?

'Oh? How d'you make that out?' she said, as casually as she could.

'Oh, just the tox report, everything was individually tested. Shame there are so many places selling Victoria sponge in Merstairs. If there was just one, we'd have them bang to rights.' Mariella smiled.

'There was that betting slip, too. Any idea what his note at the end meant?'

'The letters? Nope. Nothing yet,' said Mariella. 'But the horse was called Killing Time.'

Sarah felt a chill down her spine. 'Was it number thirteen?' Mariella shook her head. Sarah continued slowly, 'Just think, when he placed that bet, he had no idea what would happen to him only a day later. He didn't win, I presume?'

Mariella shook her head. 'Poor old thing. Nope, it came in last. All right, the pants stuff is awful, but a lot of it just seems... sad.'

Sarah decided to try her own luck a little further while Mariella was in a reflective mood. 'It's disappointing we're no further on with those letters.'

'For what it's worth, Dr Strutton thought it might actually read MT rather than anything else,' Mariella said.

Sarah sighed. 'Goodness. I was going for PB. And I thought my writing was bad! The cake, though. It wasn't made by an amateur baker. Was it actually from a local café?' she said, hoping to tempt Mariella into saying more.

'We have no idea where it came from yet. But it was definitely shop-bought. There were a few tell-tale signs,' Mariella nodded. 'The cream was piped into those blobs, not just slapped on like you do, Mum.'

'Slapped? I'm not sure that's the word you're looking for,' said Daphne, drawing herself up to her full height.

'Sloshed, then,' said Mariella, not chastened at all. 'You never whip it for long.'

'Ha, I suppose that's true, I'm always in a hurry to get to the eating part,' chuckled Daphne.

'Oh! I knew there was something,' Sarah broke in eagerly. 'There was a gold doily, under the cake. It was really preying on my mind, but you've jogged my memory. I just got a glimpse of it. I don't know anyone who has those at home. I suppose the fact that it was a shop-bought cake narrows the suspects down a bit,' she said thoughtfully.

'How do you make that out?' asked Daphne. 'Virtually every café here does its own signature Victoria sponge.'

'OK, point taken. Things were looking simple for a minute,' Sarah said wistfully.

'Aunty Sarah, you shouldn't be "looking" at this at all, not in that way you have. It isn't a riddle that needs solving. It's murder, and it's dangerous.'

'You don't have to remind me, not after last time,' said Sarah.

'Sarah's a reformed character. She's sticking to the art group now, aren't you?' Daphne said heartily.

It was the wrong thing to say. Sarah thought back to her wonky banana sketch and immediately solving the sponge mystery seemed a lot more compelling. But there was no need to alarm Mariella. Not at this stage, anyway. She smiled as meekly as she could, as though she'd learnt her lesson.

'Well, I'm not saying another thing,' said Mariella, and true to her word, she wouldn't be drawn on any other aspect of the investigation while she finished up her coffee. Then she took her leave.

'Don't make me tell you two again to stay well clear of things,' she said as a parting shot. Daphne nodded solemnly, while Sarah shook her head at the same time. Then they made the fatal mistake of looking at each other – and as soon as Mariella had disappeared through the kitchen door, both burst out laughing.

EIGHT

The evening sky was studded with stars by the time Sarah made it back next door with a sleepy Hamish. She and Daphne had managed to while away the whole day discussing the case. Daphne had grown increasingly convinced that Mr Williams had annoyed someone in the Beyond. In her view that had certainly led to his passing. Sarah was pretty sure that it was someone in the here and now who'd had it in for him, as his cake had been poisoned by a human hand. Daphne, however, remained skittishly reluctant to accept the truth. Sarah left her casting runes in the hope that one of her spirit guides would obligingly come up with clues that so far seemed thin on the ground in the real world.

* * *

The next morning dawned bright and cheery. Sarah sat with an empty bowl in front of her, having polished off some delicious granola, which she'd had with Greek yoghurt and fresh berries from the Merstairs farmers' market. She finished the last of her tea. She didn't need to start reading the next book club novel for a while. Perhaps she ought to practise her art skills – but that held no appeal. In any case, it looked as though the group was going to be without a proper model until they found a replacement, and she couldn't face drawing any more fruit. The cottage was as pristine as ever. Even Hamish looked less tufty than usual after a good brushing. She had almost no choice but to focus on the murder, she realised with a happy sigh.

She scanned through the list of fellow art club attendees in her mind. These were people who had sat in a reasonably confined space with Mr Williams for four or five weeks, since the class had started up, so they could be said to know him fairly well. If the man had died two hours before Sarah had found him, halfway through the art class, there would have been time for anyone there to give Mr Williams the poisoned cake beforehand, and then act surprised when he didn't turn up to model. Who had a motive for doing away with him, though?

She thought for a moment. It was hard to imagine Mavis of ScaleScanners paying any attention to Mr Williams outside the class, they seemed to inhabit such different worlds. She seemed so elegant, focused and intent, whereas Mr Williams, until Sarah had known better, had seemed like a slightly shambolic little old man. On the other hand, her initials were MT, so she might fit the scribble on the betting slip, and of course there had been that ScaleScanners flyer on the doormat – though that could have been the type of junk mail sent out to everyone. Passing on to Arabella Findlay, surely she had nothing in common with him, apart from the class itself. Then there was Pat. She was the oldest person in the group – Sarah felt this was probably true in all Pat's many groups – so had had the most time to develop a relationship with Mr Williams. After all, they had been living in the same small town together for many years. And her initials were PB, which Sarah still felt were the likeliest letters. Yet, despite all her salacious talk about men in general, Pat had shown surprisingly little interest in him when he'd been modelling in front of her. Penny Booth had to be a possible, too. Sarah resolved to ask all the ladies what they'd been up to a couple of hours before the class, just in case.

In the meantime, she had hit upon a brilliant way to move forward. She simply needed to test all the sponge cakes in Merstairs.

Now, who did she know who'd be a willing guinea pig, helping her test? There was one glaringly obvious candidate. As soon as the dishes had been washed up and put away, Sarah marched next door, with Hamish in tow. But, for once, she was doomed to disappointment. There was no answer to her knock.

At first, Sarah was a little alarmed. After all, the last time someone hadn't opened the door to her, it had been for the worst possible reason. But, before she started to get too worried, she remembered Daphne had mentioned a reading. She must have gone to her shop, Tarot and Tealeaves. It had to be quite some client, for Daphne to trot off so early.

Oh well, thought Sarah, turning away sadly from the door. She could still do the rounds of the cake shops herself. But a mission that would have been a laugh a minute with Daphne suddenly seemed rather ridiculous – and lonely. Did she really want to trail around Merstairs, filling herself with cake that she had no appetite for? She'd already had breakfast. She was now thoroughly regretting that wonderful granola. Cake testing on a full stomach would be an ordeal, not fun at all.

She turned to go but, just as she swivelled to face the sea, she saw a lanky figure far away on the beach, with a moving dot by his side. Of course! Charles and Tinkerbell. For some reason, she currently felt very shy with him. The way he'd dropped her hand in front of Francesca, and then walked off with his ex, not sparing her a backward glance, hadn't left her with a good feeling. Returning to a friendly footing with no expectations might prove quite hard. It made her miss the simple relationship she'd had with Peter more than ever.

Nevertheless, Sarah would still prefer to eat cake with someone, even if the terms of her interactions with that person were by no means as clear as she might like. She bustled down Daphne's path, heading now towards the beach, with Hamish bounding on ahead. He already seemed to have decoded the shapes in front of him and realised one was the dreadful Tinkerbell. Now that Sarah had become a convert to dogs, it seemed heresy to dislike one. But she felt she could make an exception for the Chihuahua.

Luckily, Charles seemed to be dawdling on the sands, while Sarah was walking at a spanking pace with Hamish surging ahead. It didn't take many moments before she was on the wide beach, and had all but caught up with him.

'Charles!' she called out merrily, and tried to be amused when he seemed to jump. 'Oh sorry, did I give you a shock?' she said.

'Um, no, dear lady. Just didn't see you there,' said Charles, trying to sound his usual languid self but seeming oddly ill at ease. He scanned the horizon restlessly. Sarah wasn't sure whether it was to spot someone he knew, or just to avoid her eyes.

Maybe this had all been a bad idea. 'Oh, well, just wondered how you are. But you're busy with Tinkerbell,' she said briskly. 'We'll be on our way. I'm giving Hamish a quick airing. Now, where has he got to?' She turned round, only to see Hamish frisking towards the water's edge, following Tinkerbell as though he was her raggedy black shadow. 'I hope he won't go in, he always stays damp for ages.'

'Not so bad, on a day like this?' Charles said, his eyes now turned to the heavens, where they rivalled the blue of the sky. It was going to be another hot day in Merstairs.

'I suppose not. He shouldn't be too smelly, he did have a

bath recently,' she added, remembering with a smile how woebegone the poor little dog had been. With his fur flattened by a good shampoo and rinse, he'd looked almost as small and rat-like as Tinkerbell herself. But not quite, she decided loyally. 'Hamish! Hamish,' she called. 'We'll just have to do the sponge tasting on our own,' she murmured quietly.

'Sponge tasting? What on earth is that?' Charles said, eyebrows raised in that lordly manner.

'Oh, nothing really... I had an idea about trying some cakes, you know, for the Mr Williams case, that's all,' said Sarah shortly. The more she thought about it, the sillier it seemed, and she didn't want to stand here and discuss it with Charles. He was obviously wishing her gone.

Charles glanced quickly from left to right, and then to Sarah's surprise he proffered his arm. 'Testing cakes? I think I can help you with that,' he said with an irresistible smile. 'Let's round up these pooches, shall we?' He gave an ear-splitting whistle and immediately both Tinkerbell and Hamish trotted up to him, as though they'd been in training for years. Sarah would have been irritated if she hadn't been so pleased. She'd had no wish to get horribly wet trying to drag Hamish out of the surf and away from his beloved. 'Now, where were you thinking of going first?'

'Um, I suppose the Beach Café is the closest,' she said, looking at the chairs spread out on the sands. Quite a few were already taken.

'We'd better get our skates on then, if that's the case,' said Charles. 'You know what the morning rush is like there.'

'You realise we're testing to see whether we can identify the source of the sponge used to kill Mr Williams?' Sarah said, to make sure Charles understood this wasn't just a jolly all-you-can-eat buffet she was offering.

'Absolutely,' said Charles. 'Anything I can do to help, count me in.'

'I wasn't sure you'd feel that strongly about it,' Sarah said tentatively, surprised by the vehemence in Charles's voice.

'Are you kidding?' he said, a grim look about his jaw. 'After what Williams did to my Arabella? The sooner we find the killer, the sooner I can shake their hand.'

NINE

Sarah was quite taken aback. Charles hadn't had this martial light in his eyes during either of their other cases. But this time, she supposed, it was personal. Very personal indeed for poor Arabella.

'OK then, Charles, good to know how you feel. But you should probably also remember...' her words tapered off.

'Remember what?' Charles turned to her, his expression still grim.

'Well, the murderer could be a lady. They always say poison is a woman's weapon.'

'Good for her, in that case. I want to pass on my warmest wishes,' he said.

At once, Sarah felt an obscure kind of jealousy burgeoning. But that was ridiculous. Whoever had committed this crime was going to prison for a long time. There were no grounds for her to envy them, even for a second.

'Incidentally, do you know what Arabella was doing before the class this time? Just, you know, for a couple of hours prior to us all meeting?'

Charles ground to a halt, and drew himself up to his full,

very impressive, height. 'Sarah Vane! Are you accusing my daughter of murder?'

Immediately, Sarah was all contrition. 'No, no – of course not. I'm trying to establish everyone's whereabouts... for elimination purposes, you know...' she stammered, blushing to the roots of her hair.

'Haha, only joshing with you,' Charles said, all affability now. 'It just so happens she was with me, in the shop. She had a couple of items to pass on to me. Left behind by that blighter Piers.'

Piers was Arabella's ex-husband, and Sarah wondered for a moment whether it was really the done thing to sell his possessions. But all was fair in love and war, she supposed. At least Arabella was in the clear as far as Mr Williams was concerned... as long as her doting father wasn't just providing her with a handy alibi.

Sarah was still a little rattled after Charles's outburst. They trudged over the soft sand in silence for a few beats, until they came to the Beach Café. Sarah sank down into her chair gratefully, suddenly as tired as though she had run all the way. Hamish curled up too and, wonder of wonders, Tinkerbell trotted over to join him, tucking herself into a tiny ball with one paw on his leg. Hamish opened his eyes wide at Sarah, as if to say, 'Do you see that? She *does* love me.' She rolled her eyes.

'Sorry, anything the matter?' said Charles.

'Oh, um, not at all. Just, um, admiring the view,' she said unconvincingly.

'Well, I'll do the honours then, shall I? English breakfast tea, and of course the cake,' Charles said.

'Yes please, Victoria sponge – but oh, don't forget to get it in a takeaway box.'

'Is that how it was at Williams's house?' Charles asked.

'No, but it was from a shop, so someone must have brought it in a receptacle, a bag, box, Tupperware...'

'I get the picture,' Charles said. 'Takeaway cake, coming up.'

'Wonderful.' Sarah sat back and closed her eyes, letting the sun stroke her face. She took a few deep breaths and felt calm again. There really was a lot to be said for the soft murmur of the waves. The occasional shrieks and laughs of children nearby were all that was stopping her from drifting off into a pleasant sleep... that, and the thought that out there somewhere was a murderer, stalking the streets of Merstairs. Or maybe on this very beach, right now.

She opened her eyes with a jolt, only to find a man peering down at her. She immediately sat up straighter – then she recognised him. It was Dave Cartwright, leader of the Men of Merstairs, whose son Albie was now in jail thanks to her. She changed her glare to a rather uncertain smile, not at all sure of the etiquette in such situations, but luckily Dave didn't seem to bear her any ill will.

'Dr Vane, isn't it? How's things? Lovely day for it,' he said. His face, with its weak chin, was already flushing in the gathering warmth of the day.

'All good – except for the terrible news about Mr Williams,' Sarah said. Might as well pump everyone she met for information, she decided.

'Oh, I know,' said Dave, lapsing into a worried frown that looked habitual. 'Mind if I...?' he gestured at the free chair at the table.

'Charles is getting some cake, but do sit down, he can find another chair when he gets back,' Sarah said.

Dave looked a little unsure, but then perched on the very edge of the seat. 'Just for a moment, then. Yes, I heard the news about the old boy. Actually, he's by way of a relative – my brother-in-law's uncle, as it happens. Funny the way things turn out.'

It was indeed, thought Sarah, wondering whether having a murderer for a child was somehow cancelled out by having a murder victim in the family tree as well. It was certainly unfortunate. 'Any ideas about what happened?'

'Oh, heart attack, I expect,' Dave said, though he looked a little shifty. Did he know what had befallen Williams, or was that expression just an extension of his usual apologetic manner? Sarah had been terrified, when she'd first heard about the Men of Merstairs, imagining a cut-throat gang at the least. But, as she had rapidly discovered, they were people who'd need satnav and a guidebook to fight their way out of a paper bag. And then require extensive counselling afterwards. Not that Sarah was unsympathetic. People's struggles were real, and she'd had enough of her own to know that compassion was the way forward.

'Such an awful thing to happen. Please do pass on my condolences, won't you?' Sarah said earnestly.

'Oh, erm, yes. I hear y-you were first on the scene, is that right?' Dave asked timidly.

'Yes, I'm afraid so,' said Sarah gently. 'He didn't turn up at the art group, so I thought I'd check in on him. As you know, he was quite elderly, and he'd had a cough. You knew he was our model?'

'Yes,' said Dave, with a grim set to his chin. 'He had some funny... ways.'

'I see,' said Sarah, deducing from the sudden extra pinkness in his cheeks that he was referring to his relative's unfortunate fondness for women's underthings. 'You've heard about that? I must say I had no idea, and I believe most people didn't know either. That coming out will be a bit... awkward, I'd imagine.'

'More than awkward, when it comes to my own wife,' said Dave, with a surprisingly cross look in his eye.

'Awkward? Oh, we can't have that, Cartwright,' came Charles's drawling tones as he approached with a loaded tray.

'Oh, Mr Diggory, I've taken your seat.' The man was all but tugging his forelock as he shot up.

'Not to worry, you stay there and I'll grab another chair,' said Charles, sliding the tray onto the table.

'No, no, I've got to get off – probably said too much already,' Dave said, lurching away with an apologetic look at Sarah. He waded through the sand like a penguin taking its first steps on land, with Sarah worrying he was going to fall. It was a relief when he made it safely to the crazy golf course where the Men of Merstairs usually gathered.

'That sounded interesting,' said Charles, taking back his seat and stretching out his long legs. 'I hope he told you the identity of the murderer, at least.'

'No such luck,' said Sarah thoughtfully. 'But I think Mrs Cartwright might be one of the many who, um, contributed to Mr Williams's little collection.'

'Not so little, in that case,' said Charles with a smile. 'Edna Cartwright is... how shall I put this? A strapping lass, yes, that just about covers it.'

'Hmm,' said Sarah, visions of very large ladies' knickers now billowing in her mind's eye. 'I must say, I'm less and less surprised someone bumped Mr Williams off.' She frowned, but then cheered up at the sight of the two slices of cake, resplendent in an open box. Charles pushed a cup of tea over to her, nice and strong, just the way she liked it.

'Well, try not to think about that for a moment, at least. After all, this is the life, isn't it?' said Charles, turning his eyes to the beach. It was a fine sight on this sunny day, the sand blindingly white, and the sea good-naturedly splashing the feet of various toddlers and intrepid bathers. 'Dogs OK?'

'They've been as good as gold,' Sarah said, looking down at Hamish rather guiltily. In fact, he'd been behaving so well she'd almost forgotten he was there. She soon saw why. Tinkerbell was now asleep with her little muzzle tucked onto his leg. He was clearly terrified to move, in case he broke the spell. He panted at Sarah very gently, almost as though he was smiling, and then went to sleep himself, a blissed-out expression on his little face.

'They're getting on well, aren't they?' said Charles, with a rather suggestive arch to his eyebrow. Sarah, who was a bit fed up with the way both dog and master blew hot and cold, confined herself to a wintry smile. Charles had not seemed particularly pleased to see her earlier, on the beach. And yet here he was, buying her snacks and seeming to hint at more. She just couldn't work him out.

'Shall we have a look at this cake, then?' she said, keeping her tone purely practical and pulling the box towards her.

'Wonderful. I'm quite peckish,' said Charles, rubbing his stomach. Then, when Sarah made no move to put the slices onto their plates, and instead studied them carefully from all angles, before prodding one with a fork, he let his mouth droop in disappointment. 'Oh, I see. You mean that kind of look.'

'Well, that's what we're here for,' Sarah reminded him as she continued to probe one of the pieces.

'Oh, all right. So, go on. What do you make of it, then?'

'On the face of it, it's pretty similar to the one at Williams's house,' said Sarah thoughtfully.

'It would be, though, wouldn't it?' Charles looked a little disdainful. 'A sponge is a sponge, after all.'

'That's where you're wrong,' said Sarah. 'You've never made one, have you?' As she already knew he'd had a housekeeper when he'd lived in Francesca's beautiful Georgian mansion, and she hadn't seen much baking equipment in his chic loft-style flat above his shop, the one time she had been there (early in the morning, and with Daphne as chaperone), this seemed a safe bet. And, sure enough, Charles shook his head ruefully.

'All right then, Prue Leith. Tell me all about baking sponges.'

'Actually, this isn't really about the process as such,' Sarah said thoughtfully, still examining the box from all angles and chopping up the cakes. 'As any sponge will be made by more or less the same method. It's the additional extras I'm interested in. You know, the frills each baker adds to make their cake special.'

'Well, both of those look special. Or they did,' said Charles, staring at the box of bits rather disconsolately.

'Don't worry Charles, it'll still all taste the same,' Sarah said. 'Go on then, have a piece,' she added, shoving the box his way.

'Sure you've finished ruining them?' he said, the look in his blue eyes belying his words.

'Just about. This cake didn't kill Williams.'

Charles, who'd been in the act of chewing one of the larger bits of sponge, almost choked.

'What?' said Sarah. 'Surely that's good news?'

'I suppose it is.' Charles took a sip of his tea and started to look a little better. 'It just reminded me.'

'But it's the whole point of the exercise, isn't it?'

'Well, for me, it was having a slice of cake in good company,' Charles said, looking at her under those heavy lids.

Sarah decided to ignore this. 'Don't you want to know why I'm ruling this cake out?'

'Go on then. Astonish me.' He smiled.

'Simple. No fresh strawberries, for one thing. The slices aren't sitting on a doily, and the piece in Williams's home was. And this jam looks like raspberry, rather than strawberry.' Sarah sat back, with a pleased look on her face, and selected a cube of cake from the box. It really was very good; light as air, and perfectly complemented by the soft, rich cream.

Charles was silent for a second, and then he spoke up. 'Have you thought, though, Sarah? Some of these criteria you're using come down to simple logistics. The cake shop, whichever it might have been, could have had loads of strawberries when the murderer was buying their slice. But today, they may have just run out.'

Sarah sat back, perplexed. 'I suppose you're right,' she said slowly. 'But I do think there are certain things about a cake which always come out the same, with the same cook. They don't call it a "signature bake" on *The Great British Bake Off* for nothing. However similar the method, everyone still has a unique style. This cake isn't like the one in that room. The crumb is, well, less crumbly.'

'Now that I come to think of it,' said Charles, after chewing vigorously. 'I think you're right about bakers having a consistent style. My old nanny had a very heavy hand. I loved her cakes, but every one of them weighed about as much as I did,' he said. 'Whereas Mrs Chivers – Francesca's housekeeper, you know – she makes a very light lemon drizzle. But somehow, I don't know, it lacks something...' Charles looked towards the sea, a little frown between his brows.

Sarah, who was secretly rather pleased that he wasn't still hankering after the sweet treats of his married life, confined herself to a neutral, 'Oh, really?' while raising her tea to her lips. 'Now there's only one question we need to sort out.'

'What's that?' said Charles, turning to face her again.

'Why, which cake shop we should go to next,' said Sarah, smiling over the rim of her cup.

TEN

Sarah and Charles were just scooping up their belongings, including their two dogs, when there was a 'Coo-ee' from the other side of the esplanade. Daphne was right in front of Tarot and Tealeaves, waving her arms around like a windmill in a hurricane.

'I think Daphne just might be trying to get our attention,' said Charles drily.

Sarah, secretly wondering if Daphne had somehow heard the words 'cake test' on the ether, maybe even via her beloved Beyond, waved back.

'Stay where you are, Daph, we're coming your way,' she said. She crossed the road with Hamish while Charles was still trying to tuck an uncooperative Tinkerbell under his arm.

'I've always wondered why such a tall man would get such a weeny dog,' said Daphne, starting to giggle as Sarah joined her.

Sarah couldn't help agreeing it was a slightly preposterous sight, but tried her best not to join in. 'I don't suppose he had much say in the matter, do you? I bet Francesca just marched to the breeders and asked for something highly strung, yappy and impossibly overbred.'

'Just like her, you mean,' said Daphne, collapsing into huge guffaws now.

Sarah, whose lips were beginning to twitch in earnest, had to turn away as Charles finally crossed over the road to join them.

'What's so funny, you two?' he asked, while Sarah concentrated hard on pretending to read a board of small ads in Daphne's shop window.

Daphne, caught on the hop, said vaguely, 'Oh, just talking about poor old Mr Williams, you know.'

Sarah, still glued to the ads, winced. Sure enough, Charles didn't seem convinced. 'I don't think it's really all that hilarious, is it?' He raised his eyebrows.

'Oh, you know Sarah. It's the way she tells them,' said an unrepentant Daphne.

Sarah, deciding she'd have words with her friend later, was about to wheel round and change the subject, when one of the rather fly-blown cards caught her eye.

Gardening services. Too busy to mow your lawn or dig your beds? I can help. Call Derek Williams on 01208 983489.

'Never mind all that, you two. Look at this. Do you think it could actually be... Surely not? Did Mr Williams place this card in the window himself, Daphne? Do you remember?'

'Well, of course I remember everyone who advertises with me, obviously. I'm a responsible shop owner,' said Daphne. Then she craned forward to see what Sarah was pointing at. 'Oh! Oh, that. Um, well, to be honest, I have no recollection of that going up at all.'

'How does the board work, Daph?' Sarah said, surveying it while Charles leant in for a closer look and then shrank back, as if he'd been stung. 'People come to you with the cards already filled in, do they?'

'Yes, and then they pay me a little bit to put them up. Just a tenner or something like that. There's no harm in it,' Daphne said defensively.

'No harm... when we now know Mr Williams stole people's underwear?'

'Well, the card doesn't say, "Give me a ring and I'll steal your knickers", does it?' Daphne snapped.

'No, but he was asking to be let into back gardens, where people's washing lines are... where they hang out their underthings...'

'Do you think that's what he was up to?' said Daphne, shocked.

'Don't you?' Sarah shrugged. 'It's, well, quite unsavoury, isn't it?'

'Speak for your own smalls,' said Daphne. It was an attempt at levity, but she was looking very anxious. 'Goodness, this is bad, isn't it? The thing is, I don't always have time to worry about the small print. I'm doing a public service.'

Sarah tilted her head at that. 'I'm not sure if allowing him access to other people's undergarments was that public-spirited, Daph.'

'Well, how was I to know?' said Daphne, sounding distressed.

'You're right, what's done is done,' said Sarah hastily, seeing her friend was beginning to look woebegone. 'And we don't know if anyone took Mr Williams up on his, erm, services. But if they did, then it might well add to the tally of people who had a motive to get rid of him.'

'It could have been a genuinely nice offer. After all, he was probably lonely and wanted to help people,' said Daphne.

'Usually, I would only feel the greatest sympathy,' said Sarah, whose fear of solitude had been acute after being widowed. 'But I make an exception for Mr Williams. With his weird hobby, he deserved to be on his own.'

'I agree wholeheartedly,' said Charles, looking fierce.

'Well, I vote we carry on with our plan. It ought to take the nasty taste out of our mouths, at least,' said Sarah, hoping to diffuse the tension a little.

'Oh? What was this? I don't seem to be in on your scheme,' said Daphne, looking from Sarah to Charles and back again.

'We've decided to test all the sponges in Merstairs, to see if we can identify where the poisoned cake was bought from,' said Charles, rubbing his hands.

In the blink of an eye, Daphne changed from anxious to electrified. 'Now that's the kind of careful, well-thought-out idea I can really get behind,' she said, a big smile illuminating her mobile face. 'Where do we start?'

ELEVEN

Perhaps Sarah, Daphne and Charles didn't really have to taste every single cake in Merstairs. They could just have looked at them in shop windows, or under glass domes, or in chiller cabinets, and made their deductions from there. But that didn't seem quite in keeping with the spirit of their sacred quest – or not according to Daphne, anyway.

While Sarah was much less able than her companions to lose herself in the tasting, and forget the very important reason why they were exposing themselves to huge numbers of (delicious) calories, even she couldn't resist the high spirits that infected the little party as they did the rounds of all the prime eateries that afternoon.

They were currently in the Mermaid Café, sheltered under the rocky outcrop of the cliffs above Merstairs, enjoying a beautifully airy sponge which was disqualified as a poison vehicle by virtue of the artistic swirl of raspberry coulis on their plates, as well as the buttercream filling and lack of doily. One reason why they were not slowing down in their quest was that they were pacing themselves sensibly, having ordered one cake between them, with three spoons. Sarah was having to fight to test anything at all, though of course she could have ruled this one out as soon as Charles had brought it over to their table. Still, she didn't want to be a spoilsport, now did she?

Daphne sat back with a satisfied sigh, licking the last smear of coulis off her spoon with evident relish. 'I think that might have been the best yet,' she said. 'Gosh, I'm exhausted.'

'There's nothing like a day's honest toil,' said Sarah, a gleam in her eye.

'Well, you can laugh, but this takes a lot of concentration. I'd put this one slightly below the Quayside Café, but just that smidgeon higher than the Blue Door Deli on the high street.'

'You do remember we're not just ranking these sponges?'

'We're not?' Daphne sat up in consternation. 'What have I been making notes for, then? Honestly, Sarah, you could have told me.' She now adopted a mulish expression.

'Well, as I haven't seen you writing a single thing down, I'm not feeling too bad,' said Sarah.

'*Mental* notes. I've been jamming up brain cells that I could have been using to channel vibrations from the Beyond for my customers.' Daphne looked most disgruntled.

'Jamming, yes, most certainly, dear lady,' said Charles, dipping a teaspoon into a pool of coulis and savouring it. 'Lots of this delicious raspberry jamming.' He twinkled his blue eyes at Daphne and she couldn't resist an answering smile.

'Well, fine,' she said. 'But Sarah, I can't give you that much more time, not if we're just going to be idling away the afternoon. Actually,' she added slowly. 'I've been thinking I should maybe rejoin ScaleScanners. Perhaps I should be going along to a meeting instead of doing this.' She looked round at Charles and Sarah as she spoke, and then seemed to be waiting for something.

'Um, really?' said Sarah.

'You're absolutely right, Sarah, I don't need to at all. Well,

I'm glad that's settled,' said Daphne, sitting back with the air of someone who'd won a long and vigorous argument.

'Oh, I wouldn't want to stop you if you felt you needed to...' Sarah said tentatively.

'I'm fond of Mavis, of course,' Daphne said, as though Sarah hadn't spoken. 'And I'd like to support her. We female entrepreneurs should stick together. She's just come up with that clever ScaleScanners app, she's such a wizard with the tech. It's just that she can be a bit, well, judgy. Obviously I always make excellent progress. You know me, Sarah, I hardly touch sweet things,' she said, wiping a cake crumb from her mouth. 'But some of the other ScaleScanners slip up sometimes and Mavis can have a bit of a go at the weigh-in. Woe betide anyone who's put on even a couple of ounces.'

'There's a public weigh-in?' Sarah raised her brows.

'Of course. That's when the scales get scanned, silly,' Daphne said. 'Mavis tells us how we're doing and we get a round of applause or not – depending on whether we've gone up or down.'

'I must say, it sounds completely ghastly,' said Charles, with the carelessness of someone who'd been as lean as a greyhound since birth, despite his apparently bottomless appetite for sponge cake.

Sarah rather agreed, but didn't want to discourage Daphne if she wanted to make healthy changes. 'I'd understand if you wanted to prioritise your meeting. But this is very important, after all. We're trying to locate the killer's cake, remember?'

'When you put it like that, it sounds quite off-putting. I don't want to get poisoned,' said Daphne, pushing her plate away.

'It's the style of cake we're interested in. I'm no keener than you to encounter any cyanide. I did explain all this at the beginning,' said Sarah patiently.

'Did you? I probably had a message coming in from the other side,' said Daphne vaguely.

'I see,' said Sarah. 'Well, all right then. It's completely your choice. But maybe if you are going to stick around, you should choose where we go next. My turn to buy the cake. Unless you don't have time?'

Sarah watched as Daphne fought various competing urges – the need to be seen as an important practitioner in clairvoyance, a waning urge to pop into ScaleScanners, and the desire to eat at least her body weight in cake, at Sarah's expense.

'Oh, very well then, just one more,' she said at length, but a smile was peeping out and her hand came down to pat Sarah's. They grinned at each other, in harmony once again.

'So, we just have to decide where. We've covered quite a lot of ground already. I think we should be strategic and concentrate on cakes filled with cream now. Anyone got any suggestions?' Sarah asked brightly.

'Well, we're almost on the doorstep, so we could just nip over to Marlene's,' said Charles.

'You mean Marlene's Plaice? The fish and chip shop?' Sarah was astonished.

'She does cakes as well. Rather good ones. With a good thick layer of cream,' said Charles enthusiastically.

'Trust you to know what all the pretty ladies are up to,' Daphne joshed him.

Sarah had never thought about Marlene's looks before – the number of shades of mauve in her shop always blinded her to anything else – but now Daphne mentioned it, she realised Marlene was an attractive woman. She was trim, with strawberry blonde hair which went well with all that purple, and large violet-blue eyes. And she was at least ten years younger than Sarah. Suddenly she remembered the way Marlene's interest had been piqued, not so long ago, when Charles had briefly been arrested. At the time, Sarah had just thought she was pouncing on an intriguing nugget of gossip, which was a vital currency in Merstairs. But maybe there was more to it than that?

'Yes, let's go to Marlene's,' she said, with a determined set to her jaw. Finding the fatal cream sponge was still uppermost in her mind – but if she could kill two birds with one stone, then so be it.

TWELVE

A couple of minutes later, Sarah, Daphne and Charles were installed outside Marlene's Plaice, with another glorious view of fishing boats bobbing on the calm seas in front of them – when they could see them, through the throng of tourists drifting past. Hamish and Tinkerbell were taking it in turns to drink out of the bowl of water at their humans' feet; Hamish spraying it everywhere, as was his wont, and Tinkerbell lapping like a tiny woodland creature. All the other tables were taken, and a harassed waitress in Marlene's purple uniform was dashing hither and thither, trying to keep everyone happy.

Just then, Marlene herself came out and made a beeline for their table. 'Can aye take your order?' It was addressed to the table in general; why, then, did Sarah feel the question was aimed at Charles in particular? He was also doing that thing which meant he was a bit embarrassed, hiding behind his menu and refusing to make eye contact with anyone. He'd been like that with her, just this morning on the beach, for reasons that still weren't clear. Hmm, thought Sarah.

'I'll have the Victoria sponge,' she said, to no one's surprise. 'And an English breakfast tea with milk, please.'

'Lovely,' said Marlene absently, scribbling on her pad. 'And you, modom?'

Daphne giggled. 'Oh, just call me Daphne, Marlene. No need to be formal with such, erm, old friends,' she added, digging Charles in the ribs.

'I'll have the same as Sarah,' said Charles, ignoring Daphne and avoiding everyone's eyes.

'Make that three,' said Daphne.

'Are you sure, you two? You don't want to... share?' Sarah asked. At this point in the day, they'd all had a lot of cake. But to her surprise, the others seemed willing to put such considerations aside and press on. For the good of the investigation, no doubt, she smiled to herself. Marlene's cakes must be really good.

What seemed like only moments later, the waitress came out with their order, and Sarah's suspicions were proved correct. The cakes looked light enough to float away. They also boasted a satisfying layer of rich fresh cream in the middle. That wasn't what had got Sarah's pulses racing, though. It was the fact that, under each slice of cake, there was something rather significant.

As Daphne's hand came out to grab a plate and Charles dived in, making as if to take one of the teapots, Sarah almost yelled in frustration, 'Stop!'

Her friends swivelled to look at her, jaws sagging slightly. There was even a slight interruption in the flow of tourists passing their table, as though the calm waters had become stormy.

Sarah looked at the blank faces in front of her and tutted. 'Don't you see? Tell me you've spotted that?' she said, pointing at one of the pieces of cake with a quivering knife.

'Yes, it looks very nice,' said Daphne, in a voice that suggested she was humouring a madwoman. 'I don't think she's used to the heat, you know,' she said in a perfectly audible aside to Charles.

'Honestly,' tutted Sarah. 'The gold doilies, you two! Under the cakes. Don't you see what that could mean?'

'Ohh,' said Daphne, picking up her plate and moving it around, like a jeweller inspecting a promising diamond. Then she put it down. 'Um, no, actually. What are you on about?'

'Well, Mr Williams's cake was on a doily. I did mention that earlier, didn't I?'

'You did,' conceded Charles, his tone languid. 'But you see, this doily surely isn't going to be the one you're after.'

'Really? Why not?' said Sarah, with a bit more feistiness than his comment perhaps deserved. But for some reason she was feeling a little out of sorts with Charles.

Charles stared at her for a second, then took his own plate. 'Well, because of this,' he said, poising his fork to shift the cake to one side. Under the table, Hamish stirred, sensing a complicated manoeuvre with food which might repay those waiting patiently for crumbs. But Charles continued without incident, shoving the sponge out of the way and revealing the doily. The golden outside was so similar to Mr Williams's that they could have been long-lost twins. But right in the centre of this one was a large purple circle, with *Marlene's Plaice* picked out in white. Sarah should have guessed Marlene would never let a branding opportunity pass her by. But then she thought again.

'There's nothing to say that the one in Williams's house wasn't like this. Sure, I thought it was all gold – but it could have had this underneath all the time, hidden by the cake.'

'But I thought you said he'd had a good bite out of it,' Charles said.

Sarah's shoulders slumped. She took herself back into that small, airless room, the horrible crime scene. And she sighed. Charles was right, the purple would have shown. Even though

Williams hadn't polished off much cake, there was enough gone to reveal some purple, if there had been any. There had not. They were back to square one.

'Nice try though, Sarah,' said Daphne, taking a lavish forkful of her own portion. 'Nearly framed your rival there.'

Luckily, the second part of her sentence was quite indistinct, thanks to the sponge, so Sarah could simply pretend she hadn't heard it. But Daphne really did take the biscuit. When she wasn't taking the cake, of course. Sarah picked at her own slice a little disconsolately. It wasn't that she wanted to see Marlene carted off in chains. Perish the thought! She only wanted to see justice done.

The whole issue of how much of the slice Mr Williams had eaten did raise a question, though. He'd only had that one bite, which must mean the cyanide had been pretty potent. She was willing to bet it must have been administered via a syringe or paste into the cream. What did that tell her?

'Sarah? Sarah! Oh, it's no good, Charles. I know what she's like when she's got that look on her face. She's wrestling with some clue or other. You should see her with *The Times* crossword sometimes. She just goes at it like a terrier and there's no talking to her until she's got the whole thing straightened out,' Daphne grumbled loudly.

'I'm not deaf, you know, Daphne,' said Sarah, with as much dignity as she could manage. 'Something just occurred to me... about the murder. I would have said it out loud but I know how squeamish you get about things.'

'Squeamish? Moi? I'll have you know I had to bury half a field mouse this morning. Mephisto left it on the doormat for me as a special present. He tries to be so thoughtful, bless him. So I've seen *everything*, believe you me,' Daphne said.

Sarah shrugged. She was only surprised the dreadful cat didn't leave the severed limbs of tradesmen dotted about as love tokens for her friend. 'OK then. Well, I'd say someone dosed one particular area of the cake with poison, and they added it after the cake was cooked.'

'Would cyanide be effective after cooking, anyway?' said Charles.

'That's a good question, I'm not sure it would still be as deadly, the compound could be affected by the heating process... Daphne, are you all right?'

'Um, yes. I think a crumb has gone down the wrong way, I feel a bit... Back in a second.' With that, Daphne shot through the door of the café, looking quite green about the gills.

'I hope she's OK,' Sarah said, fidgeting with her napkin. 'Poor Daphne, I shouldn't have taken her at her word. You know what she's like about murder. I ought to go and see how she is.'

'She'll be fine. Stay for a second,' said Charles, putting his hand on Sarah's, just as she was gathering up her bag to go after her friend.

'Oh,' said Sarah, stilled by this gesture, and looking up suddenly into Charles's blue eyes. Peter had always sweetly said her own eyes were like a summer sky – but she knew they were not a patch on the brilliant azure now gazing down at her.

Charles cleared his throat. 'Um, you know I told you a while ago that Francesca was filing divorce papers...'

'Yes?' Sarah suddenly felt breathless. At her feet, Hamish moved restlessly and she found herself hoping against hope he wasn't going to start barking up a storm. It sometimes happened after he'd been very peaceful for a while.

'Well, we've now got to the stage where... I suppose what I'm trying to say is—'

'I might have known I'd find you here, idling away the day.' A familiar voice cut through the chatter of the holidaymakers and ensured all eyes were on Sarah's table. Charles whipped his hand away as though he'd been stung by an extra-large hornet and a moment later Francesca Diggory bore down on them.

'Excuse me,' said Sarah, leaping to her feet. 'I must check on

Daphne. Charles, can you keep an eye on Hamish, please?'
Without waiting for an answer, she shot through the café door
and made for the ladies' loo.

'Well, *really*,' she heard Francesca say behind her as the
door shut.

THIRTEEN

Inside the toilets, Sarah caught her breath. All was quiet – and heavily fragranced with lavender. As well as lavender hand-wash, lavender moisturising cream and three large vases of actual lavender, the room was painted a dark shade of purple and the towels, of course, matched the theme. It was really quite claustrophobic and didn't help Sarah's gathering sense of unease about her friend.

'Daphne? Are you in here?' Sarah said. All three cubicle doors were firmly shut, and didn't have the kind of locks that showed whether they were in use or not.

The place stayed silent, save the slow dripping of a tap. Sarah was becoming quite alarmed.

'Are you OK, Daphne? Please say something if you're in here,' she said, urgency in her tone. There was nothing for another beat, and then Daphne erupted out of one of the stalls.

'Oh Sarah, you must think I'm so silly,' she said, tears streaming down her face.

'Goodness, Daph, what on earth is the matter?' Sarah said, enfolding her friend in a hug. 'There's nothing to get worked up about, is there? I thought you were feeling a bit peaky as we were discussing the, um, cake,' she said as delicately as she could, not wishing to provoke a repeat performance.

'It's not that,' Daphne said, drawing away a little and rubbing the backs of her hands over her cheeks, smearing tears and a surprisingly large amount of sooty mascara everywhere. 'I mean, of course I do have a very delicate stomach, you know,' she said earnestly.

Sarah nodded. 'Um, so what's got you so upset?'

'It's just... I'm really hopeless at this,' Daphne said, waving an arm to encompass the bathroom, her own reflection in the mirror, even Sarah herself.

'At what? I'm not sure what you're on about, Daph dear. You can't mean you're not a good friend,' Sarah said, patting her arm reassuringly. 'Because there's none better, you know that.'

'Oh, of course I know *that*,' said Daphne, now looking a bit put out. 'Obviously I have my strengths.' She drew herself up to her full height and even started adjusting her scarf, which Sarah saw as a very good sign that she was recovering her normal high spirits. But one edge of the silky material refused to cooperate, and kept hanging down. After poking at it for a few seconds, Daphne flopped forward, dropping her head and steadying herself on the basin. 'The thing is, I'm hopeless as a detective.'

Sarah did a double-take. 'Daphne! How can you say that, when we've been so successful?' At once, Daphne gave a disapproving tut. 'Well, OK, perhaps that isn't quite the way to look at it... but you have to admit we've been very effective. We've removed terrible people from the streets, we've made this lovely place safer. We've done good work, Daphne.'

'*You've* done it, you mean. You've been the analytical one, making the clues slot together... I've just bumbled around being, what was it you said? Squeamish.'

Inwardly, Sarah was cursing herself. She should never have used that word. 'Look, Daphne,' she said, thinking quickly. 'You haven't had medical training, that's all. If you had, you'd be hardened to that sort of stuff. It's not your fault.'

Daphne looked up, and for the first time in what seemed an age, a tiny smile peeped out. 'You're right. I'm usually in a more ethereal realm, that's the problem.'

'Are you? Oh yes, of course, you're totally... in the Beyond,' said Sarah. She was trying to be supportive but knew there would always be a suggestion of quizzical inverted commas when she used her friend's favourite word. 'And that's fine. If there's a spiritual dimension to our investigation, well, we've certainly got that covered with you around, haven't we?'

'Totally,' said Daphne, smiling more broadly now, and again trying to wipe the mascara off her face.

'Here, let me,' said Sarah, moistening the edge of a paper towel under the tap and giving her friend's face a quick once-over. 'You know, I did the same for Evelyn right here the other day. She'd got ketchup from her chips everywhere.' Sarah remembered her tiny granddaughter's smeary little face fondly. 'There. You're perfect now,' she said.

'Thanks, Sarah. You're a pal,' Daphne said and the two smiled at each other.

'I should think so! After all this time,' Sarah said lightly. 'Now, let's get back out there. Charles will think we've gone down the plughole or something. And Francesca arrived just when I came after you. I hope he's still in one piece.'

'That woman. When will she just decide to leave him alone?' Daphne said crossly as they walked back through the restaurant.

Sarah sighed. She'd love the answer to that particular question. In the meantime, she'd have to settle for the riddle currently facing them – which shop in Merstairs had produced the deadly sponge? If it wasn't Marlene's Plaice, despite the cream and the doily, then who on earth could it be? She decided a palate cleanser was necessary – they would focus on strawberry slices next.

FOURTEEN

Francesca was nowhere to be seen when Sarah and Daphne rejoined Charles at the table, and he was a little quiet. They paid Marlene and moved on, relying on Daphne's encyclopaedic knowledge of shops that put strawberry slices in their sponge as they left the seafront, and tried the little row of boutique cafés in the high street. They also reverted to buying one cake between three, as even Charles's enthusiasm for the task seemed to be abating. By the time they tackled the remaining scraps of one last Victoria sponge, this time bought from the Willow Pattern Tea Shop, Charles had fallen virtually silent. Sarah had felt they might make a breakthrough here, as it was the scene of the art classes, but the strawberries were much too thickly cut, and to make matters worse there was no dusting of icing sugar on the top of the sponge.

With a rather leaden feeling in her stomach, Sarah poked the last remaining crumbs with her fork and decided she had to speak up. 'There was that other clue at the murder scene, of course. The betting slip with those letters scrawled on it.'

'Now she tells us,' said Daphne with a groan. 'You mean

there was another lead we could have followed, and we needn't have eaten all this cake?'

'No one held a gun to your head, Daph. Anyway, you heard about the betting slip when I discussed it with Mariella. The letters, PB or HB, or even MT, and the number thirteen.'

'I wish you'd jogged my memory before. That's just the sort of thing I could ask my spirit guide about,' said Daphne mulishly.

'Until then, maybe we could brainstorm it together?' Sarah tried to sound enthusiastic, though she felt her own little grey cells were somewhat clogged up with jam and cream at this point. 'Do we know anyone with those initials, for example? There's Pat Buchanan, I suppose.'

'Huh, you'd love it if Pat was in trouble,' Daphne huffed. 'You've never liked her.'

Sarah held her hands up. 'If it comes to that, there are lots of other people with those initials.'

'You're not suggesting any, though.'

As usual, in response to a challenge Sarah thought harder. 'Well, there's someone in the art class, isn't there? Penny Booth.'

'Of course!' said Daphne. 'But it can't be her, can it? I've known her for ages.'

'I'm just saying, she's got the right initials... though it could have been an H at the beginning too.' Sarah frowned. 'We should check what Penny and Pat were up to before the art class, anyway.'

Daphne rubbed her stomach. 'OK. Oh, all this thinking has given me indigestion.'

'I'm not sure it was the thinking,' Sarah said, trying to ease her own tight waistband. 'I can't believe we've done all that testing and not found the right cake – or the wrong one, if you see what I mean.'

'Well, I've thoroughly enjoyed the experiment,' said Charles, but his hangdog face belied the statement. And talking of hangdogs, there were two of them under the table. Sarah had stopped Daphne giving Hamish snippets of sponge, but once a crumb hit the floor, it had been every dog for themselves.

'I've just thought,' said Daphne. 'Whoever it was could have bought a cake from one place and a doily from another, couldn't they? To throw us off the scent.'

'But you can't buy doilies round here, though, can you? I don't know when I last saw one in a shop,' said Sarah.

'Norbert's. The catering suppliers,' said Charles succinctly.

'What? There's a company here that sells them? Is it open to the public?'

'I believe so,' said Charles.

'Right. Come on then, let's go,' said Sarah, sitting up straighter and then slightly wishing she hadn't. 'In fact, the sooner we get up and get moving, the better. If we stay sitting here we'll just turn into slices of sponge.'

'Ugh,' said Daphne. 'Never mention that word again. OK, I'm in. Take us to Norbert's, Charles.'

It was a relief to be up and walking again, although the dogs were lagging behind. Sarah hoped Hamish was OK. But then her sensible side took over. A morsel of cake wasn't going to undo all the well-balanced meals he wolfed down. And the little Scottie was partial to eating things that must be far worse for his health – ancient, malodorous nasties on the beach, for instance. He'd be fine.

After a five-minute ramble back towards the centre of Merstairs, they found themselves outside Norbert's. A stack of copper-bottomed, cheffy-looking pans gleamed enticingly in the large plate-glass window, while a display of ceramic bowls in delectable sugared almond shades reminded Sarah of the beach huts on the seafront. It was going to be hard work resisting all these kitchen goodies. Sarah quickly tied Hamish up outside and Charles did the same with Tinkerbell. Both dogs were still too full to complain.

'Right, here goes. After you, ladies,' said Charles, holding the door open as Sarah and Daphne stepped inside. Immediately, Daphne veered off with a cry of joy to check out some wildly patterned tea towels. Sarah and Charles made their way more cautiously round a pyramid of glass jam jars – reminding Sarah she needed to be ready for strawberry season – to find a solitary member of staff behind the till.

'I'm sorry to trouble you, we were looking for doilies?' Sarah said politely.

'Dollies?' said the spotty youth, disengaging briefly from his mobile phone. 'Wrong place, missus. You want the toy shop on the seafront.'

'No, erm, those paper things that go under cakes, you know,' said Charles, in a bluff, man-to-man tone which strongly suggested he felt this whole business rather emasculating.

'Here, let me,' said Sarah, deciding things would go more quickly if she took over. She held her hand out for the boy's phone and quickly keyed the correct spelling into his search engine. When the page loaded, he said, 'Oh, yeah, *those*,' as though he was an archaeologist whose painstaking work had uncovered a surprising artefact from a long-dead civilisation. Sarah and Charles looked at each other patiently.

'Over there, innit?' the boy said, waving his arm in the general direction of the back of the shop.

'Right. Well, thanks so much,' said Sarah, confining herself to a mental tut. The duo made their way through a maze of roasting tins and state-of-the-art coffee machines. At the back of the shop they found folded paper tablecloths of every possible size and quite a few different colours, as well as paper napkins, plates, cups and disposable cutlery. Then, behind everything else, Sarah spotted a stack of doilies.

There weren't that many, considering the profusion of styles and hues of almost everything else. For a second, she felt rather disappointed. Then, looking more closely, she struck gold. These were exactly the same as the doily underneath the fatal slice of cake.

'Charles, do you see what I see?' she asked, then turned to him. But his attention was far away, all the way over at the front of the shop, in fact. While the employee had retreated back to his phone, and was playing music through his earbuds if the odd pecking motion of his head was anything to go by, Tinkerbell had pressed her tiny face up against the window and was busy causing multiple smears on the pristine surface with her paws. The shop door must have been well insulated, as Sarah could hardly hear anything, but from the way the dog's jaws were opening and closing, she could tell there was plenty of barking going on. 'You'd better go and sort her out,' Sarah said, resigned to making the rest of the necessary enquiries on her own.

Charles didn't need telling twice, beetling over to the door as quickly as he could. Sarah could see him outside, scooping up his little dog and cradling her to his chest, whispering soothing words to her. Much though she was reserving judgement on the pesky creature, she couldn't help but melt at seeing how devoted Charles was to his pet.

Anyway, that was beside the point, she told herself sternly as she marched back to the boy behind the till, who was now clicking his tongue in time to his phantom tune.

'Excuse me,' said Sarah, trying to get his attention. But she might as well have been invisible.

'Here, let me,' said Daphne, suddenly materialising at Sarah's shoulder with a swish of her scarf. She leant forward and tapped the lad on the shoulder, causing him to jump about a foot in the air. One of his earbuds fell out as he came back to earth and he looked from one woman to the other in startled enquiry.

'Well, now that we've got your attention... can you remember who you might have sold these doilies to, recently?' Sarah asked politely.

The boy continued to look at her as though she was speaking a foreign language.

'My friend asked if you've sold any of these lately?' Daphne repeated at a decibel level that would surely have commanded even the late Mr Williams's attention, it was so loud. Charles, outside tending to the dogs, looked up and peered through the window worriedly.

'How would I k-know?' stuttered the employee miserably.

'Well, you could use your *memory*,' said Daphne, thankfully a little less loudly.

Sarah decided it was time to interrupt. 'It would have been fairly recently, say Sunday or Monday? A single one of these doilies, or maybe even a lot of them?'

'I have no idea. You can't expect me to remember who I sell things to,' the boy said, incredulous.

'Why not? We're the only customers at the moment, and I don't suppose you've been rushed off your feet in the last week,' said Daphne trenchantly.

The boy just shrugged in response, and his fingers twitched, as though he was dying to plug himself into his phone again and blank out the irritations of the real world, currently represented by Daphne and Sarah.

Then Sarah had a brainwave. 'Do you have any CCTV here?' she asked.

The boy looked up. Sure enough, there was the tell-tale shiny lens of a camera pointing down at the cash desk. Sarah wasn't sure whether it was there to check the staff were conscious, or keep an eye on the customers, but either way it could prove very useful.

'Could we see the tapes?' she asked.

The boy shied away as though she'd requested a viewing of his underwear – fairly appropriate given Mr Williams's proclivities, Sarah supposed. 'I don't know about that. I'd have to ask Dad.'

'Do you have his number? I can give him a call,' Sarah offered, and the boy gladly gave it to her. Anything to avoid strenuous decision-making on his own part, it seemed. He looked thrilled when Sarah and Daphne said their thank-yous and departed the shop.

Outside, Charles was cradling Tinkerbell, who had a most affronted look on her bug-eyed face. Hamish, meanwhile, was looking at her with a loving gaze that seemed beautifully innocent... maybe too innocent.

'Is everything OK?' Sarah asked quickly, stooping to pat Hamish.

'Oh, er, I think Hamish there tried to get a little, erm, frisky, shall we say?'

'Really?' said Sarah. Her first thought was that her boy would surely never have tried to impose himself on anyone. He just wasn't that sort of dog. But then, he had been pining after Tinkerbell for so long... She shook her head, and realised that she should give Tinkerbell the benefit of the doubt. 'Well, I'm terribly sorry if Hamish was being less than a gentleman. I hope you'll forgive him, Tinks,' she said, making to stroke the little dog on the head.

Immediately, Tinkerbell bared her teeth and started up a bloodcurdling growl, a sound all the more terrifying coming from such a small dog.

'Oh!' said Sarah in surprise, whipping her hand away.

'Well, it's my turn to apologise,' said Charles ruefully. 'I just can't think what's got into her.'

'Francesca's probably got her trained,' said Daphne with a chortle. 'This is why I stick to cats. They're so much less trouble.'

Sarah, whose dog had suffered grievous bodily harm at the paws of Daphne's Mephisto, changed the subject – though she certainly wouldn't have put it past the mayor to encourage her dog to hate. 'Well, I vote we call the shop lad's father and ask him about the CCTV footage,' she said.

'What CCTV footage?' came a voice. There, right behind them, was Mariella, with her usual expression of mingled affection and exasperation.

'Mari, you gave me a shock! Do they teach you to creep up on people now in the police?' Daphne protested.

Mariella smiled. 'One of the many great things about being out of uniform is that I can wear these nice soft-soled shoes. I'd never tiptoe up to anyone just to eavesdrop on their secrets, even if they were the self-styled sleuths of Merstairs.'

Sarah coughed. 'Excellent that you're here, Mariella. I was just about to ask for your expert input on this,' she said, rather hoping to delegate the task of watching CCTV of the residents of Merstairs buying jam pots for an entire week.

'Hmm. So, what might I find on this tape, if I did get someone to check it?' Mariella asked.

Sarah earnestly explained their idea that the doily under the fatal slice of sponge could have come from Norbert's. Mariella looked round at each of them in turn – and then burst out laughing.

FIFTEEN

'Honestly, you three crack me up,' Mariella said when she could speak again. Sarah, Charles and Daphne looked on with varying degrees of dismay. 'Don't you think that doily was the first thing we looked into?'

Sarah felt a swoop of disappointment. 'I'd have expected that to have been the cyanide,' she said in a dignified manner.

'The lab is dealing with that side of the forensics. But I've had Tweedledum and Tweedledee – um, I mean—'

'Those idiots, yes, we know,' said Daphne helpfully.

Mariella paused for a moment before going on. 'My *colleagues* have been conducting some investigations. And they've already ascertained exactly where the doily came from. Ah, now, before you even ask,' she said quickly, as her little audience clamoured to speak. 'I will not be telling you its origin. But we have traced it and they're now squeezing all the information they can out of the sponge.'

Daphne snorted loudly. Sarah tried her best not to join in and smile at the image and she carried on. 'There was something else we thought of – Pat Buchanan and Penny Booth from the art group. Either of them might be a fit for the initials on that betting slip.'

Mariella shook her head. 'We did notice that too, actually. We're checking up on Pat, but Penny was working at the post office.'

'What about Dave Cartwright? His wife's, er, smalls, were in the collection,' Sarah said. 'He seemed very worked up about it.'

'I'd say Edna Cartwright could look after herself.' Mariella shrugged. 'But as it turns out, they were caravanning in the West Country on Monday. Any other little tips for me?'

Sarah shook her head, a little shamefaced.

'Anyway, we're up to date on the cake, thank you very much,' Mariella went on. 'So if you were doing any little investigations on that this morning, they would have been completely pointless.'

Sarah immediately felt a wodge of sponge sinking in her stomach like a stone. All their hard work – well, delicious picking at cakes – had been to no avail.

'Well, I can't hang around yammering all day,' said Mariella briskly. With that, she gave them all a little nod, said to her mother, 'I'll call you later,' and strode off down the street.

'I wonder where she's off to? Do you think we should follow her?' asked Sarah, watching as the young woman hastened away.

'No, I do not,' said Daphne, sounding outraged. 'For one thing, Mariella wouldn't like that at all. And anyway,' she added in a completely different tone, 'I think I might know where she is going.'

Sarah was agog, and even Charles lost his air of languid indifference for a moment. 'Well, tell us then,' he said, putting Tinkerbell down.

'Yes, come on, Daph, it's not like you to keep things to yourself,' said Sarah artfully.

Daphne gave her a suspicious glance. 'If I didn't know you better, I'd say you were trying to wheedle information out of me... but luckily I'm dying to tell you,' she said, flinging the ends of her scarf over her shoulders.

'Well, the suspense is killing us,' Charles drawled.

'That's the thing,' said Daphne slowly. 'I think she's gone to see the person who sold the sponge that killed Mr Williams.'

'And who would that be?' said Sarah breathlessly. 'We've been everywhere; we've tried everyone.'

'Not quite. Can't you guess?' said Daphne, an infuriating smirk playing around her mouth.

It was not often that Daphne found herself in possession of a key piece of information during the course of what Sarah would insist on calling a case. But today, the many gods swirling around her in the ether, all keeping a close and benevolent eye on her on a day-to-day basis, were truly smiling. She looked from Sarah to Charles and back again, and couldn't help clapping her hands together in excitement.

'It's simple! She's off to the supermarket!'

'What?' said Sarah, taking a step back and nearly treading on Tinkerbell. Charles, too, looked at her askance.

'I'm telling you, it's obvious. Well, I know she always picks up a few bits for the children's tea at this time of day, plus it's only round the corner – the corner she just went round!' Daphne smiled smugly. As far as she was concerned, it was case closed.

'But why would she do that? In the middle of an investigation? It seems quite unprofessional,' Sarah said, wrinkling her brow.

'Mari isn't unprofessional,' Daphne jumped in.

'I didn't mean that,' Sarah seemed to be backtracking. 'Just... it's an odd moment to pick.'

'But don't you see?' said Daphne, almost chortling now. 'I'll bet you anything she'll have gone to check out the selection of ready-made cakes they always offer at Seastore.'

Sarah and Charles looked at each other, comprehension slowly dawning.

'Why didn't you say so?' said Sarah. 'Let's go.'

* * *

Seastore was Merstairs' biggest and newest supermarket, and was built in a blocky, unchallenging style that suggested the architect had only just finished playing with Lego and didn't really see why they should stop now. There was a car park outside which would probably be full later on, but was now just smooth, empty tarmac. The automatic doors opened to admit them with a satisfying swish and the shop looked pristine. Normally Sarah would have enjoyed a browse, but after their wasted morning there wasn't a minute to lose.

'Where are the cakes, Daphne?' Sarah asked.

'You say that like I'm always loitering there,' Daphne said, seemingly a second from taking massive umbrage.

Sarah sighed to herself, and adjusted her expression accordingly. 'It's just, with all your wonderful local knowledge...'

Daphne tilted her head, accepting the compliment as her due. 'Well, I may be wrong, but I think we might just find something if we go round this corner, then up here, take a left, ignore the freezer section of course, past pet care, then ah, there we are,' she said, with a tah-dah gesture, revealing the small shelf of boxed cakes.

Sarah and Charles, both a little out of breath after Daphne's whistlestop tour, stepped forward to scrutinise the row of white boxes. Was there one here that fitted the bill?

'Red velvet, carrot, even coffee and walnut – that's your favourite, isn't it?' Charles said to Sarah.

'It is, but you're rather missing the point. There's no sign at all of a Victoria sponge.'

'But they have had them in,' said Daphne.

'How do you make that out?' Sarah asked.

'Well, you just have to look. Here on the shelf. There's a label. "Victoria sponge cake, £8".'

'Quite a bargain,' said Charles.

'I suppose so.' Sarah reflected on just how much they had paid for their umpteen slices during today's in-depth exploration. 'But we can't tell whether this was the right type of sponge because it's not here.'

'Yes, but don't get too downcast, Sarah,' said Daphne helpfully. 'Look at the other cakes.'

'They're beside the point, though, Daph. It's not like Mr Williams expired while eating a chocolate cake, is it?'

'No, but all these cakes have something in common, don't they?'

'Do they?' Sarah was feeling quite dispirited, and definitely not up to playing Daphne's silly games.

'I think Daphne's got a point, Sarah, old thing,' said Charles.

Less of the 'old thing', thanks, thought Sarah, but she did look up.

Daphne was holding two of the cake boxes out for her to scrutinise. Sarah looked listlessly at the coffee and walnut cake. It seemed a fine specimen, but at this moment she never wanted to eat cake again. The other box was even worse. She wasn't partial to red velvet at the best of times. Today the thick creamy white frosting, concealing the rich red sponge beneath, looked less appealing than ever.

'Honestly, take them away,' she said.

'But what do you notice, Sarah?' Daphne said, shaking the boxes at her.

Sarah peered. 'Nothing,' she said weakly.

'Look harder.' Daphne pushed the boxes right under her nose.

And then, all of a sudden, Sarah spotted something, and craned forward.

SIXTEEN

'It's the same doily!' Sarah and Charles said simultaneously, then grinned at each other like loons.

'All right, all right,' Daphne said. 'I'm the one who's been clever here. How about a bit of credit?' she added, with a tetchy flick of her scarf.

'Quite right, Daphne, that was brilliant, deducing where Mariella was going and leading us right to it,' Sarah said admiringly. 'I'm glad she seems to have left already, otherwise she'd no doubt be telling us off.'

Daphne was perking up considerably, like a wilting flower getting a thorough watering, when there was a dry cough from behind her. The little trio shuffled round in the cramped supermarket aisle, only to find Mariella directing an angry stare at them.

'Honestly, you lot,' she hissed. 'I could hear you from right over at the other end of the store. I was just leaving and now I've had to trail all this way back to give you what for.'

'Well, you really needn't have bothered,' said Daphne, on her dignity. 'After all, I am the parent here.'

'I'm the professional, though – and you lot are treading on

my toes,' the young woman said, looking pretty furious. Sarah
did her best to avoid her gaze, but she couldn't help remembering that Mariella had actually asked for her assistance, back
in Mr Williams's horrible cottage. Wild horses wouldn't have
made her remind the detective of that now, though.

Charles took the cake boxes from Daphne and put them
back on the shelf. Sarah spared a thought for anyone buying
those particular sponges. They had been jiggled about quite
a bit.

'Well, we really should be going, Mariella, so I'll just, um,
be seeing you later, Daphne,' Charles said, taking Sarah's arm.

'Who? What? You're not leaving me, are you?' Daphne said
in consternation. 'I'm with you two. Right, Mariella, you've
driven us out of the supermarket, so if I die of malnutrition don't
be surprised when I blame you.' With that, she turned on her
heel. 'What are we waiting for?' she said to Sarah and Charles,
giving them a shove.

Sarah took a quick look over her shoulder and saw Mariella
shaking her head at them grimly.

Outside the shop, the trio regrouped. 'Honestly, I don't
know when I've ever seen Mari that cross with me before,' said
Daphne, looking fed up. 'I mean, there've been times when she's
been a mite tetchy, like when Mephisto had a bit of a go at
Louis ages ago when he was in his pram – just his little bit of
fun – but nothing like this, ever.'

Sarah patted Daphne's arm and thought hard for a moment.
'I think the best way to get back into her good books is the
obvious one,' she said after a moment.

Charles gave a lopsided grin. 'I hope you're not going to say
what I think you are.'

'Yes, Sarah, don't you dare suggest we solve all this just to
please her,' Daphne said quickly.

Sarah shrugged. 'What other choice do we have? We've
really helped in the past. If it wasn't for us, she'd still be in

uniform, and below even Tweedledum and Tweedledee in the pecking order. But no, here she is, a fully fledged detective. And she needs us now more than ever.'

At this, Daphne gave a tiny nod, as Sarah had known she would. What mother would ever decide her child had no further use for her? Charles didn't look as convinced – but she was sure she could work on him.

'Listen, Mari hasn't come out of the supermarket yet, but she will do. Let's not linger here or we'll just get another tongue-bashing. How about heading back to the seafront and having a good long think about who, exactly, might want Mr Williams dead? We can decide how to approach anyone else called H, P, T, M or B as well.'

'Good idea, Sarah,' said Daphne, all smiles again. 'And besides, it's about time we had something proper to eat.'

'Are you kidding?' Sarah could still feel far too many pieces of sponge jostling in her tummy. 'I couldn't eat another thing.'

'Oh, but Sarah, really, you've had nothing but sugary snacks all day. I'd have thought a doctor like you would know better.' With that, Daphne swished her scarf over her shoulder and marched off towards the esplanade – and the square meal she was clearly craving.

Charles, cradling Tinkerbell in one arm, held out his other for Sarah. 'Shall we, dear lady?'

Sarah took his arm a little gingerly. They'd be going through the centre of town, and there was sure to be talk. But maybe it was time to brazen that out. And besides, they could use the short walk to discuss the case and possibly get a bit further on.

'I was just thinking about the cyanide—'

'Are you free tomorrow for—?'

They both laughed, but awkwardly. There was a disconnect, that much was unfortunately apparent. While she was happy to talk poisons with Charles until the cows came home, did she really want to chat about matters closer to her heart?

And was he in a position to make any such suggestion to her, for that matter? Francesca would definitely say a resounding no to that. Perhaps it would be better if they shelved any budding romance until Charles's marital situation was properly resolved, one way or another. The Diggorys' divorce paperwork at this point must be almost as long and complex as Magna Carta. But then, Sarah thought again about Marlene, and her lavender-coloured plates, and her yearning eyes, and she turned to Charles, resolving to answer his question properly once and for all.

SEVENTEEN

'Come on, you two,' Daphne said, sticking her head round the corner of the esplanade. 'You're taking an age.'

'Just coming,' said Sarah, her cheeks a little pink. She wasn't sure whether to be grateful to Daphne or not, for cutting her tête-à-tête with Charles short.

'We'll be right with you,' said Charles heavily.

'Are you OK, Charles?' Daphne asked when they'd caught up.

'Of course, dear lady, why do you ask?' he bit out.

'It's just that you're clutching Tinkerbell rather hard,' Daphne said, pointing to the wriggling Chihuahua.

Charles put the creature down and the dog shook herself from nose to tail while Hamish looked on adoringly. It was like seeing a man watch one of those shampoo ads, where a lovely young thing with miles of silken hair shakes it all loose in a convenient breeze.

'Well, I don't want to break the spell,' said Sarah, who clearly did. 'But we agreed we'd go somewhere to discuss the case properly, didn't we?'

'Oooh, perhaps the Beach Café?' Daphne said yearningly. 'I did hear they've changed their menu for high season.'

'I'll just be having a tea,' said Sarah.

'I think it's time I got back to the shop, wouldn't do to disappoint my customers,' Charles said, a mite shiftily. 'I'd better leave you here,' he said, with a slight bow in their direction. Tinkerbell yapped as he put on a turn of speed and disappeared up the road.

'I wonder what's got into him,' Daphne said in surprise. 'It's not as if there's going to be a queue round the block for any of his old umbrella stands.'

'No. Well, I suppose it's nice that he doesn't give up hope,' said Sarah. There was a slightly fixed set to her mouth. She was beginning to feel the situation between her and Charles was like one of Daphne's attempts to read her tea leaves – doomed to murky half-truths and misunderstandings. 'Anyway, why are we worrying about that? It's not as if we can magic up any trade for him. Let's concentrate on what we can get to grips with.'

'Yes, of course, you're absolutely right, Sarah. I could really get my teeth into a sandwich.'

'I was thinking of the investigation,' said Sarah, throwing her hands up. 'But whatever.'

* * *

Five minutes later, they were installed at a table with an uninterrupted view of the playful sea. Hamish was somewhat wrecking the mood by slurping water incredibly loudly from a bowl brought by one of the kind waitresses.

'Well, he must have been thirsty,' said Daphne kindly, patting the Scottie's tousled head when he finished gulping.

'Yes. Now we can hear ourselves think, let's just go over what we know,' said Sarah.

'Uh-oh, you've got that look in your eye,' Daphne said,

getting some sunglasses out of her capacious bag and perching them on the end of her nose. 'That, *I'm going to solve this if it kills me* face.'

Sarah gave a tight smile and took a notebook and pen from her own neat little shoulder bag. 'Now, we've got various possibilities... we think the cake itself probably came from Seastore supermarket. I imagine Mariella will be poring over the CCTV footage – or Tweedledum and Tweedledee will.'

'Gosh, I hope they won't miss anything. I wouldn't trust them to cat-sit Mephisto.'

Sarah, who had a lively dread of being left in charge of Daphne's moggy, just tapped her notebook with the pen. 'Hopefully they'll go through it carefully. So that angle is covered. Now, what we really need to think about is possible culprits. Do you have any idea who might have had it in for Mr Williams? Preferably someone with the right initials... Mavis Trussock, for example. You said she designed the ScaleScanners app, so she must be highly computer literate. That makes her one of the few around here who might know how to buy poison from the dark web... if that's what happened. Did she ever say anything mean about him? In the pub the other night she seemed to rush off pretty sharpish when Pat was mentioning his behaviour, but do you think that could have been a blind? There was even a ScaleScanners flyer in his house – I wonder if she brought it round to him?'

Daphne wrinkled her brow, which then rapidly cleared as the waitress came back into view with a groaning tray. Sarah knew when she'd lost her audience and took her cup of tea, while Daphne unloaded a large toasted sandwich, glass of fizzy orange and the pièce de résistance, yet another chunk of sponge.

'Aren't you sick of cake?' Sarah asked weakly.

'Not at all, if anything I feel more of a connoisseur after this morning's hard work,' Daphne said with a toss of her head. Her scarf slipped off and landed on Hamish, who looked quite pleased with the unexpected offering and snuggled down for a nap in the sunshine, his head comfortably pillowed. 'Oh, you look after it for me, boy,' Daphne said. 'I'm not sure about Mavis, why would she have wished Mr Williams ill? Come to that, even Hannah Betts fits the possible initials, I suppose. Oh, it's all absurd, though.'

'Let's think. No one seemed to know about Mr Williams and the underwear, until I saw his bedroom. Well, except for Pat, and I suppose Dave Cartwright, who was fuming. Then Charles was beside himself about Arabella's underwear, and he's usually so charming.'

'Isn't he just?' said Daphne with a sly smile.

Sarah ignored the smirk. 'Charles has an alibi, though. On the other hand, could all the pants be red herrings? Was there something else that caused Williams's death? Come on, Daph, you've lived here forever. Do you know much about his past?'

'Skeletons in his closet, you mean? No, I don't remember anything much,' Daphne said and frowned as she picked up a single, slender lettuce leaf and thoughtfully chomped her way through it, before carefully pushing the rest of the salad to one side. Then she took a large bite of the toastie and said, somewhat indistinctly, 'I mean, there was that whole post office business, but that was years ago.'

Sarah, who'd been just about to sip her tea, put her cup down with a snap. 'Post office business? What was that?'

'Oh, it was a massive scandal, back in the day. But it can't be anything to do with that.' Daphne waved her hand to dismiss the whole issue.

Sarah tried to take a breath, but she was too wound up. Instead, she leant forward and almost shouted at her friend, 'Are you kidding me, Daphne? Tell me about it right away.'

EIGHTEEN

Daphne looked at Sarah, horrified, and withdrew into herself, even putting her toasted sandwich down. 'Well, really, Sarah, I don't know why you're yelling at me. It's not like *I* was stealing people's mail, is it?'

'Is that what Mr Williams did? Are you sure?'

'Of course I'm sure,' said Daphne rather huffily. 'It was a huge to-do at the time, I told you.'

Sarah sat herself back with an effort and tried to drink some tea, but the cup clattered against her teeth and she put it down again. 'You didn't tell me, Daph. You haven't mentioned a word about this. And I really think you should have done.'

'But it's ancient history! I can't see why it would be relevant to what's happened now. I mean, OK, some people never spoke to him again. Mrs Jarvis, you know, the one who lives at the end of our row, well, she said she never felt right about him after he wished her a happy fortieth birthday on her doorstep one day when he was delivering the post,' Daphne said.

'He could easily have guessed it was her birthday, if she'd got more letters and parcels than usual,' said Sarah slowly, playing devil's advocate.

'Well, her point was, he might have guessed it was her birthday, sure, but how did he know it was her fortieth, not her thirty-ninth or her forty-first? She is super-sensitive about her age, even her husband never really seemed to know how old she was, but then he did get Alzheimer's, poor dear. Anyway, she wasn't the only one. Every now and then Williams would let slip a bit of information that he really shouldn't have had. Like when he commiserated with old Mr Thomas from the ironmonger's. His wife had received a timetable for her cancer treatment by post.'

'I don't understand why you didn't mention this, Daph,' Sarah said. 'If he was actually snooping on people by reading their mail, that's a proper criminal offence, as well as being super-creepy. Why did everyone tolerate him?'

Daphne shrugged. 'He retired from the post office at least twenty years ago. We're a kind lot here, we let bygones be bygones,' she said, spreading out her arms as if to encompass the whole town.

'Do you know who else this affected? Other than Mrs Jarvis and Mr Thomas?'

'Oooh now, it's going back so far. Neither Mr Thomas or his wife are on this astral plane any more, and I only remembered about Mrs Jarvis because she still moans about it. She was actually smiling when I told her Williams had been found dead. But she's a hundred if she's a day, she can't possibly have done it.'

'I wonder who might know a few more details... someone who was around all those years ago,' said Sarah, leaving out the rest of the sentence, which probably went something like, 'and was paying proper attention.' But that was a little unfair. As Daphne had already said, her nature was generous and forgiving, and she was always thinking about tomorrow rather than yesterday. A consequence of firmly believing in the Beyond, Sarah supposed.

'There's one person I can think of,' Daphne said, after screwing up her face for a while. 'But you're not going to like it.'

'I think I know exactly who you mean,' Sarah agreed, trying not to look glum. Every time Sarah had a run-in with this person, she came off second best. It was absurd. To all intents and purposes she was a dear little old lady and deserving only of respect and consideration. But the trouble was that she was rather horrible. There was nothing for it, though. Sarah swallowed her misgivings. 'Could you give her a ring?'

NINETEEN

A little before lunchtime the next day, Sarah was nursing a large tonic water in the Jolly Roger. It seemed a crime to be inside on a fine afternoon like this, when the clouds scudding across the sky looked freshly laundered, they were so white and clean. But never mind, this was important, she told herself, looking down at Hamish. He lay peaceably enough on the patterned carpet, no doubt inhaling the fumes from years of spilled pints of Merstairs Monk, the local brew. He wagged his tail to say he had no hard feelings about not being on a proper beachside walk. As long as she made up for it later.

There was a flurry at the door. It was Daphne bursting in, all scarves and bracelets. 'A large Dubonnet, please,' she said to Claire the manager as she joined Sarah.

'Pat not here yet? That's funny,' she said, sliding into the banquette seat. 'When I spoke to her yesterday evening, she said she had to meet us as early as possible as she's so busy today.'

'No sign. And we've been here for ages, haven't we, Hamish?' Sarah said unenthusiastically, looking down at her little dog. He grinned at her obligingly, then subsided back down onto his paws.

'Oh well, she'll be along in a minute. You know what she's like,' Daphne said airily.

'I suppose I do,' Sarah said tightly.

Daphne waved her hand and nearly overset her drink. 'You two just got off on the wrong foot. That'll soon sort itself out.'

'I'm not disagreeing with that diagnosis. It's just that we seem to have stayed on that same wrong foot, if that's possible without falling over.'

'You wanted to talk to someone who knows chapter and verse about Mr Williams's doings,' said Daphne. 'And she's the obvious candidate, so don't grumble to me. Didn't you want to be terribly clever and see if she was this mysterious PB from the betting slip, anyway?' she snapped.

'Are you feeling OK, Daph?' Sarah asked. It wasn't like her friend to be tetchy.

'I'm a bit worried,' Daphne confessed, her head drooping as she toyed with a beer mat on the table. 'It's little Mephisto.'

'Little' was not how Sarah would have described Daphne's hulking cat, but she knew how fond she was of him. 'Is he off-colour? Eaten a workman that disagreed with him?' she couldn't help joking.

'You can laugh, but he's not my usual cuddly boy. He just seems very... distant.'

Sarah pursed her lips. A distant Mephisto was, in her view, the very best kind. 'I'm sorry, Daphne. Anything changed about his routine lately? Is he off his food, clawing the carpet, anything like that?'

'Well, clawing the carpet, yes, but he's always loved that,' said Daphne indulgently. That explained the curiously furry look of her friend's stairs at least, Sarah decided. 'And I wouldn't say he's off his food... Mephy's just got this haughty look on his face.'

Under the table, Hamish growled very softly, which was unusual enough for Sarah to duck her head for a second and look at him in surprise. When he saw her, he gave his trademark grin. She suddenly wondered if he was now reacting to the mere name of his nemesis.

'You're a very clever boy, aren't you?' she said quietly, patting his head. Hamish folded himself up neatly again and gave her another look as if to say, 'Well, yes.'

'If I didn't know him better,' Daphne was continuing, 'I'd say he was getting a message from the Beyond. Sometimes I go a bit quiet and thoughtful when that happens to me. I just let everything go by, while I concentrate on communication.'

Sarah nodded. It explained a lot about the levels of dust covering everything in Daphne's Tarot and Tealeaves shop, the epicentre of her clairvoyancy business. 'Getting back to Pat, though, do you think maybe we should give her a ring?'

'We could, but we might do better just going to see her. She doesn't like chatting on the phone, she's got a thing about them.'

'All phones, or only mobiles?' Sarah said. 'Landlines have been around forever. She can't be that old, surely?'

Daphne shrugged. 'Well, if she was here, she could tell us. She does have a landline, that's how I remind her about book group meetings. But I only get a chance to tell her the day and then she puts the phone down. No chatting. I don't think she's got a mobile.'

'She seemed to know about the pants in Mr Williams's house. Are you sure you don't remember anything she might have said in the past about him?'

'I sometimes don't think you appreciate how much there is going on in my life,' said Daphne, drawing herself up in her seat, though the effect was somewhat ruined when her scarf made contact with one of the plastic lobsters that made up the pub's weird and wonderful décor. 'It's not just non-stop readings, I've also got my cottage to keep up, and the shop, and Mari and the kids, not to mention Mephisto. Perhaps he's feeling left out?' she said, going off at one of her tangents. 'Anyway, I don't have time to delve into Pat's past... but I suppose she did tell me a bit about the time Mr Williams was fired from the Royal Mail.'

'Well, go on then, Daph,' said Sarah, listening carefully.

'Like I said, he started to know a little bit too much about people. But then packages also disappeared. I'm trying to remember what Pat told me...' Here Daphne put her hands up to her head, in the way she had when she was receiving one of her other-worldly messages. Sarah took a deep breath. 'I think she said he made off with people's clothes.'

'Pants again?' asked Sarah.

'No, I think this might have been menswear, from the days when Pat's husband was alive.'

Sarah goggled at the idea that Pat had once been married, she seemed such a self-contained, not to say difficult, woman.

'Yes, that's right,' said Daphne, still massaging her temples. 'Pat said she opened the door to Williams when he was delivering the post, and he was wearing a sweater identical to the one she'd ordered for her husband, which never arrived.'

Sarah thought for a moment. 'Well, that's not completely conclusive. It could have been a coincidence,' she said reasonably.

'I suppose it could, have it your own way,' said Daphne.

'I'm not trying to be difficult, Daph. I just want to have something really convincing to say when we tell Mariella.'

At that, her friend smiled. 'You're right. We need to help her as much as possible.' She took a long slurp of her Dubonnet and gathered up her bag. 'Well, I suppose there's only one thing for it.'

'What do you mean?'

'Well, if Pat's too busy to come to us, we'll have to root her out. Come on then, let's go.'

* * *

It didn't take them long to walk the short distance to Pat's place in the sheltered accommodation complex. It wasn't far from their own pretty little cottages, but in many respects it was a world away. Though it was perched on the gentle sloping hill leading into town, it had been built almost with its back to the sea, and the windows on that side were tiny. Once they went through the central archway, though, Sarah realised there was method to the design – all the small apartments faced onto a central green space with benches and shady trees. Several of the benches were occupied by elderly people – who were probably not all that much older than her, Sarah realised with a shock.

Daphne didn't waste any time, but marched up to two women on one of the benches. 'Pat around?' she asked.

'Haven't seen her yet today,' said one. 'How about you, Gladys?'

The lady called Gladys looked Daphne over carefully. 'Who did you say you were again?'

'Come on, Gladys, you remember me! Mariella's mum, Daphne. Your daughter Beatrice taught Mari at the school.'

'Oh yes! Must get these specs changed,' Gladys muttered, taking the offending glasses off and polishing them on her cardigan. She slipped them back on her nose. 'Ah, there we are. Delphine, of course.'

Daphne raised her eyebrows at Sarah but thank goodness didn't say anything. Sarah chipped in. 'Where might we find Pat, then?'

'That's her flat there, end of the row. Can't miss it,' said Gladys.

Sarah and Daphne strode towards it, but as they approached, both slowed their pace. Sarah was now, under-standably in her view, quite worried about knocking on people's doors. Daphne seemed to catch her friend's reluctance, so, by the time they were facing the pale turquoise door with the silver number thirteen above it, they looked at each other as if waiting for someone else to do the honours.

'Oh, come on, we'll get nowhere like this,' said Sarah, bringing up her hand and rapping boldly on the shiny surface with the knocker. There was no reply. Again, the pair exchanged glances. Here we go again, Sarah thought to herself. 'Let's have a quick peep through the window,' she suggested.

They edged over and stood on tiptoe to look through the small, high panes – and immediately both gasped. Inside, they could just see two feet in shabby slippers sticking out from behind the sofa. Right on cue Daphne started shrieking.

TWENTY

Sarah rushed back to the door of Pat's flat and turned the knob, which gave. In a minute, she was in the living room and racing over to the prone figure, hoping against hope she was in time.

'Pat!' she yelled. 'Pat, can you hear me?'

'Course I can, what are you on about?' Pat snapped, sitting up with some difficulty.

'Pat! You're not— um, you're OK,' Sarah said, helping the old lady to her feet.

'I haven't croaked yet, if that's what you mean,' Pat said with a cackle. 'No law against lying down in me own flat, is there? Dropped a pound coin here somewhere, just having a look.'

'Here it is,' said Sarah, plucking the coin off the rug and passing it to Pat. She felt quite light-headed with relief. 'Ah, here's Daphne,' she added as her friend, very red in the face, rushed into the room.

'Thank God,' said Daphne, hugging Pat, who batted her off unceremoniously. 'You said you were going to meet us in the Roger, Pat, remember? When you didn't show up, we thought we'd come here instead. You gave us quite a turn.'

'Must have slipped my mind,' Pat said lightly. 'Well, you're here now. I haven't done my usual tidy-round, though.'

'That doesn't bother us one bit,' Daphne said, flinging out an arm and almost bringing down some of the photos that were clustered all over the walls. Sarah studied them and was surprised to see many were of what looked like musical hall performances, often featuring a lithe young woman doing the splits, the can-can and pirouetting from frame to frame, with various men in tailcoats behind her, some handsome, some not so hot. One in particular had ears like jug handles, but made up for it with a twinkly smile.

'Goodness, is that you, Pat? I didn't realise you'd been on the stage,' said Sarah.

'Course I was, did all the venues up and down the coast, how do you think I got washed up here?' cackled Pat.

'Washed up?' sniffed Daphne. 'This is a wonderful place to retire to.'

'Maybe for you, Daph. But when you've trod the boards at the London Palladium, Merstairs can seem a bit quiet. And as for talent...' Here she subsided into a hacking laugh.

'By talent you mean...'

'The geezers! Coming out of my ears, they were, when I was a star turn. I fetched up here following the love of my life. Turned out he wasn't the town bigwig he'd said he was. He was a right nasty toerag, in fact. But I stayed on here, to spite him mainly. The tales I could tell about him... Anyway, take a seat now you're here.'

As Pat had suggested, the place was none too tidy. Sarah sat down carefully. 'That's interesting, Pat, because we've come here after some information. You know the area so well, we were sure you'd know the works about what Mr Williams used to get up to.'

Pat, who'd rustled up some cups and was pouring some very stewed-looking tea from a large pot for her visitors, suddenly yelped. 'That's gone everywhere, that has,' she said, looking at a spreading pool of dark liquid on the table in front of the sofa.

'I'll get a cloth,' said Sarah, heading for the tiny cluttered kitchen just off the living room. She found a cleanish tea towel and headed back with it, mopping up the spill efficiently while Daphne and Pat milled around making things worse.

'All done now,' Sarah said, taking her seat again. 'So, about Mr Williams? I don't know whether you've heard, but there was a piece of paper in his flat with some initials on it. We thought, well, that they might be yours.'

'Oh yes? About that,' said Pat, with a curiously cunning look on her face. 'I'll just say this—'

Suddenly there was a rap on the door, and a man in overalls put his head round. 'Pat, just come to fix your waste disposal unit, you said it was on the blink. Can you show me what the problem is?'

'Righto,' said the old lady, hobbling forward to let the workman in. Then she turned to her visitors. 'Daph and Doc, I've got my hands full as you can see. You'll just have to come back later.' With that, Pat ushered them out and shut the door in their faces.

'Well, that's us told,' said Sarah, looking back at the flat as they stood outside again.

'Yes, I was enjoying that tea,' said Daphne ruefully. 'And I'm pretty sure she was going to bring out some biscuits.'

'And also, we were just about to get to the information part. You know, about Mr Williams, and those initials. She didn't say they weren't hers, at least.'

'Yes, that too, I suppose,' said Daphne. 'Oh well, let's get some lunch and we can come back later. That man will have the waste disposal done in a jiffy, surely.'

'You're right, Daphne,' said Sarah, feeling herself relax. Of course it was important to glean as much as she could about Mr Williams, in the hope that it would furnish them with clues about why he'd ended up dead. But it didn't all have to be done this minute. A relaxing break at one of Merstairs' fine cafés could be the perfect prescription.

* * *

An hour and a half later, having got on the outside of a wonderful Beach Café lunch of salad niçoise drizzled with a sumptuous amount of vinaigrette dressing, Sarah was sipping a latte and finishing off her meal with a scone smothered with cream and jam. She hadn't really needed a pudding at all, but Daphne had insisted – the word on the esplanade was that Hannah Betts's latest batch of apricot preserves was even better than the last, and simply had to be tasted to be believed.

As Sarah brought the last fragments of scone to her lips, heavily freighted with the sublime apricot concoction, she had to admit that her own jams never reached this level of silky tanginess. 'Hannah really is a marvel, isn't she?' she sighed, replete.

'She's a brilliant cook. It's a wonder she isn't distracted at the moment, I hear her niece Betsy is going through a tricky time.'

'Really?' Sarah said idly. 'She helps out here quite a lot, doesn't she?'

'Yes, that's her over there,' said Daphne, pointing to a very slender dark-haired girl who seemed to be struggling with the till. As Sarah watched, she keyed in several numbers and, when nothing happened, she tore off her apron, threw it on the floor and fled into the kitchens. A minute later, Hannah came out and took over, a frown on her face.

'Apparently she suffers from anxiety,' Daphne said in one of her foghorn whispers. 'Honestly, that generation gets in a state about getting themselves dressed in the morning,' she added.

Sarah didn't rush to judgement. 'Maybe she's got a lot on her plate.'

'Well, Hannah seems to think so. She's always giving her loads of leave, even though they're so busy. But being short in the kitchen doesn't seem to affect the cooking, does it? This jam is on another level. Heaven on a plate,' Daphne said dreamily.

'Right, well then, perhaps we should get back to the sheltered housing before we take root here,' Sarah said a minute or two later, putting her hands flat on the table and pushing her chair back reluctantly. The sun was high in the sky now and she was feeling dangerously drowsy after the delicious food. She glanced at her friend, surprised Daphne wasn't voicing an objection. Come to think of it, she'd been rather quiet since praising the jam. As Sarah looked over, concerned, Daphne stirred a little – and snored loudly. Behind her big dark glasses, she was fast asleep.

Sarah couldn't help smiling. Napping while sitting bolt upright, without the head lolling, was a skill. If memory served, it had also come in handy for Daphne during their long-ago Latin lessons, when she had declined declensions by simple virtue of being unconscious. Sarah took a quick peek under the table and saw that Hamish, too, was having a little siesta.

Oh well, thought Sarah. If you can't beat 'em...

* * *

What seemed like five minutes later, she was startled into wakefulness by a small, dry cough. She sat up, realising she'd been listing to one side, and opened her eyes.

'Must have dozed off there for a moment,' she said uncomfortably, gazing into the amused eyes of Charles Diggory. She hoped she hadn't been drooling. She surreptitiously patted her mouth with a napkin that had been left on the table, though their plates had long been cleared away.

'Hmm, yes. And looks like Daphne's still asleep,' Charles said, amusement in his tone as he swivelled to look at her friend. Her sunglasses had slipped down her nose and her hand, clutching a last crust of scone, was dangling down, where it was being busily licked by a now wide-awake Hamish. He sensed eyes upon him and stopped rather self-consciously.

'That's enough of that, I think, boy,' said Sarah, stooping down and pulling the soggy object out of Daphne's unresisting fingers. The movement was enough to disturb her friend.

'Who? Where? What was that you said?' Daphne said, struggling to gather herself.

'Um, I was just suggesting we go back and check what Pat has to say about Mr Williams. We went there earlier but she had someone fixing a kitchen appliance and we had to go,' Sarah explained to Charles.

'Not like you to abandon a job like that,' Charles said. 'I'm surprised you didn't just hang around until they'd left.'

'Yes, well, we didn't really get the chance,' Sarah explained. 'Pat more or less ordered us off the premises.'

'She does like a workman, does Pat,' said Daphne.

Sarah was rather glad her friend was still wearing her dark glasses. She felt sure that last comment would have been accompanied by a massive wink and she just didn't want to go there.

'I've shut the shop for an hour or two, I needed a break,' said Charles. If Sarah hadn't known him better, she might have assumed he'd been rushed off his feet. But it was more likely that he'd been extremely lonely in his dark and dingy antiques emporium. She couldn't blame him for abandoning ship when the weather outside was so sublime.

'If you're free for a bit, maybe you'd like to come too?' she suggested.

'Why not?' said Charles. 'I must admit, I'm keen to get this Williams business sorted.'

'Well, what on earth are we waiting for?' said Daphne,

bustling to her feet. 'Honestly, you two would sit around all day if you could.'

If Daphne hadn't accompanied this comment with a cheeky smile, Sarah might have retorted. As it was, she just gathered up Hamish's lead and made sure they'd left enough cash to pay for the meal anchored under a plate.

A few minutes later, they were approaching Pat's place again, and the same two elderly ladies were still on their bench, chatting nineteen to the dozen.

'Has that workman finished?' Sarah asked them with a smile as they passed.

'How on earth should we know?' the lady with the corkscrew curls replied tersely. 'We've got better things to do than sit around all day gossiping, you know. Here, have you heard about Mr Williams and the pants? Disgusting,' she added with evident relish.

'Er, no, sorry,' said Sarah, walking quickly on. She knew she ought to pump the old ladies for information, but she had a sudden irrational fear they knew her own undies were in that awful collection. Besides, it was high time they talked to Pat. Charles lifted his panama hat to the ladies as he passed, but also glanced at Sarah.

'Goodness, looks like the news is out,' he said quietly.

'I wonder if Pat has been talking again?' Sarah mused. It was infuriating, but it was imperative Sarah was at her most polite when tackling the old lady. She took a deep breath as all three stood in front of the turquoise door.

'I'll do the honours, shall I?' said Daphne, lifting the knocker and whacking it three times against the door.

'Daphne! You'll dent the woodwork,' Sarah said, horrified.

'Well, that will wake the dead,' Charles said with a wry smile.

But they continued to stand on the doorstep, waiting. Sarah listened carefully. There was no movement within the small flat. She tried the door again, but this time the knob didn't turn. 'That's odd,' she said. 'Do you think she's having a nap?' She glanced at the window, but the curtains were now drawn.

'Who'd sleep at this time of day?' said Daphne, blithely overlooking her own recent forty – or even eighty – winks. 'Maybe she's gone out. I'll knock again, shall I?'

'I'll do it,' Sarah said, getting to the knocker before her friend and banging slightly less ferociously. But there was still no response.

The three looked at each other. 'What do we do now?' Sarah said. 'We can't ask those ladies if they've seen Pat leaving, they bit my head off a minute ago.'

'Don't worry, I'll charm it out of them,' said Charles, adjusting his straw hat to a dapper angle and sauntering off, full of confidence. Only a few moments later, he was back looking chastened. 'I must say they're not the friendliest bunch here, are they?'

Sarah suppressed the glimmer of a smile, while Daphne looked in frustration at Pat's door.

'Tell you what, Daph,' said Sarah, inspired. 'I know Pat doesn't have a mobile but she does have a landline. Why don't you give her a ring? If she doesn't answer at least we'll be sure she's popped out. Maybe one of her neighbours will know where she might have gone at this time of day. Then we can just meet her wherever she is.'

'Great idea,' said Daphne, taking her bag off her shoulder and rummaging in it. 'Oh, you hold it will you, while I look. This is the trouble with getting organised,' she said crossly. 'I spent ages applying my new system to this handbag yesterday and look where it's got me.'

Sarah obligingly took the not inconsiderable weight of the bag while Daphne rooted around in its interior. Eventually she struck gold. 'Aha! There it is. Just where I put it, too.' Now she squinted ferociously at the screen and stabbed out Pat's number.

There was a pause, and then all three of them heard the distinctive warble of a phone inside Pat's flat. The sound went on and on. Four rings, five... six...

'That's funny,' said Daphne. 'I wonder why she isn't answering?'

It might just have been the proof they'd sought that the old lady had gone out. But the feeling of dread trickling down her spine warned Sarah this could be something much more sinister.

TWENTY-ONE

'Oh my God!' said Daphne, loudly enough to make the ladies on the bench crane over to see what was going on. 'What's happening? Where's Pat? Has she been abducted?'

Sarah put her arm round her friend, and was attempting to calm her, when a thin, dark-haired man of around thirty came round the corner.

'Hello, hello, what's all this? Little problem?' he said, his dry moustache quirking up at the corners as his eyes shifted rapidly between them. He smoothed his striped tie nervously. A slightly skew-whiff name badge on the lapel of his navy suit said *Ted Ackroyd, Manager*.

'Um, Mr... Ackroyd,' said Sarah. 'We have reason to be a little concerned about Pat, she was in earlier, and didn't say anything about going out. And now there's no response when we knock and we can hear her phone inside.'

'Aha, I see. Pat. It would be her of course.'

'What do you mean?' Sarah asked.

'Oh, nothing. Just not one of our more... peaceful residents,' Mr Ackroyd said, fiddling with his moustache. 'She's had one or two troublesome visitors, too.'

'Visitors?' Sarah said. 'I wonder, did a man by the name of Williams ever come round at all?'

Mr Ackroyd stared at Sarah. 'I can't possibly tell you that. There's all sorts of client confidentiality issues. But at least I've got one complaint sorted out. People were saying washing was going missing from the communal area. That's been dealt with,' he added with a sly smile. 'Anyway, you're relatives, are you?' he asked, looking hopefully at Sarah, Daphne, Charles and the dogs.

'Um, we're just here to see Pat,' Sarah replied, feeling a tad impatient. 'I really think we should check she's OK right now.'

'I see,' said Mr Ackroyd. 'But I do have a letter to pass on to her family. Would that be you?' His little eyes gleamed.

'No. But we might be able to get a message to them?' Sarah said, hoping he'd say more.

'It's just that there have been... incidents, with the staff. This might not be the best accommodation for her, if you know what I mean,' Mr Ackroyd said, looking particularly weaselly. 'Anyway, she's probably just out.'

'Well, I'm sure you're as concerned as we are about where she is right now,' said Sarah, who wasn't at all. She felt rather sorry for Pat, if this awful man was trying to evict her from her flat.

'You know, it could look *very* unfortunate if we don't check inside to make sure she's OK,' Charles said firmly. 'You wouldn't want any other residents to start talking about neglect.'

Mr Ackroyd swallowed and fingered his moustache some more. 'I'll just ask a member of staff to run and get the master key,' he started, fishing in his pocket for his phone.

'Why not get it yourself? It would save a lot of time,' Sarah said earnestly.

Mr Ackroyd gave her a rather cross look, then loped off reluctantly to do her bidding.

'I must say, you two are good with these jobsworths,' said

Daphne loudly. Sarah hoped Ackroyd hadn't heard, he'd be even more obstructive if he had. But it seemed Daphne had timed her comment well, as the manager reappeared obligingly only a short while later with a pass key in his hand.

It didn't take long for him to open up the turquoise door, but for Sarah every second seemed like an age. If Pat had fallen ill, as she very much feared, then time was of the essence. But when it eventually swung back, Sarah realised almost at once that it was already too late. As soon as she took a step over the threshold into the stuffy flat, she smelt the whiff of bitter almonds which had struck her so forcibly at Mr Williams's house.

She didn't hesitate, pulling Mr Ackroyd back by his arm. 'Don't go in there. It's a crime scene. I'll take a very quick look but you should ring the police now.'

'Do you mean an ambulance?' Ackroyd said, his jaw sagging. 'What do you mean, I can't go in? I'm the manager, I'll have you know.'

'And I'm a doctor,' said Sarah, pushing past him, her hand covering as much of her nose and mouth as she could manage. She didn't need to go far into the tiny flat to see what she had been dreading – Pat, sitting upright on the sofa, her eyes blank and staring, a piece of red velvet cake on a plate in front of her with a single bite out of it. Poor Pat. There was nothing Sarah could do. She was entirely beyond help now.

Sarah shut the door behind her, then turned to Daphne, who was trembling and had gone as white as a sheet. She put her arms round her and held on tight as her poor friend started to sob.

Ackroyd was on the phone.

'Is that the emergency services?' she asked. He nodded wordlessly and she put out her hand for the mobile. 'Hello, Dr Sarah Vane here. Please let the police know they'll need a mortuary van. Yes, it's another case of cyanide poisoning.'

Sarah's mind was whirring as she helped Daphne away from Pat's front door. A second death! This was horrific. And, though she'd not been Pat's biggest fan, the poor old lady had truly not deserved this awful fate. She shook her head, scarcely able to believe what she had just seen.

Her main thoughts, however, were for her friend. Daphne had spent so much time with Pat, in her innumerable hobbies, from the book group to the crafting club. They'd enjoyed many little suppers together, though Sarah had been baffled about what they had in common. Well, that was all at an end now.

'Are you OK, Daphne old thing?' said Charles, taking her friend's other arm.

'Of course she's not, Charles,' Sarah couldn't help but snap. It was a horrendous and very stressful situation. 'Let's try and get her to that bench.'

The two ladies who'd been sitting there jumped up as the group approached. 'Here, what's going on?' 'Pat all right, is she?' they twittered.

Charles and Sarah exchanged significant glances, then Daphne burst into speech. 'Dead! She's dead, dead I tell you,' she said, almost as though she was having a vision – whereas what she had just witnessed had been cold, hard reality.

'Goodness me,' the frailer of the two ladies said. 'Come on, Gladys, we'd better tell Dee, Blanche, Tina and Maureen. But not Pamela, she's such a gossip.'

'Wait a minute, before you go,' said Sarah, settling Daphne down on the bench with her bag and a packet of tissues. 'Did you see a workman leaving Pat's place, not long after we left the first time?'

'Workman?' The first lady shook her head. 'Did you see anyone, Lou?'

'Or... Mr Ackroyd, the manager?' Sarah added quickly.

Lou shrugged. 'How long ago?'

'Say, two hours?' Sarah calculated quickly, thinking about

the time she'd spent having a lovely lunch with Daphne, and then, for goodness' sake, falling asleep in the sun. It had been very enjoyable, and she was sure this was what she was entitled to do, in her retirement. But she couldn't help bitterly regretting it. They should have been back in Pat's flat, getting the truth out of her about those blasted initials. Now, instead of hearing the old lady's promised nugget of information about Mr Williams, all they had was another corpse on their hands.

That sounded pretty brutal. In fact Sarah was very shaken up about the death. It was shocking, talking to someone one minute and seeing their lifeless corpse not long afterwards. She was really kicking herself over what had happened. She was even starting to wonder whether the workman himself had been a sinister figure. Had he realised what Pat was just about to say, and taken swift action to silence her?

Or could it have been the dreadful Mr Ackroyd? He'd more or less admitted he wanted to force Pat out. Had he found a way to get rid of her, by copying the method used by Mr Williams's killer? He had a pass key so could easily have let himself in. Or had he actually murdered the old man too? He'd said that odd thing about an issue with the washing having been sorted out. Was Williams stealing people's underwear here as well, and to stop it, had Ackroyd killed him? Sarah's head was spinning.

'Trouble is, my memory isn't what it was,' said Lou, looking confused. 'Who did you say you were again?'

'Never mind,' said Sarah, turning back to Daphne. There was a little more colour in her cheeks now. 'That's right, just take deep breaths. You'll feel better soon.'

'I won't! I'll never get over it,' Daphne said, shaking her head vigorously.

Charles sat down and put a clumsy arm round Daphne. 'Terrible shock for you, dear lady. I'm so sorry.'

Daphne sniffed wetly into Charles's pristine linen sleeve, and Sarah could see him trying his best not to recoil.

Then Daphne seemed to pull herself together. 'Who has done this terrible thing, though? That's what I want to know,' she said, clenching her fist. 'We've got to catch this person. They can't just go around killing my friends. They've got me to answer to now!'

TWENTY-TWO

While Sarah appreciated Daphne's stirring speech, she hadn't expected her to leap to her feet the moment it ended and run out of the sheltered accommodation before either Sarah or Charles had time to react.

'Follow her,' said Charles quickly. 'I'll stay here and have a word with Mariella when she gets here. You can leave Hamish with me.'

'OK, thanks,' said Sarah, shouldering her bag and dashing after Daphne.

Luckily, Daphne had run out of steam shortly after leaving the complex. Sarah found her doubled over next to the sea wall, her hand pressed to her side.

'That's right, just stay there for a moment or two,' Sarah said, coming up to her. 'It's lactic acid causing that stitch, it'll clear soon,' she said. 'Where were you on the way to, anyway?'

'The obvious place, of course. If you're so clever, you'll have guessed it by now,' said Daphne, her face pink from her exertions.

'There's no need to be angry with me, Daph,' Sarah said, rather hurt that her friend was taking all her emotions out on her. 'I vote we go to Seastore. That looked like a slice of the red velvet cake they had there yesterday. If we can just find someone who remembers who they sold it to – Mr Ackroyd, that workman, or just someone with the right initials—'

'Drat!' said Daphne angrily. 'That was *my* idea.'

'Well, a very good one it was too,' said Sarah soothingly. 'Are you OK to make a move now?'

Daphne straightened up carefully. 'Yes, yes, I'm fine. Right then, let's get on with it,' she said, with a determined look on her face.

The shop wasn't far away. There were more cars parked outside than yesterday, so Sarah hoped it wouldn't be too busy. Inside, however, it was quite empty. 'I wonder where all the car owners are?' she asked as they made their way to the cake aisle.

'Oh, people just leave their cars here before getting the train, it's so close to the station,' Daphne said. 'Look, there's one of the red velvet cakes left.'

'But that's not good, Daph. It would be better if it was all gone, that would mean someone had definitely bought it from here.'

'It looks identical, though, doesn't it?' Daphne said, examining the cake through the clear window in the box.

'Hard to tell exactly, until it's cut into,' Sarah said.

'Do you mean we'll have to buy it and eat it to make sure?' Daphne said, perking up briefly. Then she realised what she'd said. 'Oh. I'm not actually sure I could face a red velvet cake ever again. This business is really affecting my appetite. Maybe that's why I'm not... quite myself.'

'Well, the coffee and walnut cake is still innocent until proven guilty. Let me get one of those and we can have a slice back at home later over a nice cup of tea.'

'To think, I'll never have tea with Pat again,' Daphne said, her eyes suddenly welling up. 'Oh dear.'

Sarah patted her shoulder. 'It's awful, Daph, it really is.

Whoever did this needs to be put behind bars... as soon as possible. Let's talk to the shop manager now, and then we'll go and think about how on earth Pat connects with Mr Williams. And what she was going to say to us. Could someone have known what that was, I wonder? Apart from the maintenance man, that is?'

'I hope you're not expecting me to have many answers, Sarah,' Daphne said, sagging suddenly as the reality of Pat's death hit her. 'This has knocked the stuffing out of me. I'm not sure I'm up to much.'

Sarah patted her shoulder comfortingly. 'Of course not, Daph, it's been an awful shock,' she said. 'Don't you worry. I'll just ask whoever's in charge here – if we can find anyone.'

Both looked round somewhat wildly for a member of staff, but as usual when needed all the assistants melted away. Finally, Sarah marched up to the till, which was still manned – Seastore didn't quite run to self-service machines yet.

'I want to buy this cake, and also have a word with the manager,' Sarah said to the girl at the checkout.

'Riiiight,' said the girl, chewing gum with all the enthusiasm of a Friesian cow enjoying a mouthful of prime grass. 'Dunno 'bout that.'

'Listen, it's an emergency,' said Sarah, looking at the girl earnestly.

The girl considered for a moment, moving her wad of gum from one cheek to the other. She looked around the shop pointedly. Then she spoke again. 'Thing is, he's not here, is he?'

'Well, where is he? We need to talk to him about your red velvet cake,' Sarah said.

There was another pause as the girl chewed carefully. 'That's a coffee and walnut,' she said at length.

'We know that,' said Daphne, clearly holding onto her temper by a thread. 'Can you ring the manager? Right now? My friend has just been killed and we think it was your cake that did it.'

It could have been the tone that Daphne said this in, or possibly the volume, but a couple waiting behind them thought better of their purchases at this point, dumping their basket of groceries and scurrying away.

'I told you all those cakes and pastries were bad for you,' the woman muttered to her husband as they left.

The girl behind the till seemed to snap into a different gear at last, reluctantly taking out her gum and throwing it in the bin by her feet. She then pressed a button under her till and spoke into an echoing, crackling intercom. 'Mr Hertz to the tills, Mr Hertz to the tills.' Then she sat back, as though she had performed an immense feat.

Luckily, they didn't have long to wait before a stout man with a shiny face emerged from the back of the shop. 'What is it now, Gina? Can't I leave you unsupervised for ten minutes?'

As he smelt strongly of cigarettes, Sarah deduced he'd deserted the shop floor for a smoking break and wasn't at all happy at getting his fix interrupted.

'These ladies have got a problem,' Gina said, waving a hand at Sarah and Daphne.

'Madam and, er, madam. Can I help you?' Mr Hertz said in a way that suggested he thought it extremely unlikely.

'Yes, you can,' stormed Daphne. 'Your cake killed my friend,' she said, her face working as she collapsed in tears again.

Sarah handed her a tissue and took Mr Hertz to one side. 'Do you have a room somewhere where we could discuss things? I'm sure you don't want customers hearing all this, now do you?'

Mr Hertz, looking as though his day was rapidly going to pot, jerked his head towards the back room. 'This way,' he said in resigned tones.

Gina, left in peace again, unwrapped another stick of gum

and chewed thoughtfully as she watched the women walk away. Then she looked at the straggle of shoppers still waiting to pay. 'Next,' she said, in unenthusiastic tones.

In Mr Hertz's cubby-hole of an office, just off the warehouse-like area where the supermarket stock was kept, he threw himself into his swivel chair and looked on as Sarah and Daphne decided which of them would get the one remaining seat. Sarah prevailed on Daphne to sit and she did so, her tunic billowing out. She then blew her nose lavishly. Sarah propped open the door with the waste bin to allow a bit of air to circulate as the smell of cigarettes was very pungent, something she noted was both unhealthy and probably illegal.

Sarah spoke up. 'Mr Hertz, we won't waste your time—'

'Good, because I am very busy,' he interrupted rudely.

'Look,' Sarah began again, refraining from commenting on the fact that the man's desk was bare, the shop was pretty empty and he'd been skulking in this room smoking for what smelt like a lot more than ten minutes before they'd arrived. 'One of our friends has just died, after eating your red velvet cake. I'm sure you don't want to get the blame for that, do you?'

The effect of this statement was electrifying. Mr Hertz went from defensive to stunned but helpful. 'You're kidding! We had those coppers in here the other day pawing over the cake aisle, and looking at the security footage, but they got nowhere. Then they said they needed to take the cakes away for "inspection", but I wasn't having that, not without a proper chit. That cake you've got there, have you paid for it?'

'Not yet,' said Sarah, putting the box down on the desk. 'But we intend to. Mind you, the longer this business takes, the less I feel like eating it, how about you, Daphne?'

Daphne nodded, but she was still in a world of misery, dabbing at her eyes. 'Pat loved this shop,' she said with a sob. 'I can't think why.'

'Yes, well,' said Sarah hurriedly, thinking insults wouldn't help them much at this stage. 'Perhaps we could see whatever footage you have from this morning?'

Mr Hertz's gaze slid from Daphne to Sarah and back again. 'Why on earth would I want to show that to you two? The police are going to be here demanding it any minute, and they're not going to be happy...'

'Yes, and may I ask what you thought about the officers you dealt with?' Sarah said, looking at the man earnestly. 'Were you impressed? Do you think they'll get the job done before the reputation of Seastore is completely trashed? You don't seem to have an awful lot of customers in today, I notice. That must be because the news about the Victoria sponge has got out. I bet the Co-Op at the other side of town is awash with shoppers as we speak. You're a small, independent store, not a company with multiple outlets. If people find out you weren't very helpful about the red velvet cake that killed Pat, it could damage your reputation and have a very serious effect on your trade.'

'Pat? The old bid— erm, the lady who used to help Bill Turbot out with the Scouts?'

Sarah couldn't help shuddering. Pat's crush on the late scoutmaster had been quite unsavoury, in her view. 'Yes, that's her. Poor dear Pat,' she added rather hypocritically. 'Very popular in the town, as you know. The last thing you want is a boycott by her friends. That's everyone at the sheltered accommodation, not to mention the book group and the crafting club. Oh, and all the regulars at the Jolly Roger pub.'

Mr Hertz seemed to reflect on that. 'All right. Well, I suppose I'll have to look the footage out for the police anyway, when they get here. Won't do any harm to show you two first. After all, it's not as though you can do anything with the information, is it?' he said, laughing heartily at the very idea that Sarah and Daphne were capable of anything constructive.

'How dare you? I'll have you know that Sarah and I have

solved not one but two awful— ow, Sarah, why did you just tread on my foot?' said Daphne.

'Oops, must have stumbled,' Sarah said, widening her eyes at her friend in a bid to stop her flow.

Mr Hertz got to his feet. 'Well, if we're going to do this, we might as well get on with it before the afternoon rush,' he said hopefully, though as they left his office and passed through the shop again it seemed more deserted than ever. Gina was happily blowing bubbles behind her till, but stopped when Mr Hertz gave her a filthy glare. 'I hope you've paid for that gum, young lady,' he said. 'This way, please,' he said, showing them into an even tinier booth at the front of the shop which Sarah hadn't noticed before.

Inside it was a rather surprised security guard, who had been finishing off what looked like a large early tea of Pringles, washed down with a two-litre bottle of Fanta. Daphne looked at it enviously, while Sarah tried not to calculate the sheer quantity of E numbers he must be ingesting.

'All right, Ron?' said Mr Hertz to the guard, who was now gasping as a crisp had gone down the wrong way.

'Take a mouthful of your drink,' said Sarah in matter-of-fact tones.

Once he had done that, Ron smiled broadly at her. ''S'better, thanks.'

'Right,' said Mr Hertz. 'Now, let's get on with this.'

Sarah definitely approved of his sense of urgency. She wasn't sure she could bear to be in the booth for much longer. It was no doubt snug with one large guard in it, but with three others crammed in, the word 'poky' was being redefined.

'What you after, then, guv?' Ron asked, stowing his food below the desk and wiping the crumbs off onto the floor. Sarah couldn't help thinking what a shame it was that Hamish had missed this moment. She hoped he was OK with Charles.

Hertz looked askance at Ron's attempt at a tidy-up, but

confined himself to saying, 'We need today's footage. From about what time, ladies?'

'Well, probably from about your opening time, until, what time did we leave Pat, Daphne?'

Daphne hiccoughed at hearing her late friend's name and buried her face in her rather battered tissue.

'Um, it was around twelve, I think,' Sarah said, filling in the gaps herself.

Ron, who'd been looking from Hertz to Sarah, red-faced, now interjected. 'But sir, you know those constables took everything.'

'I know they've removed the previous tapes, Ron. To view at headquarters, they said.'

'Yeah, but no,' Ron said. 'They've had the lot. The equipment and all.'

Hertz looked stunned. 'But why on earth did they do that? It leaves us without any CCTV in the store.'

'I said to you at the time...' Ron started, but Hertz waved an arm to silence him, and accidentally whacked the side of the booth.

'Ouch. All right, all right,' he said crossly.

'You signed a bit of paper saying you were OK with it,' Ron continued inexorably.

'I said all right, I've remembered,' said Hertz, now as brick red as Ron.

'So you mean there's no CCTV footage from this morning at all?' Sarah said, flummoxed.

'You heard the man,' said Hertz, folding his arms crossly. 'Ron, get on the phone to those two coppers and get our stuff back here now. People will be killing each other with our cakes all day long at this rate!'

At this, Daphne sobbed again and Sarah decided it was high time they were on their way. 'Well, many thanks for your help,' she said, backing out of the booth, smiling at Ron and ushering her friend out. 'We'll just have another word with Gina on our way home,' she added.

Once she'd left the booth, Daphne perked up a little. 'Thank goodness, my energy streams have room to breathe again,' she said. 'Can we please go now?'

'Of course,' said Sarah. 'I just want to ask the girl on the till something,' she said, bustling over.

'But why?' Daphne wailed. 'I really need to sit down. I'm in mourning, you know.'

'Won't be a second,' Sarah said brightly. 'Just hang on.'

'But what can she tell you? She's too busy chewing to say anything useful,' Daphne said in her carrying voice.

'Shhh!' Sarah said quickly. 'I've just realised. There's no CCTV, thanks to Tweedledum and Tweedledee. But I bet Gina was on the till this morning. She could have sold the red velvet cake herself. I only wish it had occurred to me earlier.'

But when Daphne and Sarah reached the till, there was a problem. Gina was nowhere to be seen, and another girl was sitting in her seat, wearing an identical Seastore tabard and also chewing away on gum as though her life depended on it.

'Um, we were hoping to speak to Gina,' Sarah said.

'Tea break, innit?' said the new girl. 'Buying that cake, are we?'

'What?' Sarah had forgotten she was still clutching the boxed-up coffee and walnut cake. 'Oh, er, yes please.'

'That'll be eight quid, love,' the girl said, chewing idly as Sarah fished out her purse and waved a card at the reader.

'Where will Gina be taking her break?' Sarah asked, tucking the receipt away. 'Round the back?' she pointed in the direction of Mr Hertz's office, expecting there to be some staff quarters nearby.

'Nah, she'll be at the arcade, won't she?' said the girl. 'Can't miss it, on the seafront. The one with the slot machines.'

'Right. Thank you so much. Come on, Daphne,' Sarah said, plucking her friend by the sleeve.

'Where are we going now?' asked Daphne plaintively. 'Can't we sit down?'

'Not for a bit,' said Sarah as patiently as she could. 'You want to find out what happened to Pat, don't you? This is our chance. Whoever bought that cake might have known the CCTV wasn't working. Maybe that's why they came back to Seastore. But Gina *sold* the cake. Don't you see, Daphne? She has to know who the killer is.'

TWENTY-THREE

Sarah marched Daphne along the streets until they reached the esplanade, the jewel in Merstairs' crown. But today, her attention was a long way from the matchless views and she didn't spare the wheeling seagulls a single glance. Her focus was entirely on finding the amusement arcade, a throwback from the days before international travel, when the combination of seaside and slot machines had possessed a heady glamour.

'I think it's about halfway down here, isn't it, Daph? I've never been in but you can hear the whizzes and bangs of the machines from the street. I suppose it's like a cut-price casino, full of fruit machines.'

'Dreadful place,' said Daphne with a sniff. 'That's one sort of fruit you'll never talk me into having more of. Such a dark and dingy place, when here we are with all this fresh air,' she said.

'I know exactly what you mean,' said Sarah, as they passed Daphne's own shop, Tarot and Tealeaves, whose windows were so grubby it was impossible to see what went on inside. 'Some people like it that way, I guess,' she said.

'But why on earth would you have a tea break in a place like this?' said Daphne, balking as they reached the threshold of the arcade. 'Poseidon's Palace', proclaimed a sign in glaring, jagged gold letters. The doorway was just an open space, but it still felt like entering a deep, dark cavern as they went inside. Everything – walls, floor and ceiling – was painted black, while the machines lined up everywhere crashed and flashed and bleeped, pulsating with colour and life. 'I can't hear myself think,' said Daphne in a deafening screech, which really didn't help.

Sarah, letting her eyes become accustomed to the darkness and the cacophony of dings and bongs, looked around carefully. There weren't many people in here, despite the initial hectic impression given by the noise and neon lights of the machines. There was a sort of control booth right at the back of the place, and a few knots of teenagers clustered around what were presumably the most exciting games. Was Gina somewhere there?

'Let's see if we can find who we're looking for,' she said, grabbing Daphne's arm and urging her onwards.

'But we stand out like sore thumbs in here,' Daphne said.

'When has that ever stopped us?' Sarah said bracingly. 'Come on.'

She knew why the normally bouncy Daphne was feeling a little daunted. Everything about this place was designed to disorientate, to get people to focus on the machines, to forget time and every other consideration while pouring their money into the ever-hungry slots. It definitely wasn't meant to appeal to ladies of their generation, and simply by appearing in the doorway they bumped the average age of customers up by about fifty years. But that was not important. They had to find Gina, and the faster they did that, the sooner they'd be out – and hopefully a little further on in the investigation, too.

They approached the first group of youths, stumbling

slightly over the machine leads snaking around in the darkness as they went.

'This is a health and safety hazard,' Sarah couldn't help noting, then realised it made her sound even older and more out of place. 'Um, we're looking for Gina?' she said, tapping one youth on the shoulder.

He was crouching over a machine that was blaring out a fake machine gun rat-a-tat-tat and he flinched visibly as she touched him. Then there was a whole chorus of 'Oh no, man!' and on the screen there was a brief explosion, then everything went blank before a tinny theme tune started up and a skull and crossbones flashed onto the screen. 'My turn now,' said another of the boys. The ousted competitor turned on Sarah in disgust, then saw Daphne.

'Aunty Daph!'

'Fabian! Darling,' said Daphne, engulfing the lanky boy with his shock of blond hair in one of her biggest hugs. When he finally emerged, blinking, she introduced him to Sarah. 'This is Mariella's husband John's sister's boy. Well, we're in luck finding you, aren't we?'

'Lovely to meet you,' said Sarah. 'Sorry about the game.'

'No worries. Was my best score... but whatevs,' Fabian said graciously.

Then Sarah ruined their new accord. 'No school today?'

'Um. Free period,' mumbled Fabian.

Sarah smelt a rat. If this had been one of her girls, she would have conducted a fierce examination of timetables and teaching strategies. But she brushed all that aside. 'I'm so glad we've run into you,' she said. 'We're looking for Gina... Gina from Seastore. Do you know her?'

'Course,' said Fabian. 'Gina! Gina, over here. People to see you.'

Gina, who must have spotted Sarah and Daphne by now and was probably keeping a purposefully low profile, detached herself from the little clump of spectators around the game and walked reluctantly towards them.

'Yeah?' she said, moving her gum from one side of her mouth to the other.

'Gina, we were chatting in Seastore earlier, you might remember?' Sarah began carefully.

'Hmm,' said Gina, neither confirming nor denying.

'We wondered if you'd given any thought to what we were talking about? Someone buying a cake early this morning...' Sarah continued gently, when Daphne broke in.

'Look, Gina, my friend Pat was killed this morning. She ate a piece of red velvet cake and then she died. Do you want to be next?' she said, staring at the girl. Even in the dim lighting, Sarah could see her reacting. She swallowed automatically in shock, and the gum must have gone down. She coughed a little, but then regained her composure.

'No one is saying you had any responsibility for what happened,' Sarah put in quickly. 'We just wondered if you could remember who you served.'

Gina looked at Fabian, and then back at the group round the machine. 'Let's go outside,' she said, much to Sarah's relief. 'My break's nearly over anyway.'

The warmth and brightness of the esplanade came as a welcome respite from the relentless mechanical cocoon of the arcade, as did the wonderful normal seaside sounds of birds cawing and toddlers laughing. Sarah rather hoped she'd never have to set foot in Poseidon's Palace again.

'Is there something you didn't want to say in front of your friends?' Sarah asked the girl gently.

'No. It's not that,' said Gina, though there was definitely a hesitation in her manner. 'It's more... did you know there's quite a lot of shoplifting in Merstairs?'

Sarah and Daphne looked at each other in surprise. It was

such a well-heeled little community. Surely there weren't that many people in need?

'Who shoplifts?' Sarah asked, feeling a little sceptical.

'Don't get me wrong, and I know your daughter is in the police,' Gina said, nodding at Daphne, who preened.

'Everyone knows my Mari,' she said graciously.

'Yeah. But the other cops... well. Let's just say they make things a bit easy, if you know what I mean.'

'I'm not sure I do?' said Sarah.

Gina squirmed a little. 'It's just that... it isn't hard to get things past them, is it? I mean, no one's scared of being questioned by that pair.'

Sarah winced inwardly. How awful that Tweedledum and Tweedledee, the bobbies on the beat that communities were always said to value so highly, were actually increasing crime in Merstairs.

'But you do also have a security guard at the shop, Ron, I think he's called?' Sarah said, hoping this might make a difference, even if the Merstairs police were – Mari excepted – worse than useless.

'Don't get me wrong, Ron's great,' Gina said. 'But he can't be everywhere. Not all the time. And the cops just took our CCTV away, too.'

'I don't understand this. Are you saying you didn't sell the cake this morning?'

Gina nodded.

Sarah looked at her blankly, and then something clicked. 'Aha! Because it was stolen instead?'

'Eggsackerly,' said Gina succinctly, chewing away on a fresh piece of gum.

'Good grief,' said Sarah.

'That rather puts a spanner in the works,' said Daphne.

'But hang on a moment,' Sarah said, thinking hard. 'Do you know who's doing the shoplifting?'

'That's where it gets a bit... tricky,' said Gina, chewing more slowly.

'Why's that, Gina? You can tell us,' Sarah said, with what she hoped was a dependable smile.

Gina shifted from foot to foot. 'I feel bad saying it. But it's the biddies, isn't it?'

'Biddies?' said Sarah, trying not to feel affronted at the term. She was sure some people would be all too happy to stick her and Daphne in this bracket, being women past the age of sixty.

Gina looked down, and dragged her foot along the pavement, edging a fallen ice cream cone into the gutter. 'It's them in the sheltered housing. You know, down the way,' she said, nodding her head in the direction they'd come from.

'Wait a minute,' said Sarah, finally cottoning onto something. 'The housing where Pat lived?'

Gina nodded miserably.

'So you're saying...?'

'I don't get this,' said Daphne. '*What* are you saying? Just spit it out, girl.'

Gina just looked at her, eyes wide.

Sarah sighed, and spoke up. 'She's saying Pat stole the cake herself. That's right, isn't it?'

Gina nodded slowly, while Daphne's mouth opened in a perfect O.

TWENTY-FOUR

Sarah and Daphne leant on the railings, looking out to sea, as Gina scurried back to the supermarket so she wouldn't be late for the rest of her shift.

'I just can't believe it,' said Daphne.

'What, exactly?' Sarah asked gently.

'Well, either thing, really. That Pat was a thief, or that she committed suicide.'

'Pat was full of mischief, though, wasn't she, Daph? I wonder if, at some level, she thought Seastore owed her a cake or two after a long life of shopping there. And Gina and the other girls on the till probably turned a blind eye. They know the residents are trying to scrape by on tiny pensions, they feel sorry for them, I expect. Not that I'm condoning it,' Sarah said, putting her hands up. 'But as to suicide... I don't think that's what happened.'

'But you heard Gina,' Daphne said, brows arching in surprise. 'Pat pinched the cake herself. She just stuffed it up her top and sauntered out. She *must* have been responsible.'

'Not at all,' replied Sarah. 'Someone else in her flat could have administered the cyanide, by putting it into the cake. All Pat had to do then was eat it.'

'So... assisted suicide?'

'Not if she was unaware that the cake had been doctored. That would make it just good old-fashioned murder.'

Daphne shivered. 'Well, for once I think murder is the best option. I don't like to think of Pat killing herself.'

'She didn't have any reason to, did she? She wasn't ill... or not *that* ill, anyway,' Sarah said, thinking back to the woman's hacking cough and bent back. 'I know it's an awful phrase and the older I get the less I like it, but I suppose she'd had a good innings.'

Daphne sniffed. 'Pat couldn't stand cricket. And she wouldn't thank you for saying that. She was full of life.' She dabbed her eyes with the tissue Sarah handed her.

'Well, all the more reason for saying it wasn't suicide,' Sarah said, patting her friend on the back. 'Come on then, we'd better get back to the sheltered housing. We've left Charles there with Hamish, remember.'

'Oh, all right then, not that I ever want to go near the place again. Poor Pat, dying there, in a den of thieves,' Daphne said, her voice wobbling.

Sarah didn't point out that Pat had been firmly in the thief camp herself, if not thief-in-chief. She wasn't quite sure how she felt about this new piece of evidence of Pat's character. Maybe it had just been an expression of the free-spirited side of her nature, or perhaps she'd been counting on the fact that no one would try and prosecute an old lady for the theft of a cake. The cost-of-living crisis undoubtedly played a part, too. A cake for £8 might be cheaper than a couple of slices in a café – but it was still a lot of money if you were on a pension. And, if Pat had spent her life treading the boards, Sarah rather doubted she had any great financial cushion in place for her later years. Performing was a precarious profession at best. At worst, it was just shorthand for unemployment.

And were Pat's friends back at the accommodation also involved? If so, that was a bit more worrying, as it put the shoplifting on a bit more of an organised criminal footing. There was also the troubling conundrum of how the poison had got into the cake, if Pat had pinched it herself. Sarah wondered about this as they walked back to find Charles. She remembered that Mariella had initially aired the idea of suicide with Sarah, when they'd been confronted with Mr Williams's body. It seemed like months ago, though it was still less than a week. Was Pat's death now evidence of a strange new pensioner trend in doing away with yourself? But that really didn't seem at all likely. It had to be the signature style of the murderer, rather than anything Mr Williams or Pat would have signed up to voluntarily.

Sarah hadn't known Mr Williams that well, but the last time she'd seen him he'd been in fine spirits and his questionable behaviour over the years didn't suggest someone who had ever suffered from a major depression. Likewise Pat. They had seen her hours before her death when she had been cackling with pleasure over her wicked past.

Daphne suddenly stopped dead in her tracks. 'I just can't believe Pat is gone! She was the most vibrantly alive, positive, truly radiant soul...'

Once again, Sarah was left feeling she'd missed something as far as Pat was concerned. One shouldn't speak ill of the dead, and all that, but 'radiant' was not the word she would have used.

'It's awful,' she said, urging her friend onwards. They'd nearly reached the building.

'She was as happy as the day was long.' Daphne shook her head.

Sarah could get behind that statement, at least, remembering those epic bouts of chuckles, which inevitably ended up in coughing fits. Her mind was ticking over rather fast now. If Pat hadn't been suicidal, then someone had placed the poison in her slice of cake at some point after she'd stolen it and brought it home to her sheltered accommodation. Top of Sarah's agenda now was finding out who had visited her that morning. And there was, of course, at least one person that she and Daphne both knew of.

'Ah, here we are. And it looks like Mariella's beaten us to it,' she said, seeing the policewoman's familiar car at the kerb.

Once inside the courtyard, it was clear that the police had been busy. Pat's turquoise door was still open, but now had yellow and black incident tape across the entrance. Charles and Hamish were sitting on the bench in the centre, but they were hemmed in by elderly lady residents, all watching the proceedings like birds on a telegraph wire, heads bobbing and bright eyes taking everything in.

Charles hailed them as soon as he spotted them. 'What ho!' he said, waving just in case they hadn't noticed him from two feet away. Hamish looked similarly thrilled to see Sarah, darting away from Charles and leaping up at her in a way that had been strictly prohibited since day one of puppy training. She forgave him, though, because his greeting was so loving – and she was just as pleased to see him.

'Keeping an eye on things?' Sarah asked Charles, as he tried to prise himself off the bench without dislodging too many of the ladies, who all seemed very sorry to see him go.

'Er, trying to,' Charles said ruefully. He'd obviously had quite a time of it. 'Between Pat and that Williams man's disgusting habits, those good ladies have been talking my ear off. Any developments?'

'I'll leave Daphne to get you up to speed,' said Sarah. She was weighing up her chances of success if she tried moseying over to Pat's to get Mariella's attention. After all, she did have a titbit of information to pass on. It would only be public-spirited of her to have a go, wouldn't it? 'Hamish, find Mariella,' she whispered to the little dog, inspired by what had happened at Mr Williams's house when she'd had to dash after him. She felt a little naughty but told herself that in a murder enquiry sometimes you had to bend the odd rule.

Hamish padded quickly over to the turquoise door. The incident tape was much too high to be any sort of impediment to an inquisitive little Scottie, and he disappeared inside straight away. Sarah ducked under it to follow him. 'Excuse me,' she called out loudly in the hall. 'Just coming in to get my dog, he's run away,' she said crossing her fingers.

Mariella stomped out from the living room into the hall, and put her hands on her hips. Hamish sat at her feet, looking at her admiringly, then turned his head back towards Sarah as though to say, 'Found her! Easy peasy.'

'Aunty Sarah—'

Sarah held her hands up. 'Before you even start, I just think you ought to know that Pat stole the red velvet cake from Seastore this morning. And when we left her flat, a man in overalls had just arrived to fix her waste disposal unit.'

Mariella stared at her impatiently, so Sarah burst into speech again. 'Don't you see, Mariella? He's one of the men you need to look for. There's a very good chance he's our murderer.'

TWENTY-FIVE

Mariella, her red hair tucked behind her ears, looked at Sarah with a bemused expression on her face.

'You mean this chap?' she said, moving slightly and revealing the man in overalls, large as life, in the middle of Pat's crowded living room, being questioned by Tweedledum. There was nothing about his stance that suggested he was a killer at bay. On the contrary, considering he was in the middle of a crime scene, he seemed quite relaxed, though the room still had the strange atmosphere of a place where something awful had happened. It was an effect heightened by the hushed scene-of-crime officers fingerprinting surfaces and sorting through Pat's belongings.

'Listen, Dumbarton, I'll take this over,' said Mariella, striding over to where the officer was talking to the workman. 'Come with me, sir.'

'Are we going to the police station?' the man asked. His face was tanned, with white lines around his eyes suggesting he was usually smiling. He flexed his arm, reaching for his phone, and Sarah noticed his muscles and his large hands with black-ringed nails. 'Only I'll have to tell the wife.'

'Not now, sir, we're just going to have a little chat. If you could come in here with me for a second,' Mariella said, opening a door which turned out to be Pat's bedroom. The cosy-looking bed, smothered with crocheted throws which Pat must have made with the crafting group, seemed unbearably poignant to Sarah. She stood with her back to it and the three of them made an unspoken move towards the window, where the thick net curtains were moving in the breeze.

Along the windowsill was a row of china ornaments that Pat had clearly prized, shepherdesses with shy smiles fixed on pretty painted faces. They didn't seem much in keeping with her brash character, but they were beautifully dusted, unlike the rest of the flat. Now their simpering gestures and porcelain skirts swished on into eternity, while their owner lay cruelly murdered.

'Right then, sir, I understand you met this lady this morning,' Mariella said briskly, gesturing towards Sarah.

Sarah smiled, hoping not to betray the nerves she was feeling. This man could be a double murderer, after all. His overalls, genuine though they seemed to be, smeared lightly with what looked like brick dust and a few daubs of paint, would be easy enough to pick up in any DIY store. Dressing as a workman was a perfect disguise for anyone wanting to prey on the elderly. Everyone needed maintenance work done, after all. Throw on a high-vis jacket, grab a clipboard, wear a boilersuit, show a confident demeanour and you were in.

But pointing away from Sarah's neat murder theory was the fact that the man didn't seem nervous at all, and the little insignia on his breast pocket matched the signage of the sheltered accommodation. That, in itself, wasn't a let-out – but it did mean, Sarah imagined, that he would have been thoroughly vetted when they'd taken him on, for things like a murderous hatred of elderly people and a propensity to poison them.

The man nodded at Mariella. 'Yes, we weren't exactly introduced as such... but this lady was in the flat this morning when I came over. She left pretty quickly when I arrived, with her friend with the funny thing on her head.'

'OK,' said Mariella, pressing her lips together. 'And can you explain what you were doing in Pat Buchanan's flat in the first place?'

'Of course, yes. The manager, Mr Ackroyd, asked me to check on Pat, I mean Mrs Buchanan. She was complaining, er, saying that her waste disposal unit wasn't working properly.'

'Complaining, you said?' Mariella pounced. 'Did Mrs Buchanan often complain?'

'I'm sure I can't say,' said the workman with the ghost of a wink. 'You'd have to ask Mr Ackroyd about that,' he added.

Mariella nodded. 'All right, I will. When was the last time you were in this flat?'

'Yesterday,' said the man promptly. 'That time it was the basin overflow.'

Mariella frowned. 'And the time before that?'

'Day before yesterday,' the man said with the merest hint of a sigh. 'Dripping tap.'

'I'm beginning to see a pattern,' said Mariella. 'Did Pat, er, Mrs Buchanan, call you out a lot?'

'She did, yeah,' he said, with a slight shrug.

'More than other residents, let's say?'

This time he merely gave a lopsided smile. 'It wasn't my fault.'

'Why would you say that?' Mariella leapt in. 'These all seem like valid minor problems with Pat's flat.'

A shadow passed over the workman's face, and Sarah decided to rescue him. 'Did Pat, erm, try and get a bit friendly with you?'

He crinkled up his eyes. 'It was only a bit of fun, I suppose, but it could get wearing.'

'Pat was sometimes like that,' Sarah said. 'She took a fancy to people.'

'Right,' said Mariella. 'Yes, of course. So, you started to find it annoying?'

Instantly, the man dismissed the idea. 'No, oh no, nothing like that. Just part of the job.'

'Hmm,' said Mariella, giving him an assessing glance. 'I wonder if you could come down to the police station later on today, just to give us a proper statement. As you've nothing to hide.'

'Sure,' he said, clearly not best pleased. 'Am I free to go now?'

'Yes. See you later,' said Mariella.

Once the man had left the room, Sarah said tentatively, 'You don't think he'll do a runner, do you?'

Mariella laughed. 'Certainly not. I know where he lives, and where his mum, sister and aunt live. He's OK really, bit of a lad maybe. It sounds as though Pat was giving him a hard time. You know what she was like with her crushes.'

Sarah certainly did. It took a lot, not to say a crowbar, to brush her off. 'Of course, that does give him a motive to... get rid of her.'

'He had a whole box of tools with him this morning, including several hammers that could have done for an old lady like Pat in a second. I can't really see him tampering with a dainty cake and feeding it to her, can you? For one thing, he'd have got oil all over it with those dirty great mitts of his. It really would have shown on that white icing.'

Sarah nodded her head. She had noticed the state of his nails straight away. 'But if you're right, it's back to square one again. I really thought we had a likely suspect there.'

'Well, if you think about it, eliminating him does get us a little further on,' said Mariella thoughtfully. Sarah almost held her breath; for once, the detective seemed to be forgetting that Sarah wasn't on her team. 'Someone else must have had access to Pat's flat, after he'd gone.'

'Yes!' said Sarah. 'And I know just the man! He's the other one I've got my eye on. Come on, it's this way,' she said, urging Mariella out into the passageway.

TWENTY-SIX

'This is all very well, Aunty Sarah, and I appreciate your enthusiasm, but where on earth do you think you're taking me?' Mariella puffed as Sarah came to a halt outside another door.

Sarah took a second to get her own breath back. 'Don't you recognise this office? Oh, but you might not have had time to catch up with him yet. It's Mr Ackroyd, the manager of this place.' Mariella looked blank, so Sarah continued in a whisper, in case he heard. 'He has the master key, so he could easily have got into Pat's place, and he more or less admitted to me earlier that he's desperate to get her out of the sheltered accommodation. Plus he said something about dealing with a complaint about washing going missing. I think that might be connected with Mr Williams.'

'With his murder, you mean?' Mariella looked intrigued.

'It's worth looking into. And he really seemed to dislike Pat.'

'Why did he want her gone, did he say?' Mariella asked, hand raised to knock on the door.

'I think it was the usual – problems with her latching onto the staff. He'll tell you, I'm sure. Um, there could also have been some issues at Seastore,' Sarah said, not sure whether it was quite the moment to discuss the cake thefts.

'Hmm, we've had no luck with the CCTV there, thanks to... well, never mind about that,' said Mariella, clearly deciding not to drop her colleagues in it. 'But it has to be working here, surely. They must keep an eye on things in case a resident has a funny turn. We'll ask Mr Ackroyd for the footage and see how things go from there. Let me do the talking.'

Sarah wanted to pinch herself. This sort of involvement was just what she'd wanted, ever since things had first started happening in Merstairs.

'Right. After you,' she said, gesturing to Mariella and trying not to seem too eager.

Mariella made as if to knock, then turned to Sarah. 'Not a word to him about your suspicions, mind.'

'Don't worry. I quite understand,' said Sarah earnestly. She really didn't want to spook either Mr Ackroyd, or Mariella, at this critical juncture.

Mariella paused for a second longer, then rapped at the door in an unmistakably authoritative way. It was immediately cracked open, and the weaselly features of Mr Ackroyd peered round at them.

'Yes?' he said, looking over their shoulders.

'Can you let us in, please,' said Mariella, keeping her tone light and reasonable, yet still brooking no nonsense. 'We need to discuss some things with you.'

Very reluctantly, Mr Ackroyd opened the door a little wider and the two women went in. The office wasn't large, but it was reasonably comfortable, with a desk facing a window onto the courtyard, a comfortable office chair, two visitors' seats and a heater, which was mercifully off on this hot day.

'Well, since you've insisted on coming in, what can I do for you two lovely ladies?' Mr Ackroyd said, sitting himself down and spinning from side to side, fingering his moustache. 'I'm rather busy at the moment dealing with the police, if you must know. I don't have time to talk to residents' families right now.'

'A little respect would be nice, for starters. I *am* the police. Detective Mariella Roux of the Merstairs force, to be precise, and this is Dr Sarah Vane.'

'We met earlier,' Sarah put in helpfully.

Mariella gave her a quelling look. 'We'd like to see your CCTV footage covering the area around Pat Buchanan's flat, ideally from midnight last night to now.' She crossed her arms.

'Oh. Oh right,' said Ackroyd with a cough. 'Well, I'll just have to get that checked. Excuse me one moment.' He looked expectantly at the women, as though waiting for them to leave his office. Mariella gazed back at him while Sarah watched with interest. After a couple of beats, he picked up the phone on his desk and dialled.

'Mike. Yeah, listen. The CCTV in the passageway, opposite the courtyard, you know? Ah right. Yes, that's what I thought. All right, thanks for telling me.'

Ackroyd looked at Mariella with an expression almost of triumph on his face. 'Sorry, lo— um, detective. It's broken.'

'What? You're telling me your CCTV isn't functioning?'

'I reported it to the council last week. The guy I just rang was supposed to fix it but, as you could probably hear, he hasn't got round to it. He's rushed off his feet.'

Mariella and Sarah looked at each other. Outside, the courtyard was full of elderly people eager for news. Daphne and Charles were both still on the bench while Hamish was being petted from all sides. There was absolutely no sign of activity from any staff.

'Rushed off his feet, is he?' Mariella said drily. 'Riiight. I understand you also have a pass key that lets you into all the flats.'

Ackroyd shifted nervously in his chair. 'So? I need it in case someone's taken ill.'

'Was Pat "taken ill"?'

The manager stared at Mariella. 'Here. What are you saying?'

'It's a simple question. Were you in Pat's flat this morning?'

Mr Ackroyd's eyes darted from left to right. Then he seemed to have an idea. 'Ask her,' he said, pointing rather rudely at Sarah. 'She'll tell you.'

'Well, we met him outside Pat's place,' Sarah admitted rather grudgingly. 'But—'

Just then, Ackroyd's phone rang again and he held out his hand for silence and picked it up importantly. 'Manager speaking.' He turned to Mariella. 'I'm sorry, this is going to take some time.'

'All right, but I'll be questioning you again,' Mariella said very firmly. 'I'd like to see you down at the police station tomorrow afternoon at four. Come on, let's go,' she added to Sarah.

Sarah didn't need much urging. The little office was growing stuffier by the minute, and judging from the aroma, Mr Ackroyd hadn't changed his socks that morning. They shut the door on his affronted face.

Outside, they both drew deep breaths and took stock. 'So Ackroyd wasn't actually in Pat's flat?' Mariella said.

'Well, Daphne and I met him outside. But he could easily have been in there earlier. We need to check for fingerprints.'

Mariella frowned. 'We?' Then she continued. 'There've been two sets of CCTV out at crucial moments. You'd almost think—'

'There's someone doing this deliberately,' Sarah rushed to finish her sentence. 'Someone who knows where the cameras are and can disable them – like the manager, for instance. I think it would be worth our while asking the people on and around the bench,' she said. 'They're not as reliable as CCTV, I grant you, but they do have a very lively interest in people's comings and goings, and they'd certainly recognise Mr Ackroyd.'

'They'll be keen to remember, once the penny drops that the killer could strike again,' said Mariella with a determined look on her face

'Well – probably best if you don't go saying that to them,' said Sarah carefully. 'The last thing we need is mass panic in the sheltered housing. We just want to treat this like an interesting bit of scandal – the stuff they like best.'

'All right then, I suppose you know this sort of age range best – not that you're quite there yet,' said Mariella swiftly. 'Erm, no offence.'

'None taken,' said Sarah, biting back a smile and only glad Mariella was letting her help out. 'Hopefully someone will have seen something.'

'It won't be as good in court as CCTV footage would have been. Any lawyer could easily pick holes in this sort of testimony. People living here are in need of help and their memories are probably as leaky as sieves,' Mariella said. 'But you're right, it's all we've got to go on now.'

Sarah put a hand on the detective's arm to stop her. 'Do you want to do this formally, though, Mariella? Take everyone down to the police station, like Ackroyd and the handyman? Or is it a good idea just to ask a few questions in a more relaxed setting?'

'A setting where you can get your tuppence worth in, Aunty Sarah? Go on, then. I suppose we can do it here for now. And if we do get any useful information then I can whisk people off to make a proper statement that they can sign.'

TWENTY-SEVEN

Sarah tried to keep a jaunty swing out of her step as they approached the bench, but it was hard. It would be very wrong to say things were going well when someone had just died, but she just needed a grain of evidence against Mr Ackroyd to bring the whole case to a close.

It wasn't long, however, before she felt as though they were taking two steps back for every tentative toe they put forward. First up for questioning were Gladys and her friend Lou. While Daphne and Charles held the rest of the group at bay, Sarah and Mariella ushered the ladies onto a pair of slightly rickety garden chairs just out of earshot.

'Well, this is nice, isn't it?' said Gladys, settling herself more comfortably into the seat. 'Lovely view of Mr Pickles's place at number seven. I say, Lou, you can almost see his gladioli from here.'

'Very perky,' said Lou, giving her friend a nudge. Mariella and Sarah exchanged a glance.

'Well now, ladies, if you could just bring your minds back to this morning,' Mariella said in a businesslike tone.

'Yes, lovely weather, isn't it? But we can't stop long chatting with you, dear,' said Gladys firmly. 'It's going to be time for dinner in a minute and I want to tell Della at number four about Mr Williams and the girdles before that.'

'We'll be very quick,' said Sarah, hoping that was true. 'We just wondered... you remember seeing me and my friend this morning? We popped into Pat's place.'

'You and the police lady?' said Gladys suspiciously.

'No.' Sarah was patient. 'Me and Daphne, look she's over there.'

'So she is,' said Gladys, waving enthusiastically. 'Told my cards once, she did. An absolute fandango.'

'...Erm, a fiasco, you mean?' said Sarah tentatively, not wishing to offend Mariella.

'That's the one!' Gladys said, shaking her head.

'Well, moving on, let's concentrate on Pat, shall we,' said Sarah as brightly as she could. 'So, you saw me and Daphne go into her flat. Did you see anyone else?'

'No. No one at all.'

'And you, Lou, anyone? Take a moment to think if you need to.'

'Well, there was a lot going on,' said Lou carefully. 'There was the maintenance man popping in, but that happened every day really. Well, Pat had a bit of a thing for him, we all knew about *that*, though it was clear he only had eyes for m— oh, I shouldn't say really,' she said, lowering her eyes modestly. 'Anyway, it was quite busy in the courtyard so a bit difficult to see what was going on. And of course I wasn't studying Pat's door, was I, Gladys?'

'What? No, definitely not, whatever Pat might have said. Ridiculous, claiming you were jealous, Lou.'

Sarah pricked up her ears. It sounded as though there might have been some sort of rivalry between Pat and Lou for the affections of the handyman. But something else had caught her attention. 'You said it was busy in the courtyard. Why would that be? Was Mr Ackroyd involved?'

'What? No, he keeps out of the way, too much like hard work for him. It was because of tonight, of course,' said Lou. 'What a shame Pat will miss it,' she added in tones of unmistakable satisfaction.

'What's happening tonight?' Mariella asked.

'Oh, it's our gala evening. Entertainments, quizzes, snacks, the whole works. It's the biggest night of the year,' said Gladys with a rapt smile.

'I didn't see any preparations,' Sarah said in surprise.

'Come at the wrong moment, then, didn't you, love? There were people traipsing in and out, bringing supplies and putting them in the community hall. That's where we meet for all the big events,' Gladys said.

Sarah and Mariella looked at each other again. Mr Ackroyd hadn't mentioned any of this. 'Shall we go along and have a quick look at the hall?' Sarah said to Mariella in an undertone.

Mariella gave Sarah an exasperated look. 'I think we'd better.' She turned back to the women briefly. 'We'll see you in a minute, ladies.'

They got up and walked over to the manager's office, but before they reached it, a lady carrying a mop and bucket came round the corner. 'Where is the community hall, please?' Sarah asked.

'Oh, I've just come from there,' the lady said. 'It's looking a treat. Just beyond the last of the flats, there. Yes, that one with the turquoise door. Go past it and turn left.'

Sarah waved to Daphne and said they'd just be a minute, and she and Mariella hurried off. Sure enough, round the path and less than a hundred yards from Pat's place, there was a long low building with a cluster of brightly coloured balloons attached to its door, one of them already semi-deflated. They walked in, and Sarah looked around in surprise. The decorations were amateurish, it was true, with a 'Congratulations' banner hanging at a slightly wonky angle and the red paper tablecloths a little askew, but everything looked welcoming and cheery. There were a few crashes and bangs from the side of the room, so she and Mariella walked further in and peered round the door.

There were two young women unloading loaves of bread from a plastic tray, and another putting catering dishes of what looked like lasagne into a large fridge. Over at the sink, someone was busily rinsing glasses. Everyone was wearing blue hairnets and white overalls, disconcertingly like the outfits sported by SOCO teams. Just then, the woman at the sink turned round and Sarah stared in surprise. It was Hannah Betts, from the Beach Café.

'Hannah! Fancy seeing you here,' said Sarah with a broad smile.

'I didn't know you had family here,' Hannah said, drying her hands.

'I don't, just, er, visiting a friend. How about you?'

'I'm helping out at the annual shindig,' Hannah said with a small smile. 'My mum used to live here, you know. My Betsy and I used to look in on her all the time. Until she passed away.'

'Oh, I'm so sorry, I didn't realise.'

'No reason you should have known,' Hannah said lightly. 'It was before your time. But I like to help out here when I can. Just in her memory, you know.' She sighed.

'And how is Betsy doing?' Sarah said, remembering her troubles with anxiety. 'I hope she's feeling better.'

'She's OK, I think, poor girl. It's been one thing after another. But I'm hoping she'll soon be feeling a lot more like her usual self.'

'Well, it's very good of you to pitch in, when you must have so much to do in the café.'

'Oh, I like to keep busy,' Hannah smiled. 'Mind you, I'm

having to rewash everything. Doesn't look like the place has even been dusted since last time,' she said, shaking her head. 'All right, there, Mariella?'

'Yes, all good,' said Mariella. 'I'm really glad you're here, we're trying to establish who was where earlier on. You know, when Pat was killed.'

Hannah dropped the glass she'd been rinsing, and it smashed in the sink with a loud crash. 'Pat? You mean... I thought she'd just had a heart attack or something.'

'I'm afraid not,' said Mariella evenly. 'You haven't heard the details?'

'I've been stuck in here for hours, I've been up to my eyes,' Hannah said, looking shocked. 'No one's told me a thing. You mean... it was like Mr Williams?'

Mariella raised her eyebrows. 'Why would you say that?'

Hannah blinked. 'Oh, I don't know... well, you said she'd been killed. *Was* it like Mr Williams? I'm confused now.'

'I can't really give out any details,' said Mariella. 'But I am keen to know what you saw and heard this morning. In fact, is there somewhere we could go and talk?'

'Of course! Anything to help,' said Hannah. 'Though I probably won't be much use, I've been working in here the whole time. Gill, if you wouldn't mind clearing this up? I don't know what came over me,' she said to one of the women bustling around, pointing at the mess in the sink. 'Be careful, of course. Use the heavy-duty gloves, and wrap the shards up in newspaper,' she said, as the woman nodded.

Hannah followed Mariella and Sarah into a small cloakroom, which smelt musty but at least had a bench and a couple of chairs they could sit on. All the pegs were empty now, but presumably if there were events in the winter months the residents could muffle up before leaving their flats to keep warm on the very short journey over here.

Sarah took one end of the bench and after a moment's

thought Mariella sat down on it, too. That left Hannah with a chair. She subsided onto it, looking strained. 'I can't believe this about Pat,' she said, shaking her head.

'Yes, coming right after Mr Williams,' Sarah said.

'Dreadful business,' the café owner said heavily.

'And you had no idea what had really happened until now? Didn't you see the police cars? Notice the constables going round to all the flats?' Sarah said, a little surprised.

Mariella looked over at her. She shook her head very slightly and Sarah fell silent. Mariella was right, this was her show, not Sarah's. She ought to consider herself lucky to be sitting in on this, not draw attention to herself and risk being chucked out.

'I suppose I just assumed they always did that when there's a death in the sheltered accommodation,' Hannah said, not seeming to notice the power struggle going on in front of her. 'And I was too busy getting things set up. You know how it is. Everything has to be organised and ready to start by five o'clock.'

'I thought it was an evening gala?' Sarah couldn't help chipping in.

'It is.' Hannah shrugged. 'People round here go to bed early.'

Sarah and Mariella both smiled at that. 'So, this is probably a silly question, but did you see any unusual activity in the courtyard at any point?' Mariella continued.

'I've mostly been stuck in here,' Hannah said. 'Not this cloakroom, obviously, but the hall and the kitchen. There's a lot to sort out. There've been loads of people coming and going, including my staff of course.'

'Is it a hot meal?' Sarah asked.

'There's a choice. Soup, salad, sandwiches and some cakes for later.'

'Cakes?' Sarah couldn't help cocking her head at Mariella, but Mariella just compressed her lips and shook her head once more. Sarah resolved again to remain silent. Or to try her best, anyway.

'They all love a bit of my cake, so I just do a few of my specials,' Hannah said.

'I see,' said Mariella, making a note. 'And what would they be, just for the sake of interest?'

'Oh, you know, Victoria sponges always go down well, then today I've got a coffee and walnut or two and a lemon drizzle.'

Mariella scribbled away, then Hannah spoke up again. 'Oh, and a red velvet, of course. I thought people might like something a bit different.'

Sarah tried to stop herself giving Mariella a significant look but from the way the detective studiously avoided glancing her way, she thought she'd probably failed.

'Did any of your serving staff discuss what had happened at all? The fact that Pat had died?'

'I heard it at some point, and I was sad of course, but... well, that sort of thing does happen here. Everyone's over a certain age, when all's said and done. It's awful but, well, it's part of life, isn't it?' Hannah shrugged sadly.

'Did you see Mr Ackroyd, the manager, at any point?'

'That's the funny thing,' Hannah said slowly. 'I did see him – right outside Pat's window. It looked like he was peering in, or something. But when I came past he just smiled at me and hurried off. So I don't know what that was about,' she added, looking from Daphne to Sarah.

'He didn't say anything?'

'Not that I heard. I might have had my earbuds in, though. I try not to get distracted when I'm at work,' she said. 'Now, I'm really sorry, I want to help all I can, but I do have to get on. The gala won't be the same without Pat, of course, but I suppose the show must go on,' she said.

'Just one more thing,' said Sarah cheekily, before Mariella could reply. 'There were some initials written in Mr Williams's handwriting in his house, they might have been HB. The same as yours. Do you know what that could have been about?'

Hannah looked blank for a second. 'HB? That's a kind of pencil, isn't it? No idea,' she shrugged. 'Is that all? It's just that I've got so much to do.'

Mariella smiled at her. 'Of course, Hannah. You carry on. We can't have the gala being disrupted – though I suppose Mr Ackroyd might still feel he ought to cancel it out of respect...'

'Oh, he's said he won't do that,' said Hannah hurriedly. 'Instead it's going to be a sort of memorial.'

'That's a lovely idea,' said Sarah.

'Mm,' Mariella agreed. 'Well, we know where you are if we have any more questions,' she said, smiling at Hannah and shutting her notebook.

Once Hannah had gone and closed the door after her, Mariella and Sarah were left looking at each other. 'What do you make of all that?' Mariella said to the older woman.

Sarah was silent for a moment. 'Do you think that could be right, HB referring to pencils? Mr Williams did go to the art group every week.'

'Yes, but he wasn't drawing, was he?' said Mariella.

'No... There's something needling me, but I can't quite work out what it is,' Sarah said, frustrated.

'I agree,' said Mariella. 'Well, I've got a lot more helpers to interview, and I'd better see if Gladys and Lou have remembered anything.'

Sarah was sorely tempted to ask to stay, but decided it was better not to push her luck. 'I'll leave you to it, then. I ought to keep an eye on Daphne, she'll be finding this hard to deal with. Shall I send the next person in?'

'No, don't worry about that. I'll pop out when I've got my notes in order,' Mariella said.

Sarah dithered, with her hand on the doorknob. She was torn. She badly wanted to stay at the centre of the investigation, but Hamish and Daphne needed her. 'Well, just give me a ring if there's anything I can do,' she said hopefully.

Mariella gave her that wry look again. 'Will do, Aunty Sarah.'

She half-turned the handle, then looked over her shoulder at the detective. 'Do you get the feeling we're missing something? Something we should be following up on?'

This time Mariella simply rolled her eyes. 'Always. Don't worry, it's all in good hands. We'll get to the truth in the end, one way or another.'

Sarah left the room but then came to a halt again right outside. Mariella's soothing words were all very well, but they lacked a sense of urgency. And could the detective really promise she'd find the killer before they struck again?

TWENTY-EIGHT

Sarah took Daphne, Hamish and Charles home, and spent the evening patiently listening to her friend's lamentations about Pat as they all ate a takeaway fish supper in her kitchen. It was one of the cheeriest spots in the cottage. The red and white checked tablecloth and array of sparkling china arranged on the dresser could normally be relied upon to raise Sarah's spirits. Charles was usually an uplifting presence, too, even with the uneasy state of affairs between them. But tonight he was all but silent, Daphne was sunk fathoms deep in gloom and even Hamish seemed subdued, though that could have been because Daphne hardly dropped a single chip on the floor.

'All right, you lot, that's enough of that,' said Sarah forcefully, bundling up the chip papers and shoving them into her bin. She got out a bottle of crisp Sauvignon Blanc from the fridge and reached down three glasses. 'I know you told me you didn't want any wine, Daph,' she said quickly, forestalling her friend's objections and pouring it out. 'But I think a little something might cheer us up, tonight of all nights. We need to drink to Pat. And also to finding whoever did this.'

After a second's hesitation, Charles raised his glass, and

then Daphne followed suit. They mumbled the toast and sipped. Daphne still looked pretty downhearted, but Sarah felt the atmosphere lifting. It was always better to focus on action, in her view.

'Let's look at what we've got so far,' she continued. 'Mr Williams was poisoned by a piece of Victoria sponge from Seastore, and in his house was a huge quantity of women's underwear.'

'But the pants might be nothing to do with his death,' Daphne piped up. 'No one really knew what he was up to, after all.'

'Someone could have found out his secret, though. What about Pat, for instance?' said Sarah.

'Well, I suppose that's the thing,' said Daphne slowly. 'She did seem to know all about it. Remember, she mentioned it in the pub right after you found Mr Williams. And Pat *loved* a secret.'

Sarah thought back to the times when she'd encountered the elderly lady. It was true, she'd always been chortling over some bit of gossip or other that she probably shouldn't have known in the first place. Funny that Sarah had spent quite a bit of time worrying over the state of Pat's lungs, when it looked as though it was what was stashed in the old lady's mind that had proved fatal. 'Do you think she knew something else about Mr Williams? But what could that have been?'

'Let's think about what Williams did for a living. He was in the post office, and left under a cloud,' said Charles thoughtfully.

'Yes, because of all those rumours that he stole the post, or read it before delivering it,' Sarah put in.

'Could he have strayed across something really important back then? The sort of secret that no one wanted to get out?' Charles said.

'Well, he could have done, but that was all so long ago. He

must have retired twenty years back. Why would anyone kill him now, for something that happened years ago?' Sarah sighed, and went to the fridge. She got out a couple of punnets of gorgeously flavoursome Kent strawberries from a local farm for them to munch on while thinking things through. 'I suppose people have long memories around here?'

'Or perhaps that stuff isn't relevant at all. Perhaps it's just that Pat saw something she shouldn't have,' said Daphne slowly.

'Did you see Pat, after Mr Williams died?' Sarah asked.

'Well, we both did, didn't we? This morning,' Daphne said, pressing a tissue to her eyes.

'Of course. But apart from that. Did she say anything at any point that you thought sounded odd?'

Daphne laughed through her tears. 'This is Pat we're talking about! Of course she said odd things.'

'Odd things about *Mr Williams*, Daphne. Do try and remember.' Sarah tried not to sound cross, but this was pretty vital.

Daphne put a hand to her head, and for a moment Sarah thought they were due another trip to the Beyond. 'She did say something. Now that I really think about it. Last time we were at the Jolly Roger together.' She stopped and dabbed her eyes. 'One of the crafting gang kept fiddling with her bra strap, saying it was really uncomfortable. Well, we were all girls together. And then Pat said it was just as well Mr Williams wasn't around, he'd soon have it off her.'

Sarah boggled at Daphne. 'And you didn't think to mention that? It's such a gross thing to say, too.'

'The thing is,' Daphne said. 'Pat did say the strangest things... no one took much notice.'

Sarah shrugged, and looked over to Charles. 'Sounds like she definitely knew what he was up to. Have you got any thoughts?'

'Just that it's lucky someone else got to him before I did,' said Charles, shaking his head. 'But I was just wondering about the cakes. I mean, the Victoria sponge was from Seastore, we're clear on that...'

Daphne sat up a little straighter. 'But what about Pat's red velvet? Gina at Seastore as good as said Pat pinched it this morning. It must have been tucked away in her kitchen when we were in the flat.'

'And Hannah did say she'd brought some red velvet cake with her, for the gala tonight, which is now a memorial gala if that's a thing,' said Sarah. 'But the cake in Pat's flat was on a doily that was just the same as the one under Mr Williams's slice. So I'm pretty sure it was from Seastore. Of course there's no proof as their CCTV equipment was taken away.'

'Wait a minute,' said Daphne. 'So the red velvet from Hannah is more of a – red herring?' Her shoulders started shaking and Sarah realised she'd gone from grief to hilarity pretty quickly. It was a relief, of a sort – but maybe that was enough of the wine.

'You could say that,' Charles started to say, but then Sarah remembered again that half-finished feeling she'd had in the interview with Mariella.

'There is something niggling away at me about all that,' she said. 'I just wish I could get it to come to light.' She frowned down at her hands, which were now a little pink from the strawberry juice.

'In any case, and forgive another play on words, but Pat's death wasn't a case of someone seeing red with the red velvet cake, was it? It was premeditated. Just as the Victoria sponge was,' said Charles.

'Yes,' said Sarah slowly. 'So we're looking at someone who's got the capacity for long-range planning, someone who's not afraid to act when something goes wrong. Whoever killed Pat moved fast, in between our chat with her this morning and then the arrival of the gala staff.'

'It could have been someone who worked at the housing complex all the time. That would make it easy for them to slip in and out of Pat's flat without anyone noticing.'

'Well, we did initially wonder about that workman, but it wasn't him,' said Sarah absently. 'My money's still on Mr Ackroyd. I'm not sure he's the daring type, he's such a weasel of a man. But he was definitely on the spot... would he really kill one of his own residents, though?'

'OK, well, I think we're starting to go round in circles now,' said Charles, suddenly bustling to his feet. 'Let me give you a hand tidying up, Sarah, then I'll see Daphne home next door.'

'Oh, there's hardly anything to be done,' Sarah said. 'I'll just pop the dishwasher on and it's all taken care of.'

Daphne, meanwhile, remained where she sat, the glum look stealing back onto her face. 'I just don't know if I'll be able to sleep, all alone,' she said, a little shamefaced.

Sarah immediately sat down again. She pressed her friend's hand. 'That's absolutely fine, Daph. You can stay the night here. You know I keep a bed made up for my girls. I think I've got a spare toothbrush. Will Mephisto be OK?'

'Oh, yes,' said Daphne without a second's hesitation. 'He'll be hunting at the moment, he probably won't be back till dawn.'

Under the table, Hamish gave a little shiver, and looked very glad he was safely indoors.

Charles seemed a bit disconcerted at having his plan derailed, and Sarah suddenly wondered if he'd had the intention of heading back to her house after seeing Daphne to her cottage. Well, she'd never know now. It was destined to remain a mystery – and if Sarah had anything to do with it, that was the only one that would be plaguing her. The poisoned cake business, and whatever was nagging at her from the interview with Hannah, was going to become clear in the still watches of the night, she just knew it.

TWENTY-NINE

Sarah woke up before dawn, with Hamish sitting heavily on her chest, and was quite cross about both things. Worse still, no great revelation had struck her in the early hours. She had slept badly, and when her eyes had closed, a parade of figures from the photo gallery in Pat's flat had pirouetted through her dreams. She knew she'd missed something important when she'd been talking to Mariella, too, but she couldn't for the life of her put a finger on what it was.

There was nothing more frustrating than half-remembered pieces of crucial information. There was only one known cure for this level of irritation, in Sarah's experience – a good long walk on the beach.

She dressed quickly and tiptoed past the spare room door, heartened to hear the sound of Daphne's rhythmic snoring. At least her friend was getting some proper rest, which would help her in the struggle to put Pat's death behind her.

Downstairs, she got Hamish's lead, hushed his excitement about the prospect of a walk, and was through the door in the blinking of an eye.

As soon as she was outside, the breeze started tousling her

hair and she looked towards the sea to gauge what sort of a day they'd be getting. The clouds were thready and fluffy and moving fast on a vast blue backdrop, and the waves coming up to meet them were similarly frisky. The horizon stretched for miles, and she and Hamish were the only ones out on the beach at this hour. It was the perfect moment to clear her head and get her thoughts in order.

But, try as she might, and no matter how much the breeze buffeted her, her recollections just wouldn't snap obligingly into place. There were shards of thought chasing each other, but none seemed to join up into anything remotely resembling a revelation. She concentrated hard. There was definitely something about Pat's past on the stage that was preying on her mind. She must have met so many people as she toured the coast – had one of them suddenly popped up again and bumped her off? It seemed so unlikely, but might be worth looking into.

Then there was the interview with Hannah. She cast her mind back to the sheltered accommodation cloakroom, where the café manager had explained how she was setting up the gala. Her staff were moving about purposefully, clattering the chairs and tables. The delicious aroma of the large tubs of snacks and salads wafted as they were brought out of the large fridges and checked over by Hannah. Then there was her comment that she hadn't seen anyone much around as she'd brought her supplies through the courtyard to the reception room, and that Mr Ackroyd had appeared but hadn't said anything to her. Then she said that Ackroyd had suggested the gala become a memorial.

Wait a minute.

The memory unspooling in Sarah's mind came to an abrupt halt, almost as though someone had pressed pause. Had Hannah spoken to Mr Ackroyd or not? It didn't make sense.

Was this the glitch that Sarah had spent so long pondering over? It didn't seem much, now she'd finally dragged it out of her subconscious. The sort of tiny mistake anyone could make. Hannah obviously had spoken to Mr Ackroyd, however briefly. She had just forgotten, in the shock of Pat's death. It was understandable. Now Sarah needed to speak to Ackroyd too.

She called to Hamish, who'd been having a high old time auditioning bits of driftwood for the important role of a stick to be clenched in his mouth for the rest of the day. He was not amused at being interrupted, but when Sarah turned to walk back without him, he realised that to carry on ignoring her would be folly. He'd almost got her properly trained, but every now and then there were moments like this. He couldn't be cross with her, though. Most of the time, she was a wonderful companion.

By the time they got back to the cottage, Sarah had a spring in her step and a renewed sense of direction. She just needed to make sure Daphne was on board with the next phase in the investigation, then they could get moving with it all.

THIRTY

The windows of Sarah's cottage sparkled in the sunlight, reflecting a beautiful collage of all the bedding plants that had survived Hamish's attentions, as she walked up the path. She opened the front door, rather hoping she'd be met by the aroma of brewing coffee, but there was nothing doing. Perhaps Daphne was still asleep.

She put Hamish's lead back on its hook and dropped her keys into the bowl on the little table by the door and pottered through into the kitchen. But the first thing she saw was Daphne, head down on the table, weeping.

'Oh Daph! Maybe I should have got you up and you could have joined me and Hamish on our walk. It's done me the power of good,' Sarah said, sitting next to her friend and putting an arm round her.

Daphne said nothing, but the weeping tailed off and left her sniffing.

'Here, let me get you a cup of tea and some breakfast,' Sarah said. 'Things will look brighter then.'

'Will they, though?' said Daphne, levering herself upright

with an effort and peering around with bleary red eyes. 'Poor
Pat, I feel as though her spirit is hovering around us,' she wailed.

Sarah looked over her shoulder quickly as she bustled to the
bread bin. 'Well, I rather hope not,' she said as she cut two
healthy slices from one of the Seagull Bakery's famous raisin
loaves. She fed them into the toaster. Pat hadn't been her
biggest fan when she'd been walking the earth; the last thing
Sarah needed was the poor old lady giving her a hard time from
the afterlife. She knew it was absurd, but she couldn't help
listening out for a spectral cackle. Thank goodness, the only
sounds she could hear were the gulls outside and Hamish indus-
triously chewing on his bone in his bed by the stove.

'I won't be good for anything today; my psyche has taken such a
knock. You know, I hardly got a wink of sleep, tossing and turning all
night long,' Daphne continued. 'When something like this rips the
curtain between us and the Beyond, sensitive souls like me, prone to
insomnia, well, we really suffer.' She shook her head sorrowfully.

Sarah would have been a lot more sympathetic if she had
not heard Daphne earlier, making a noise strongly suggestive
either of a lumberjack sawing through a tough chunk of wood –
or a very deep and refreshing sleep.

'Well, you might feel a tiny bit better after this,' she said,
putting a lavishly buttered slice of toast in front of her friend,
together with a large mug of tea.

Daphne looked at the plate through half-closed eyes. 'Oh, I
really couldn't possibly manage a thing,' she said in martyred
tones, adding faintly, 'And isn't there any jam?'

Sarah hid a smile as she went over to the cupboard and took
down the apricot preserve. 'Hannah Betts's finest,' she said.
'You know you love this one.'

As though on autopilot, Daphne slathered her toast,
munched the whole piece down, finished off her tea with a sigh
of satisfaction, then started to look wistful and half-starved

again. Sarah, who'd scarcely finished a corner of hers, got up and put two more slices in the toaster.

'So I was thinking...' she said as she poured Daphne another cup of tea.

'That sounds ominous,' Daphne said, her voice a little stronger.

'It's just that we don't want to lose momentum, do we?'

'Don't we?' Daphne didn't sound so sure.

Sarah tried a different tack. 'Say you stayed in all day. Say you thought hard about Pat, about what she went through. Would that change anything? Would it make you feel better?'

Daphne thought for a while, fortified by her second and third slices of toast. 'Well, I suppose not. In fact, I feel quite down just imagining it.'

'Exactly,' said Sarah, leaning forward eagerly. 'I think we should get out and about, doing the most useful thing we can for Pat now.'

'Burning offerings and saying incantations to light her passage to the next world?'

'Um, no. I was thinking of going to see Mr Ackroyd again.'

'That awful little manager man? Why? I don't see what else he can tell us – and he didn't seem to like us much yesterday either.'

'We can't let that get in the way, Daph. I really think he might be involved. When Mariella and I spoke to Hannah she didn't seem sure whether she'd spoken to him or not. Maybe he was moving around more than he said he was – in which case, he could have got into Pat's flat, couldn't he? Hannah said she saw him peering in through the window. Perhaps he was waiting for his chance... After all, no one would really notice him coming and going as he's in charge of the whole place. What could be more natural than pretending to drop in on a tenant – one he just happened to want to get rid of?'

Daphne shrugged a little listlessly. 'Could he do that, though?'

'Well, yes. He has access to the master key, we know that because he let us in to Pat's when we couldn't, um, raise her. He probably knew when the workman finished in the flat, he must have a schedule of who's doing what where. He certainly knew how often Pat called that poor man out. He was perfectly placed to go in there and get Pat to eat the cake.'

'Well, to be fair, no one would have had trouble getting Pat to polish that off. She did love a sweet treat,' Daphne said, picking up the crumbs of her toast with a moistened finger. 'That apricot jam was lovely, by the way. You don't have any spare jars, do you?'

Sarah smiled at Daphne. That was more like it. 'If you come and help me ask a few questions here and there, then I can probably help you out. Of course, you could always ask Hannah herself.'

'Oh yes. But she's probably sold the lot by now, it's so good.' Daphne straightened up. 'All right, you've talked me into it. I'll just get dressed and then we'll get on with it.'

'Wonderful,' said Sarah. A moment later she was left in the crumb-strewn kitchen, with Hamish diligently tidying up under the table. She stacked the dishes in the sink for later. At last, she felt they had a good chance of making some progress. And she couldn't help wondering what on earth Mr Ackroyd would have to say for himself.

THIRTY-ONE

Sarah, Daphne and Hamish made short work of the walk to the sheltered accommodation. On a day like this, it was pure pleasure to be out, and Hamish's tail was wagging so furiously that it was a wonder he didn't turn into a little helicopter and fly all the way there.

Once they strolled into the courtyard at the centre of the place, though, the atmosphere seemed to change. The sky was just as blue, the seagulls were as loud. But everything seemed a lot drabber inside than it had been out on the coastal road.

It wasn't so surprising, Sarah reasoned. After all, there had been a murder here only yesterday. But then, death must come often to this place. The residents were, by definition, elderly or frail. Perhaps the party had given everyone hangovers on top of everything else.

There was only a solitary resident sitting on the bench in the middle of the courtyard today. After exchanging glances, they walked over and sat down. The elderly lady surveyed them with bright eyes and a smile, but her knuckles suddenly showed white as she gripped her stick.

'How are you this morning?' Sarah said, hoping the bland question might break the ice.

'Old enough to know not to talk to strangers,' the lady said. After three attempts, leaning ever more heavily on her stick, she got herself upright and then shuffled off fast to a flat near Pat's. Her turquoise door was still emblazoned with crime scene tape, which probably wasn't doing much to add to the general jollity.

Just then, Mavis Trussock came round the corner. Daphne called out to the woman, who was looking as chic as ever in a pale pink linen top and white trousers. But she didn't seem to hear, and hurried out through the courtyard and onto the road with her head down.

Sarah shrugged. 'Well, no one seems to want a nice chat. I wonder what Mavis was doing here? I'm still dying to ask her why one of her leaflets was in Mr Williams's cottage.'

'Oh, I think one of her aunts lives here,' Daphne said. 'And those flyers of hers get everywhere. A bit like the icing on a cream bun.'

'Hmm, there could be more to it, though. Anyway, shall we go and look at the hall where the party was last night, see if there's anyone there to talk to?'

'OK,' said Daphne. 'But I thought you wanted to talk to Mr Ackroyd. Why not go straight to his office?'

'I don't know,' said Sarah slowly. 'I just have a feeling it might be better this way?'

'Well, I'm all for trusting your instincts,' said Daphne. The aqua cheesecloth number she had on today billowed slightly as she got up. Sarah rather wished she'd chosen a different colour, as it toned with Pat's door and that seemed an unlucky coincidence. Then she mentally shook herself. She was being absurd, letting all these signs and symbols infect her rational mind.

'Right. Off we go then,' Sarah said.

They reached the hall without seeing another soul. 'I

wonder if it was such a late night that everyone's just staying in bed,' Daphne said.

'Maybe,' Sarah said, not adding that maybe they were frightened stiff. She opened the door to the hall, but again it seemed deserted.

Most traces of last night's jollifications had gone. The balloons had been taken down, as had the banner. All the tables were clean and had been arranged in neat straight lines, presumably waiting now for the next big event. Here and there, though, Sarah spotted a stray napkin that hadn't yet been swept up, and there was a pile of the big plastic catering pallets stacked on the table nearest to the door.

Just then, there came a crash from the vicinity of the kitchen. It was rather chilling, in the big empty space, and Daphne clutched Sarah's arm hard.

'Ouch!' Sarah bleated.

'Sorry,' whispered Daphne, just as someone called out tentatively.

'Anyone there? Hello?'

'I think I recognise that voice,' said Daphne. She bustled forward and Sarah followed until they were standing in the doorway.

'It's Betsy, isn't it? From the Beach Café? You haven't been here all night, have you?' Daphne asked.

Betsy, who'd been at the sink, turned round with her rubber gloves still on, looking flustered. 'Oh, er, no. A few of us just nipped back to clear up about half an hour ago. I'm the last one left, I always seem to take ages,' she added unhappily.

'Were you here for the party, last night?' Sarah asked.

'What? Oh, not really. I was in the kitchen just helping out.'

'It's very nice of you to do all this,' Sarah said. 'You must have your hands full, what with working at the café as well.'

'Yeah. I've got to go over to the arcade later too.'

'Really? Oh, joining all the other youngsters at the slot machines?' said Sarah.

Betsy gave her a rather nervous look. 'No, we've got an arrangement with Mavis Trussock. She's got loads of storage round the back, and it's close to the café. I've got to pick up the napkins and stuff.'

'Are you sure you're OK sorting this lot out? You look a little... tired,' Sarah said sympathetically.

The girl managed a smile. 'I like to help out here, in memory of my gran.'

'Oh yes,' said Sarah. 'I heard she was a resident.'

'Yeah, we wanted her to keep her independence,' Betsy said sadly.

'Absolutely,' said Sarah. 'Sheltered accommodation is a great solution,' she added, fervently hoping it was a path she'd never have to take herself.

'Well, if there's nothing else...' said Betsy, looking stressed. 'I need to get back to the café as soon as I can.'

'If you're sure we can't help?' Sarah said politely, as Daphne goggled at her side, obviously hoping for the no which Betsy instantly gave.

'Thanks, but I'm nearly there now,' she said with an unconvincing smile.

'Oh, you haven't seen Mr Ackroyd this morning, have you?' Sarah asked as she turned to go. 'We just want to ask him a couple of things.'

'No, I haven't seen a soul,' said Betsy. 'It's been as quiet as the grave round here. And I must get on,' she said in a rather shrill tone. Sarah and Daphne retreated, looking at each other in surprise. The girl was clearly at the end of her tether.

THIRTY-TWO

Sarah, Daphne and Hamish left the hall quickly, closing the doors carefully behind them. Sarah was rather thoughtful.

'What do you make of that, then?' asked Daphne. 'I don't think she should be working at all, let alone in hospitality.'

'You're probably right,' Sarah said. 'She really seems on edge... still, let's concentrate on Mr Ackroyd for now. He's our prime suspect, after all.'

'Well, if he touched a hair of Pat's head, he'll have me to answer to,' said Daphne as she marched along.

There was still no one in sight as they made their way to Mr Ackroyd's office, and the courtyard and rows of windows from the residents' flats seemed even blanker and bleaker than before. They both slowed down and looked around.

'I don't like the fact that there's no one on the benches,' said Daphne. 'Where are they all?'

'Still enjoying that lie-in, I expect,' Sarah said, though she shared Daphne's uneasy feeling. 'Mr Ackroyd will know what's going on.'

But, when they got to the manager's door and knocked, there was no answer.

Sarah and Daphne's eyes locked. 'Shall we?' Sarah asked.

Daphne hesitated. 'You don't think...?'

'Look, we can't assume people are dead every time they don't open their doors to us,' Sarah said heartily, turning the doorknob sharply. She stepped forward cautiously, then swayed in place. If she hadn't still had a hand on the door, she would have fallen. Then she immediately held out an arm to stop Daphne going any further. 'Go and call Mariella. Now,' she said in a strangled voice.

There was no slice of cake on Mr Ackroyd's desk. But the manager was still definitely dead. His staring eyes as he lay splayed across the desk, the soft drip-drip of blood pooling on the floor, and the preternatural stillness in the small office all told that story loud and clear. To be on the safe side, Sarah stepped forward a little and examined him as closely as she dared. Nope, life had definitely been extinguished.

Good heavens, what on earth was going on in this place? Another death... it was beyond belief. She hadn't particularly taken to the man, but this was an abomination. And a huge shock. She'd been intending to confront him, and put it to him that he had been perfectly placed to kill Pat. He had also known of Mr Williams's thefts from the sheltered housing washing line, so had a motive there as well. In fact, she'd been quite hopeful she was going to wrap the whole case up. And now here she was, recalibrating all her ideas, and also feeling the pity and disbelief she always experienced looking at a dead body. Ackroyd's moustache, so preposterous in life, looked sad and limp in death. He hadn't been old. In fact, compared to those in his charge, he had been a spring chicken. She shook her head over the terrible waste of a human life.

Meanwhile, Daphne ran up and down outside the office with Hamish in tow, yelling incoherently, her hair flying. Hamish seemed to think it was all some new kind of game and was quite enjoying himself. Sarah could see a few of the elderly residents popping their heads out of their front doors at last, most of them just nodding and smiling uncomprehendingly, as though Daphne was putting on a performance for their benefit. It surely wouldn't be too long, though, before they realised what she was trying to say.

Sarah stepped out of the office, and shut the door carefully. As Daphne passed, red in the face, she stuck out a hand and grabbed her arm. Before her friend had time to start gabbling again, Sarah shook her head firmly. 'Daphne. Did you hear what I said earlier? Ring Mariella. Now.'

Something about the firmness of her tone cut through Daphne's hysterics and she was soon pressing the buttons on her phone, held in a somewhat shaky hand. 'Mariella? It's happened again,' she wailed when the call connected.

Sarah held out her hand for the phone. 'It's Sarah here. Your mum's a bit upset... Yes, well, I'm very sorry to say...' Here she broke off as her voice shook. She took a breath to steady herself and then continued a bit more strongly. 'I've just come out of Mr Ackroyd's office. You have to come immediately. You'll need Dr Strutton again, I'm afraid. Yes, he's dead.'

At this, Daphne started wailing again.

'Got to go,' Sarah said to Mariella. Then she turned to Daphne. 'Look, we can't upset all the residents. You're going to have to calm down a little, or else I'll have to take you into Mr Ackroyd's office to sit quietly. I'm sure you don't want that.'

Daphne started gibbering again at the thought.

'All right,' said Sarah. 'Do you think you can just stand here with me until the police come? Or you could go straight home and put the kettle on, and I'll come when I can,' she added, rather hoping Daphne would go for the latter option. She could murder a cup of tea right now. Though perhaps that wasn't the best phrase to use.

'Go? Now? And leave you here in your hour of need? Oh, I couldn't possibly do that, Sarah. What kind of a monster do you think I am?' Daphne's outrage at the suggestion was palpable, and something about this seemed to be transmitting itself to the elderly ladies, who had now come out of their flats and were gathering in a knot in the courtyard, looking more and more jittery and alarmed.

'Smile,' Sarah said, pasting a wide grin onto her own face. 'Let's just look as though everything's perfectly normal.'

'Normal?' shrieked Daphne. 'Three people! Three have died,' she continued, though luckily the shriek had left her little breath for the second part of the sentence, so the word that cut through to the elderly folk watching was 'normal'. After some discussion, people started going back inside their flats, to Sarah's great relief.

Without so much of an audience, Daphne seemed to regain some control. 'Do you think this... this *thing* happened while we were here?'

Sarah rather doubted it. It was hard to tell without touching Mr Ackroyd, but his eyes had looked a little filmy, as though they'd been staring sightlessly for a while. On the other hand, the pool of blood was still liquid. But she knew better than to mention either detail to her friend.

'That's going to be a matter for the pathologist. We just need to stay here until Mariella arrives.'

'Why can't we leave now? Why do we have to be responsible? Surely that's a job for the manager... Oh—' Daphne fell silent as she realised what she'd said. 'What about the other staff members?'

'Everyone's a suspect, Daph, at this stage. Safest to stick it out if we can. But if you're feeling a bit woozy then no one would think any the worse of you for leaving,' Sarah said gently.

'Woozy?' Daphne seemed to take offence at the term. 'I'm perfectly fine, I tell you,' she said, fanning her flushed cheeks with her hands. 'I'm... just worried about little Hamish. Where is he?' she looked round.

Hamish, who'd trotted off to get his tummy tickled by some of his fans amongst the residents, looked up at his name but showed no signs of wanting to provide Daphne with an excuse to retreat. Perhaps it was just as well that they soon heard cars pulling up outside and doors slamming decisively. A moment or two later, Mariella appeared in the courtyard, looking focused and intent. The constables Tweedledum and Tweedledee were bringing up the rear, stumbling over their boots as usual. Both were rather red in the face.

Mariella marched over to Sarah and her mother, her hair streaming out behind her. 'Goodness me, you two,' she said, shaking her head. 'I don't know what to say at this point. Aunty Sarah, you'd better just show me what we're dealing with. Mum, perhaps you could have a word with my colleagues, let them know when you arrived, what you saw and so on.'

'Oh, but surely I should be with you two?' Daphne protested, giving the constables a look of disdain.

'In the office with the late Mr Ackroyd?' Sarah said gently.

Immediately Daphne blanched. 'Perhaps it would be better if I stayed outside. Someone's got to keep an eye on Hamish, after all,' she said.

'That's the spirit, Daph. Thank you, I know he'll be in good hands.' Sarah patted her friend's shoulder and turned away. 'Shall we?' she said to Mariella, girding her loins. Though Mr Ackroyd wasn't a particularly terrible sight, there was always something about confronting a dead body that was daunting.

Mariella put on forensic gloves and shoe covers. 'Too late for you, I suppose?' she said to Sarah.

Sarah shrugged. 'Well, of course I had no idea what we'd find when I went in. And then, when I saw him...' She swallowed briefly and carried on. 'I just stepped towards his desk to make visual observations, I didn't touch a thing.'

'Hmm, well that's something. But perhaps you should just start wearing a forensic suit all the time,' said Mariella, her hand on the office door. 'It might save us a lot of effort eliminating traces.'

'I am hoping not to make too much of a habit of this,' said Sarah, taking a last breath before going into the small room.

'Are you?' Mariella asked drily before she turned to the task in hand.

The scene was just as disquieting as before. Mr Ackroyd was lying flat across his desk, his head turned to the side so his expression of mild surprise, fixed now for all eternity, was easy to see. The bloody patch on the carpet hadn't grown considerably, which told Sarah that it was some time since the poor man's heart had stopped beating.

'Is Dr Strutton on her way?' she asked Mariella quietly as the detective approached the figure.

'Yep. She made the usual joke about this being a BOGOF – you know, a "buy one, get one free" offer, like down at Seastore. Poor Pat's still on her table as we speak.' Mariella rubbed her gloved hand over her face. 'I don't mind telling you, Aunty Sarah, I really want this to stop. Mr Williams – well, with his weird hobby, some might say he got what he deserved. Pat hadn't done a thing, though. Oh, she wasn't everyone's cup of tea, I know that,' she said, looking at Sarah intently. 'I know you didn't particularly get on.'

Sarah thought for a moment. 'It wasn't that I didn't like her...' Then she shook her head. 'Well, all right then, I wasn't a particular fan. She just had a rather inappropriate way of objectifying people. Wait a minute, I wonder...'

'What is it?' Mariella asked.

'Just that there were some morality issues about both Pat and Mr Williams, I suppose. The underwear thefts, the way Pat used to, well, if she'd been a man, people would have said she was lecherous. Women don't often have that predatory side to their natures, do they?'

'Or maybe they don't usually show it,' Mariella said

thoughtfully. 'Do you think someone could have decided they were, I don't know, too morally flawed to live? Some kind of virtue vigilante?'

'Well, don't go giving that name to the newspapers, they'd love it,' said Sarah, shaking her head. 'If that were the case, and that's a big if, then I wonder where Mr Ackroyd here fits in. Did he have any, um, strange habits?'

Mariella shrugged. 'Not as far as I know. They'd hardly have put him in charge of the town's sheltered accommodation if he had, would they?'

Sarah wondered. You never knew these days. Perhaps Mr Ackroyd had just been better at keeping his secrets than Mr Williams and Pat. 'Does he have a wife? Children?'

'Someone who'd know the real him, warts and all, you mean? I'll get onto it,' said Mariella. 'It's frustrating, I was going to interview him at four today. Anyway, in the meantime, anything you'd like to tell me about this death?'

'Well, as you can see, there's no poisoned cake here,' said Sarah. She moved towards the body carefully and pointed to his back, indicating the gash in the man's shirt. 'It looks to me like a straightforward stabbing. I say that, but there's one interesting thing about it.'

'What's that?' Mariella said, narrowing her eyes.

'He was stabbed in the back. And this isn't a large office at all. He trusted the person enough to allow them to get behind him, and then they attacked.'

'And the weapon?' Mariella was looking around.

'As far as I can see, there's no sign of it. But whatever was used, it was driven in with force.'

'Why do you say that?'

'If you look,' Sarah said, leaning a little more closely towards the body, 'you'll see the wound is deep and the edges aren't cleanly delineated, but it's not particularly wide. It looks like a five-centimetre gash, so at a guess it's probably a knife that's between fifteen to twenty centimetres long. Not a hunting knife or anything fancy, I'd say. But clearly it was plenty long enough. It appears the knife was driven in, then almost jiggled around in place, as though the perpetrator was trying to make sure they'd done the job properly. And by that, I mean that they wanted to kill the man.'

'Would that be difficult to do? Could anyone have done it?'

'Are you asking if it was a man or a woman?' Sarah asked. Mariella nodded. 'That's a difficult one. I'd say in general it is always easier for a man to kill than a woman. They are just stronger. They have considerably more grip strength than a woman at any age, and women's muscle power then falls right off a cliff when they reach menopause. So statistically, it's more likely to be a man. But having said that, there's still nothing to say that a fit, healthy woman couldn't have done this. Judging from the depth of the wound, though, I'd say they either got lucky with the angle, or they know something about anatomy.'

'What makes you think that, Aunty Sarah?' Mariella asked.

'Because, unless I'm very much mistaken, this man has been stabbed right through the heart,' Sarah said quietly.

THIRTY-THREE

Once Dr Pamela Strutton had arrived and taken charge of the body, and the SOCOs had started processing the crime scene, Sarah joined Daphne and a very cosseted Hamish in the courtyard.

Daphne seemed a lot calmer now, thank goodness, but the sheltered accommodation residents had been told exactly what was going on, and were looking pretty stunned at the news. Mr Ackroyd might not have been a beloved figure, but he'd still been many decades younger than most of those sitting in the courtyard. Though nobody was bandying about the word 'murder', the residents weren't slow to catch on to the fact that it was a suspicious death and there were a lot of pale, shocked faces. Neither Mr Williams nor Pat were the hot topic of conversation any longer. Sarah whizzed over to Mariella again for a quick word.

'It might be a good idea to get the residents' doctor out here, just in case anyone is badly affected by the news. Nasty shocks at this age aren't the best idea,' she told the policewoman. 'I'm sorry to dump that on your plate as well. Oh – and also,

Hannah's niece Betsy was in the kitchen earlier. She might have seen something.'

'Thanks,' Mariella said, then added, 'It's a shame you're not still practising medicine. I could just get you to give everyone a once-over.'

Sarah gave her a sympathetic smile, at the same time counting her lucky stars that she wasn't on call. She'd have had no objection to helping in normal circumstances, but today she was very glad she'd left such responsibilities behind her.

The residents were being interviewed in turn by Twee-dledum and Tweedledee. The constables had faces like thunder as they collected numerous accounts of breakfasts prepared, eaten and washed up by elderly folk in total ignorance of the violence being done only metres away from their flats. The fact that they were all now severely rattled by recent events didn't help matters – and a fair few of them were suffering from forms of cognitive impairment as well. For once, Sarah felt a certain amount of sympathy for the constables. They really had their work cut out.

'Come on then, Daph. Thanks for looking after Hamish for me. I hope he was a good boy,' Sarah said, reaching down to pat the little dog.

'He was a treasure. All the residents love him so much. He really brought some joy to a place in sad disarray,' said Daphne heavily.

'How are you feeling about everything?' Sarah asked her sympathetically. 'Would it help if we went to the Beach Café to talk things over?'

As usual, the promise of a slap-up meal did a lot to lift Daphne's spirits and, if she were honest, Sarah too felt herself brightening up at the prospect. She hadn't taken to Mr Ackroyd, it was true, but finding him dead had knocked the wind out of her sails. There was a reason why there was always food on offer after a funeral: the simple act of breaking bread together after a death was somehow an affirmation of the power of the human spirit. No matter what, life goes on.

When they got to the Beach Café, there was a huge queue at the counter, which Sarah joined while Daphne and Hamish went to find a table. Neither Hannah nor Betsy was in sight, and she caught a glimpse of one of their regular helpers working the till rather laboriously.

Even though the line of people was pretty slow-moving, she didn't really mind. It was a gorgeous day and the view of the Kent coast over her shoulder was unchangingly magnificent, no matter what shenanigans were occurring on dry land.

Inevitably, the Merstairs rumour mill was already going strong and Sarah heard several versions of the latest tragedies while waiting her turn, shuffling forward in the queue every now and then. Pat had run amok and killed Mr Ackroyd. Mr Ackroyd had been having a fling with Pat and his wife found out. Mr Ackroyd had seen who'd killed Pat and the murderer had no choice but to get him out of the way... She was amazed at the ingenuity people displayed. The whole queue was also in uproar about Mr Williams.

'I always knew he was shifty. There was something untrustworthy about those ears,' said the woman in front of her. Then Sarah felt a tap on her shoulder.

When she turned, she caught sight of dark-haired Mrs Booth from the art group. Without her official post office tabard, the forty-something mum cut quite a glamorous figure, her pale skin and lustrous hair complemented by the rich dark turquoise top she was wearing. She bustled up to Sarah. 'Dr Vane, you always seem to be in the thick of these things... you must know what's going on. Is it true that Pat and Mr Ackroyd were in some sort of murder-suicide pact? And what about all this underwear business? Pat mentioned it... and you know what happened to her.'

Sarah looked at Mrs Booth, horrified. Mariella would be

furious if she gossiped about the investigation. 'I've really no idea about all that...' she said, playing for time. 'But weren't you, um, helping the police with their enquiries about Mr Williams? You probably know so much more about the investigation than I do,' she added.

As she'd hoped, Mrs Booth immediately shrank away. 'Oh, that was all a terrible misunderstanding,' she spluttered, eyeing the queue worriedly in case anyone had heard.

Just then, it was finally Sarah's turn to be served. To her surprise, Betsy had taken over the till, her pretty face red and shiny.

'You made it back quickly,' Sarah said, after giving their order.

'Yeah. So that's a vegetarian breakfast, a latte and an espresso, right?' Betsy said, not quite meeting Sarah's eyes. Red blotches seemed to be appearing on the poor girl's neck as she spoke.

Sarah suppressed a sigh. The girl clearly didn't want to talk about what had happened at the sheltered accommodation – and who could blame her – and as a result she'd got the order completely wrong. Sarah went over it again carefully, making sure Daphne's essential full English breakfast and cup of tea were firmly on the list. Hannah was right to be concerned about her niece. The girl seemed on the brink of tears, but finally they got things straight and Sarah was relieved to be able to turn away. She kept her head down as she wove her way back through the throng to get to the table Daphne had found. She didn't want to talk about Pat, pants or the poor manager if she could help it.

The table was perfectly placed, affording them a fantastic view of the waves. A couple of hungry seagulls perched nearby, in the hope of scraps. Hamish was giving them his best 'Not if I can help it' look from under the table. The avid expression in the birds' eyes reminded Sarah of Mrs Booth and her questions.

'You'll never guess what I've just been asked,' she said as she took her seat. But when Daphne looked at her with sorrowful eyes, she realised it wasn't the moment to share Merstairs' finest conspiracy theories. Her friend was genuinely grieving Pat, she was horrified by the death of Mr Ackroyd, and she was as allergic as ever to idle chat about murder. 'No, don't worry, it's nothing,' Sarah said hastily. 'Has Hamish been a good boy?'

This was a question they all knew the answer to, and Hamish rolled over under the table to display a fine fluffy tum for all to admire.

'Well, what a handsome chap,' came a drawling voice, and Sarah looked up to see Charles, standing silhouetted against the bright sun. Somehow this made his eyes look all the more piercing. 'May I join you ladies?'

Despite herself, Sarah felt the swooping of butterflies in her stomach. Stop it, she told herself. It wasn't seemly, she was a recent widow, and in any case she had so much on her plate with the murders. But the butterflies refused to listen, and continued to loop the loop.

'Of course, Charles,' said Daphne with the first glimmer of a smile Sarah had seen all morning. 'Draw up a chair, if you can find one. This place is in a muddle as Hannah's not here.'

'Oh? Oh yes, there's Betsy at the till... whoops, she's dropped someone's coffee. Oh, and a sandwich. Dear me. Hannah having a day off, is she?' asked Charles, putting his hand to his brow to shield his eyes as he looked around for a spare seat. It was hard to spot one as there were now so many people milling around, meeting the queue which was snaking through the centre of the café.

'I suppose so. What a day to choose. Oh, you might not have heard what's happened, if you've been stuck in your shop,' Daphne said, falling silent and plucking anxiously at her scarf.

Charles knew better than to cross-question her, and just looked enquiringly at Sarah instead. 'I'll tell you when you've found a chair. I think someone's getting up over there,' she said, pointing to a corner of the café.

Charles immediately swooped and moments later he was installing himself at their table. 'Don't think I'll bother joining that queue. I'll just order when they bring your food,' he said.

'Goodness knows when that will be,' Daphne said restlessly. 'It's taking forever, isn't it, Sarah?'

'It's certainly been longer than I hoped,' said Sarah. She was keen for Daphne to get a meal inside her. And at this point, she was pretty peckish herself. But then she saw a harassed-looking waitress coming towards them with a tray. 'Ah, this is us now,' she said, waving a hand at the girl.

Just as it looked as though the waitress was going to stop at their table, a lordly arm came out. 'I think that's our food,' said a very familiar voice. It was none other than Francesca Diggory, mayor of Merstairs and Charles's very nearly but unaccountably still not quite ex-wife, who had just arrived and was sitting herself down at a table that had magically become clear. A moment later, she was tucking into an order that looked suspiciously similar to the one Sarah had placed, what seemed like an age ago now.

Daphne stared at Charles, who seemed to shrink in his seat. Sarah could hardly bear to look at him. He was at his worst when anywhere near his ex. She seemed to have the same effect on him as kryptonite on Superman.

'Well, I'm not going to sit here and let this daylight robbery happen,' said Daphne, half-rising to her feet.

'Wait a second, Daph,' said Sarah quickly. 'I wonder if I could diffuse the situation.' Before waiting for an answer from either of her friends, the warlike one or the craven coward, Sarah approached Francesca's table. The mayor and a slightly colourless woman, who Sarah recognised from the Jolly Roger's book group, were tucking into heaped plates of the Beach Café's famous all-day breakfast.

As Sarah watched, Francesca speared a particularly deli-cious-looking snippet of bacon, dipped it in the runny yolk of her fried egg, and popped it into her mouth. Her friend was shovelling up scrambled eggs as though there was no tomorrow.

'Funny, Francesca, I wouldn't have thought a full English breakfast was very "you",' said Sarah. 'Full of saturated fats, nitrates in the bacon, plus are those eggs actually free range? It's so difficult to tell.'

Francesca chewed carefully and finished her mouthful. 'Very tasty,' she said. 'Well, it's heartwarming to see the plain townsfolk are so interested in their mayor's welfare. I'm very grateful to you indeed,' she said with an on-off patronising smile. 'I don't mean to be rude, but what are you doing at my table?'

'You hijacked our order, as you know,' Sarah said patiently.

'What, you mean all these naughty fats and suchlike? Surely a goody-goody like you doesn't want to eat this,' Francesca said, scooping up a little egg, chewing and making much of how excellent it was. 'Spectacular. Oh, in case you're wondering who this is accosting me, Beatrice, this is Sally. She's one of my husband's bits on the side.'

At this, Sarah rolled her eyes. 'One day you'll really go too far, Francesca. Beatrice, we have met, in the book club, as you'll no doubt remember. We'll make sure you get the bill for our meals, anyway,' she said. She was about to turn to go, when a warm hand came down on her shoulder. She looked up in surprise.

'Ah, good day, Francesca. As you'll know, I've signed those papers you sent me and lodged them with my solicitor. We are no longer married, and I'd be grateful if you stopped harassing my friends,' Charles said.

Sarah winced a little inwardly at the 'friends' part, but then Charles carried on. 'And you must also lay off my girlfriend,' he said boldly, his hand now slipping down from Sarah's shoulder to her waist.

Sarah tried her best to keep her expression neutral, but she couldn't help the flush of pink that mounted to her cheeks. On the one hand, it seemed to smack of the playground being claimed as a 'girlfriend' in this way. But she had to admit she did feel some satisfaction. Poor Francesca's face had fallen a mile, and Beatrice was now doing her best to hide rather a large smirk – maybe not such a great friend after all.

Sarah turned away. She didn't want the worst side of her nature to get the better of her. However horrible Francesca was, her jealousy was proof that she still had strong feelings for Charles, even if they came out in odd, self-defeating gestures like her inability to stop attacking Sarah every time they met. More to the point, Sarah had not consented to being Charles's girlfriend at all. They hadn't had a conversation about it, let alone gone on a proper date. It wasn't on for him to make a declaration in public, before all the interested eyes and ears in the Beach Café, without running it by her first.

She shrugged off Charles's hand and went back to sit with Daphne, feeling an uncomfortable whirl of emotions.

Daphne, who'd seen the tense exchange but had been too far away to hear anything, was refreshingly direct. 'So, care to tell me why Francesca is still eating my food?'

Sarah couldn't help smiling, despite her inner turmoil. 'Did you expect me to grab the fork out of her hand, Daph? Anyway, I suppose it's just about possible that she ordered the same thing as us – though I've never seen her eat anything like it before.'

'And what was Charles up to over there? Why's he still talking to her?'

'How should I know what Charles is doing?' said Sarah a little more tersely than she needed to.

At that moment, a much-needed distraction arrived in the shape of the waitress, who had another laden tray in front of her. As she put down the teapots, cups and plates, she whispered to Sarah, 'I'm so sorry, I think there could have been a mix-up in the kitchen. We're all just friends of Betsy's helping out as best we can, to be honest. To put things right, we'd like you to choose a slice of cake from the display after your mains.' She smiled brightly as she said this, and went away clearly feeling all was now right with the world.

Daphne, it was true, had a faraway look on her face at the prospect of free cake. But for Sarah, all it had done was bring up the issue of the murders again. The Victoria sponge, the red velvet... and now the stabbing. What was the connection between the three? And why had the careful premeditation of the first two deaths changed into the hasty and finesse-free death of Mr Ackroyd? She was a suspect down, now that he was out of the frame forever... though was there any possibility that Hannah's jittery niece Betsy could have had something to do with his death? But there was surely no connection between her, Mr Williams and Pat. Then for the first time, a frightening new thought struck Sarah. Were there, could there be, *two* murderers at large in Merstairs?

THIRTY-FOUR

Sarah knew herself well enough to realise she was now using the murders as a displacement activity, keeping her brain busy and preventing herself from dwelling over-much on Charles and his grand gesture, which had fallen so flat. She was back in her cottage, with a full teapot and her best mug in front of her, Hamish in his basket and a plate of freshly baked chocolate chip biscuits at her elbow. She also had a pad of paper and a pen out, and was gazing into the middle distance while trying to think hard about all that had happened in Merstairs since that fateful art class, when she had discovered Mr Williams's body. Unfortunately, she kept seeing the hurt look in Charles's blue eyes as she had stomped away from Francesca's table in the Beach Café.

She was delighted to be interrupted by a ring on the doorbell, and got up almost before Hamish to answer the door. She wasn't quite so thrilled to see that it was Charles standing on her doorstep.

'Listen, Sarah, I just wanted to explai—' he started, when there was a loud call of 'Coo-ee' from over the hedge.

'Is that you, Charles?' said Daphne, popping up with weeds

clutched in both hands. 'Just sorting out my path. You know how I love to keep a tidy garden.'

As Daphne was scarcely visible through the overgrown shrubs on her side, both Sarah and Charles stayed tight-lipped at this.

'Well, if you're having a confab about the, um, dead people situation, then I'm coming over. I've had a brilliant idea,' Daphne continued, undaunted by the rather charged silence. She threw down her weeds and a second or two later was rushing up Sarah's path, today's maroon scarf fluttering in the breeze. Once she'd reached Charles and Sarah, who were still standing like dummies on the doorstep, she stopped. 'Well, come on then, are we going in or what?'

Sarah blinked, and stepped back to let them both precede her into the kitchen. Daphne quickly made herself at home, reaching down two more mugs from the dresser and pouring the tea. 'You might want to put some hot water in the pot, Sarah, there isn't quite enough for you,' she said, a biscuit already in her hand. 'Now, where were we? Oh, I see you've drawn up a list of possible suspects here,' she said approvingly.

Sarah moved over to the kettle and switched it on, standing with her back to the sink with her arms crossed. Charles, looking a little pinker than usual, had his eyes fixed on Hamish, who'd left his basket and was rolling under the table in a four-paws-in-the-air welcome.

She sighed inwardly. Well, this was very awkward, but no doubt she'd got through stickier situations – even if the memory of them escaped her right now. She sloshed more water on the tea leaves and sat down, putting a biscuit on a plate for Charles and adding milk to his tea. He looked up from petting Hamish and smiled at her tentatively, and she couldn't help smiling back, her heart melting at his evident diffidence, so unusual in a man who normally seemed to have everything sorted out to his liking. His declaration earlier had been ridiculously premature, it was true, but she couldn't help finding him rather appealing. She waited to feel the usual stab of guilt over Peter, but for once it wasn't there. Oh, he would always be her first love, and she missed him in her very bones. But who knew what the future would bring?

'If you two have quite finished mooning over each other, maybe we should get down to some work,' Daphne said archly.

Sarah tore her eyes away from Charles's. 'Yes, Daphne, what were you saying about having a clever plan?'

Daphne gestured with her second biscuit. 'Well, I thought we could set a trap. You know, like you baking these earlier with your windows open. You knew I'd have to come round to try one.'

Sarah's mouth fell open. 'It's a hot day! Oh, never mind. What sort of trap? And who on earth do you think we might catch in it?'

'More to the point,' Charles spoke up. 'Isn't this an incredibly dangerous idea? This person – I know you never like to use the word murderer, Daphne – has struck three times now. And on the last occasion, I understand the methodology was different. I think it's called escalation, isn't it, when, um, these types start to get erratic?'

'Oooh that's impressive, Charles, escalation. What a great word,' said Daphne, seemingly blind to the meaning behind the term. 'Did you get that from Mariella?'

'No,' said Charles, looking uncomfortable again. 'I saw it on an American telly series, NCIS. It's rather good actually.'

Charles's evident embarrassment was rather endearing, Sarah decided. She'd found the interior of his flat rather intimidating, with its arty books and air of monkish concentration. The news that he wasn't above watching a bit of TV was quite welcome – especially as she herself was partial to the odd crime drama.

'I agree,' she said, after taking a sip of her tea to allow

Charles time to recover. 'It could well be escalation. But there is another possibility. There could be two separate, er, perpetrators at work.'

'You mean like Hannah's niece, Betsy Styles? We saw her just after Mr Ackroyd died, and she seemed very on edge,' Daphne said.

'Good detective work, there, Daph,' said Sarah encouragingly. 'But I've been thinking about that. Mr Ackroyd had been dead for a while when I saw him, and I think Betsy and the others had only been in the kitchen for about half an hour. That lets her out.'

'You sound disappointed,' Charles remarked.

'Not at all,' said Sarah quickly. 'I'd hate to think of that overwrought teenager doing something so awful. I do want to get this awful business sorted, though.'

'Perhaps it's two people working as a team? But one of them lacks the finesse of the other,' said Daphne.

'Yes, that could be a solution, too,' Sarah said slowly. 'Is that what you wanted to talk about?'

'No. It's just that you forced us to spend such a long time testing all those cakes,' Daphne said plaintively. Sarah's mouth dropped open, but her friend hadn't finished. 'Maybe we would have been better off thinking about the poison instead?'

Sarah sat back at the table. A variety of different replies occurred to her, some of them less than polite. Then she took a deep breath, and spoke. 'I actually think that would be a really good idea, Daphne.'

THIRTY-FIVE

Daphne looked as pleased as punch, and clapped her hands together, forgetting she was still clutching a biscuit. Hamish pounced before Sarah could stop him and gave the floor a thorough going-over.

'Have you considered how you'd like to investigate poisons, then?' Sarah asked Daphne.

'Hmm.' Daphne thought for a moment, absent-mindedly scooping up another biscuit to help her along, then chewing on it while apparently deep in thought. Sarah looked at her expectantly. 'What? Oh. Nope. No idea.'

'Biscuit, Charles?' Sarah asked, pushing the rapidly emptying plate towards him. 'I expect Mariella will be looking into purchases on the dark web – as far as anyone can. It's all encrypted and anyone operating one of those sites will be very keen to cover their tracks,' she said.

'Is there any other way to get cyanide, though?' Charles mused.

'You can actually make it at home,' Sarah ventured.

'Really?' Charles sounded astonished.

'Oh yes. What do you think people used to do a hundred years ago, to get rid of pests? They'd make it themselves.'

'But what from?'

'It's in all kinds of things. Cigarette smoke, vehicle exhaust fumes, fruit pips, almonds of course, some types of beans...'

'You're kidding!' Daphne looked thunderstruck. 'You mean it's all around us?'

'Oh, I forgot, there's some in spinach too,' said Sarah. 'I once did a study on poisons at the GP practice, I thought it might come in handy. This is the first time it's been of any use and of course I've forgotten most of it.'

'You seem to have an excellent memory to me,' said Charles warmly and Sarah smiled.

'Are you saying if I eat a lot of spinach and have a bag of almonds, I'm risking cyanide poisoning?' Daphne said.

'Absolutely not,' said Sarah reassuringly. 'You need to extract the cyanide to make it usable.'

'And that's really difficult, is it?' Daphne asked hopefully.

'Well... perhaps not as tricky as you might think,' Sarah admitted. 'So while you're unlikely to die by accident from cyanide poisoning, I'm beginning to think it wouldn't be too difficult for this person, given their level of cunning, to arrange it.'

'But as you said before, all the planning doesn't fit with the death of Mr Ackroyd.'

'Yes,' Sarah shook her head like a plumber assessing a boiler that had been tinkered with by a rival. 'Something went badly wrong there. Either it was someone else, or our original careful planner got rattled and had to act very quickly – too swiftly to use their usual skill at covering their tracks.'

'I don't like this,' Daphne said, with a quaver in her voice. 'It sounds as though this person is getting completely desperate.'

'I think they might be,' Sarah said, trying to sound as calm as possible. 'But that could work in our favour. If they're not thinking as clearly as they were, they're much more likely to make mistakes. And then we might be able to get on their trail.'

'Just as long as one of their "mistakes" isn't bumping off the amateurs shambling along after them,' said Charles thoughtfully.

'Mm.' Daphne was quiet for a moment. 'We need to look out for someone who's made bulk purchases of things you can make cyanide out of. But how can we do that?' She threw her hands up. Hamish looked round hopefully but there were no more flying biscuits in the vicinity this time.

'That has to be a job for Mari. She's got a lot more resources than we have. And people will be more helpful towards her, too,' Sarah said.

'I'm not sure they'd be very accommodating towards those dreadful blockheads she has to rely on,' said Charles with a huff.

'You mean Tweedledum and Tweedledee? No, I know. Poor Mariella. I did ask her to suggest to DI Brice it was time to get some new blood on the team, but he told her there's a recruitment freeze,' Daphne said. 'Also, I think it might have backfired a bit because she said they've been even meaner to her since then.'

Sarah shook her head. It was a mystery to her how either man had passed the stringent tests required to join the police. She supposed they had their uses under normal circumstances, when the most pressing crime in Merstairs would probably be a seagull swiping an abandoned chip. But at the moment she felt the population was not being served at all. No wonder amateurs like her felt the need to step in.

While Charles finished the last biscuit but one and Sarah made a fresh pot of tea, Daphne gave Mariella a call. Sarah wasn't entirely surprised that her helpful suggestions about checking out large-scale purchases of cyanide-producing food items didn't go down terribly well.

'Honestly, Mum,' Mariella's cross voice blared out of the phone – and she wasn't even on speaker. 'I do think you need to leave the running of this to us. Just concentrate on the Beyond, why don't you?'

'Mariella! I don't much care for your tone,' Daphne remonstrated. 'You know it's unwise to be dismissive of the spirit world. And besides, I'm just trying to help.'

'Sorry, Mum,' Mariella replied much more quietly. 'It's just... well, I suppose all this is getting to me. Three deaths now. It doesn't look good if we can't make any progress.'

Daphne now fiddled with the phone so Sarah and Charles could hear properly. 'Brice is even saying if we can't break this soon, they'll call in the big guns,' Mariella went on.

'Scotland Yard?' Daphne said in excited tones.

'No,' said Mariella glumly. 'Canterbury.'

THIRTY-SIX

'Tea is all well and good, but I'm awash with the stuff now,' said Daphne a little later. 'What we need is a proper dinner. Did you hear, Claire at the Jolly Roger is going to be doing food? Today's the trial run.'

Immediately, Charles perked up like a dog that had heard the rattle of the treats bag. 'What do you say, ladies, shall we make a move?' He picked up his straw hat and looked ready for the off.

While Sarah couldn't quite believe Merstairs needed another place to eat, she was all for making sure it was up to the area's high standards. Within five minutes, she had gathered her handbag, a light cardigan in case it became chilly later, and Hamish's lead. Then they had to wait for almost twice that time while Daphne tracked down various stray possessions like her mobile phone and her scarf, which she turned out to be sitting on. Eventually they were all ensconced down the road in their favourite banquette seat at the pub, gazing with slight perplexity at the laminated menus that Jamie the barman had plonked on their table.

'Langoustine? With curry sauce? I'm not sure about that,'

said Daphne. 'Here, you quite like a Thai curry, Sarah,' she said helpfully.

'Not with a garnish of pineapple and pasta,' Sarah said. 'This is all a bit odd, isn't it?'

'It's like they've cut out meals from various menus, thrown them all up in the air, and seen where they land,' said Charles. 'I might have the steak pie with noodles.'

'I think it's too warm to eat a pie, for me,' Sarah said. 'I'll have the salad and ratatouille. What about you, Daph?'

'I'm going to have the sausages. You can't go wrong with those, even with this grapefruit garnish they mention,' she said, waving down Claire and giving their orders. They were soon enjoying a round of their usual drinks, while Hamish had a bowl of water under the table and a couple of the dog biscuits Claire kept for very good boys.

'So, now we're here, and we're settled, any more thoughts on our conundrum?' Sarah asked.

Daphne groaned. 'You just don't give up, do you?'

'Well, I couldn't live with myself if there was another, erm, incident, and we hadn't done our level best to stop it,' Sarah said. 'So, where are we? I keep coming back to Mr Williams. Everyone was reasonably friendly with him in the art class, wouldn't you say, Daph?'

Daphne took a big sip of Dubonnet as she thought hard. 'I suppose so. People were cordial, I would say, rather than pally.'

'Well, I was quite friendly, but I was in the dark about his more questionable habits,' Sarah said ruefully. 'What about Mavis from ScaleScanners, was she on good terms with him?'

Daphne shrugged. 'You have to remember, I had my mind on higher matters when I was there.'

'Of course, the Beyond,' said Charles, with a commendably straight face.

'No,' said Daphne, a little put out. 'Bananas. Or Mr Williams, of course. Whatever we were drawing that day.'

'What about Mrs Booth, from the post office?' Sarah asked next.

'Well, she only came when her days off allowed,' Daphne said thoughtfully.

'But could she have known about Mr Williams's terrible reputation, from when he was a post office worker himself?'

'What, and revenged herself on him for letting her employer down, so many years after the event?' Daphne sounded a little incredulous.

'I suppose you're right,' Sarah said. 'That does sound a little unlikely. But there is another person we haven't completely cleared yet,' she said, peeping at Charles.

Charles looked at her, uncomprehending... then a light dawned in his eyes. 'You don't mean—? Not Arabella? But I told you she was with me in my shop for a couple of hours before the art class that Monday.'

'Were there any customers in the shop, who could vouch for that?' Daphne asked. Sarah was glad her friend had raised this. After all, a father and daughter giving each other alibis was not exactly watertight.

Charles looked a little shifty. 'It's hard to say. I don't keep track of everyone who comes in, you know. There is such a thing as data protection.'

Sarah wasn't sure if he was shielding his daughter, or whether he just didn't want to admit he hadn't had a single customer in his shop during that entire period. 'Well, we need to speak to her anyway,' she said briskly. 'She is the leader of the group so presumably she was the one who booked Mr Williams as the model and had to have dealings with him... despite the fact that, all the time, he was filching her underwear...'

Her voice tailed off as Charles continued to stare at her, his patrician features taking on a stern aspect. She now knew what it would have felt like, a few centuries ago, if she'd been a peasant annoying this particular lord of the manor.

'You cannot be serious,' he said, in tones of great finality.

'We have to consider everybody, Charles, surely you can see that?' said Daphne, who'd got to the end of her drink and was now making dreadful slurping sounds with her straw.

'Let me tell you, my daughter would never, *ever*... The idea is unthinkable.' He crossed his arms over his chest and gazed into the far distance, obviously too cross to look at or speak to either of his companions.

Sarah and Daphne exchanged a glance and Daphne gave a waggle of her lavish eyebrows. Charles, when in high dudgeon like this, was actually rather funny, and impossible to take seriously. But it wouldn't do to let him see that they found him amusing. Poor man, thought Sarah. She was sure she'd be just as defensive if her own daughters were coming under suspicion.

'Well, moving on from that...' Sarah started diplomatically.

'No. No, you're right. We should make sure everything's above board. I can't have you two believing that I'm shielding a murderer. Especially you, Sarah, as you're always going on about clearing people's names,' Charles added with a bit of a sniff. He got out his mobile, keyed in a number, then put the phone on speaker and slapped it down on the table.

Sarah and Daphne listened to it ringing, then all of a sudden it was picked up. 'Dad? What's up?' came Arabella's voice. 'I'll have to be quick, I'm just getting supper for the twins.' Sure enough, in the background, Sarah could hear the wailing and whining of overtired, hungry children. In a way it was reassuring. The one time she'd bumped into little Max and Calista with their granny, Francesca Diggory, at the recent Whitsun fair, they'd been dressed in absurdly posh outfits and behaving frighteningly well. It was good to know they were normal children under all that fuss.

'We won't keep you,' Charles said grandly. 'You're on speaker with Sarah and Daphne, by the way,' he said. Oh dear, thought Sarah. Now Arabella was bound to be even frostier with her at the next art class.

'I see,' snapped Arabella. 'Well, what can I do for you all?'

'So sorry to disrupt your evening, hopefully we can clear things up really quickly and let you get back to your children,' said Sarah. 'As you may know we're looking into—'

'Oh, for goodness' sake, Sarah, she doesn't need a great long rigmarole,' Daphne broke in impatiently. 'Where were you on Monday, Arabella, right before art class? We just want to be sure you weren't anywhere near Mr Williams, you see,' she said.

There was a pause. 'I have talked to the police about this, you know,' the young woman said, with the air of someone hanging onto their patience by a thread.

Just then, a little voice called out, 'Mummy, Mummy, he's hit me again!'

'Ugh,' said Arabella. 'Right, long story short, before the art class I was setting up in the café for at least half an hour. Before that, I was at Dad's shop, as I'm sure he's told you. If you want proof, apart from both our words, there must be CCTV footage of my car. Oh whoops, I forgot. You're not entitled to see it, as you're *not the police.*' With that, the line went dead.

'Well, thanks, ladies. Looks like I'm going to be off her Christmas card list for a while after making her go through that,' said Charles grumpily.

'Oh, I doubt it,' said Sarah. 'If she's anything like my daughters, she'll forgive you – right around the time she next needs an emergency babysitter.'

'Ha! She's got you there, Charles,' said Daphne.

'And we're now able to clear Arabella from our enquiries. It's a win.' Sarah tried her most impish smile, but Charles was still looking cross. 'It's only routine, after all, Charles,' she added.

'Oh... fair enough, I suppose,' Charles said, allowing a bit of a twinkle to reappear in those blue eyes. 'Sorry to have been a grump. No one likes to have a family member under the spotlight.'

'Absolutely,' said Sarah in relief, raising her glass in a toast to Charles's change of heart. 'I agree it's not ideal. But you see how easily we got through all that?'

Daphne chortled. 'Yes, so painless, just a huge hissy-fit from Charles. But anyway, perhaps we can talk about cheerier things now.'

For a second, Sarah racked her brain. There didn't seem to be anything else in her life at the moment, apart from the murders. And, of course, the upcoming return visit from her daughters. She really wanted to have this awful poison business wrapped up by then.

'Naturally, Daphne, whatever you'd like. After you, dear lady,' said Charles, who was now very expansive, possibly to make up for his tetchiness earlier.

Both Sarah and Charles were now focused on Daphne, waiting for her to introduce a new topic of conversation. But, after a few seconds, she threw down the beer mat she'd been picking at. 'It's no good, is it? There's nothing else going on at the moment apart from... this ghastliness.'

'I'm sorry, Daph. I know how hard all this is for you,' Sarah said gently.

'Especially in here, actually,' Daphne piped up. 'I keep expecting to see Pat. She was such a fixture. The book group meetings, and of course the crafting... and even when it wasn't one of our clubs, she was often sitting on one of the stools by the bar, just chatting.'

Yes, thought Sarah. Though Jamie, the new barman, was possibly relieved that she was no longer distracting him from his work. She'd taken rather a shine to him in the last couple of weeks. He was another one whose whereabouts needed checking, she decided.

'Shall we have a refill, while we wait for our food?' Sarah

asked her friends. The consensus was hearty assent, so Sarah picked up her glass and Daphne's, and went over to the bar. Jamie was behind it, arranging bags of crisps and cutting a lemon into thin slices.

'Sorry, Jamie, could I just ask you something?' Sarah said. At his surprised nod, she asked quickly, 'I just wondered if you were here in the pub yesterday morning, from about ten to twelve? I, er, well, I thought I saw you near the sheltered housing,' she said, crossing her fingers surreptitiously.

'Me?' Jamie frowned in surprise. 'Don't think so. I was here for the brewery delivery. Quite a few kegs, this time, now we're into high season. Claire needed a hand getting them sorted. Then I was working till three.'

'Oh, my mistake. I'm getting so short-sighted,' Sarah said, hoping she was doing a good impression of a daffy pensioner. 'I just wanted to get another round,' she said, sliding their glasses across the counter.

'Coming right up,' said Jamie, as he fetched their drinks.

* * *

An hour later, the trio was out on the pavement, admiring the last streaks of purple, pink and orange in the sky as the sun set.

'Well, that meal was... memorable,' said Charles.

'I think "terrible" is the word you're searching for,' said Sarah. 'In my view Claire needs to go back to the drawing board with that menu.'

'Yes.' Daphne shook her head. 'The fruit with my sausages was a step too far,' she said sadly.

'Never mind,' said Charles, rather absent-mindedly. 'Are you cold, dear lady?' he said to Sarah, fixing her with a meaningful look and sweeping off his jacket to drape it over her shoulders.

Sarah, who hadn't actually been chilly, glanced at him and shrugged inwardly. He looked rather as though he was working up to another dinner invitation, she thought. Well, he needed to take his courage in both hands and get on with it. At this point, they'd had more false starts than an under-fives egg and spoon race. She smiled in a noncommittal way, then felt bad that she wasn't giving him more encouragement. 'Thank you, that's lovely,' she replied.

Daphne looked from one to the other. 'Oh, for goodness' sake you two, are you going to go on a date, or what? The suspense is killing us,' she said, jiggling Hamish's lead. Hamish sat on his haunches, seeming to grin up at Sarah and maybe even give her his blessing.

Sarah risked a glance at Charles. He was looking rather as though he'd been hit in the face by a large haddock. She tutted inwardly. Then he opened his mouth to speak. This was usually the moment at which they were interrupted by Francesca having one of her Diggory-digs, but for once Sarah could see clearly from one end of the esplanade to the other and there was no sign of the woman. The silence stretched anyway, and she began to feel extremely uncomfortable.

'Well, let's not stand here. We're tired. Let's talk about, um, all that, later,' she said firmly.

Daphne shook her head, clearly disappointed at this cop-out. But when Sarah peeped at Charles again, she was rather miffed to see that he looked quite relieved to be let off the hook. OK then, it's like that, is it, she told herself a little crossly, as she settled her bag more comfortably on her shoulder and took Hamish's lead back from Daphne.

'Oh, um, I've just remembered something, it's really important, I must just dash back to the flat,' Charles said. Sarah handed him back his jacket and in an instant he was gone, loping along the road like a stork, his long legs making short work of the distance.

'Right, well, just the two of us, then,' said Sarah, biting her lip.

Immediately, Daphne took her arm. 'Don't be sad, Sarah. It'll all work out in the end, you see if it doesn't. My spirit guide, Pongo, has always foretold a happy ending for the pair of you.'

Sarah tried her best to look thrilled at this news, but in fact she was sure it was pretty much the death knell as far as her fledgling relationship with Charles was concerned, given the reliability of Daphne's connections in the Beyond. Oh well, she thought to herself. It was far too soon after Peter, anyway. It was for the best. She tried to console herself with this thought – though part of her did wonder why doing the sensible thing often hurt so much.

THIRTY-SEVEN

On an impulse, Sarah and Daphne stopped at Marlene's Plaice for a herbal tea before heading home. Sarah hadn't forgotten that Marlene was apparently one of Charles's flirts. She was beginning to think Merstairs must be littered with ladies that he'd dallied with or 'led on', as people used to say, before chickening out of making anything more meaningful out of the situation. Part of her wanted to ask Marlene about her experiences with the man, but she rather dreaded seeing a smug smile on the woman's pretty face, which might hint she'd got a lot further than Sarah had.

In fact, Sarah told herself sternly, she had probably just misconstrued Charles's behaviour all along. He'd never meant for them to reach the next stage, whatever that might even be at their advanced ages. His ex, Francesca, was a massive handful, that was clear to anyone who met her, and he was also obsessed with his shop full of dusty old tat. She'd thought he was as intrigued as she was about all the mysteries swirling about Merstairs, but maybe she'd got that wrong, too. She'd just been a fun companion to enjoy the odd drink with, that was all.

'Sarah? Sarah! Are you listening to a word I'm saying?' said

Daphne rather crossly, waving her hands in front of her friend's face. 'Honestly, I'm getting more sensible chat out of Hamish than from you at this point. And he's been asleep for the last five minutes.'

'Sorry, Daph,' Sarah said. 'I was miles away. I was thinking about, erm, the case. It's just so hard to see what's going on.'

'I know,' said Daphne. 'A lot of mixed messages. I'd find it confusing, too. And of course you've been out of the game for such a long time, too.'

'Game? I'm not sure I'd call finding a triple murderer a game...' Sarah said, wrinkling her brow.

'Oh, I see, you really are talking about Mr Williams and all that. I thought you were just using that as a cover for worrying about what Charles is up to,' Daphne said, giving Sarah a clear-eyed look.

Sometimes Sarah forgot how empathetic her friend could be. It was a skill that must come in handy when she was interpreting people's Tarot cards for them. You could gather a lot about a person by their demeanour, their dress, their general air, and then convince yourself and others that you were channelling the Beyond... Well, Daphne was using all her abilities on Sarah tonight, and she wasn't entirely sure she loved it.

'All right then,' Sarah said, trying to hide her exasperation. 'What do you think Charles means by all this? You know him a lot better than I do.'

'Are you sure about that?' said Daphne, with a suggestive waggle of her eyebrows.

'Well, if you're going to be silly,' said Sarah huffily, taking a sip of the peppermint tea that had been going cold while her attention was elsewhere.

'I think Charles is very keen on you,' said Daphne more earnestly. Sarah immediately felt a little brighter. 'But...'

Why did there always have to be a but, Sarah thought to herself. 'Well, go on then,' she said.

'He was married to Francesca for umpteen years. That's going to take a lot out of a man. He's not even divorced yet.'

'Oh, he is though, he signed the papers and returned them to his solicitor.'

'That's news,' said Daphne, raising her cup to her lips. 'But even so, he's only just become free.'

'They split up years ago, though, didn't they?'

'I think it was only a year before you arrived here,' Daphne said. 'Not that long, anyway. And it's hard, getting into another serious relationship when one's just fallen apart. In such a public way, too. As you'll have seen, Francesca never lets an opportunity go by to humiliate him.'

'Right. Yes, I completely understand all that. But I haven't been pursuing him at all. Far from it.'

Daphne patted Sarah's hand. 'Of course not. You aren't made that way. And it's not long since Peter...'

'Exactly,' said Sarah a little forlornly.

'I think Charles is very tempted, but he knows you're a "serious relationship" kind of girl, and he might not quite be ready for that. Sometimes he thinks he is, sometimes he knows he isn't.'

Sarah sighed. 'I think you've hit the nail on the head, Daph. He keeps getting cold feet.'

'Which is such a shame, when the weather's so lovely and warm, even at this time of night,' Daphne said with a little chuckle.

Before she knew it, Sarah was smiling again, too. There were worse things in life, she supposed, than having an on-off admirer.

Things like having three unsolved murders on her hands.

THIRTY-EIGHT

Sarah was a little surprised to wake up, refreshed, eight hours later in her bed, with Hamish curled on the floor by her side. She'd expected to toss and turn all night long, there was so much on her mind. But perhaps the weight of worries had worn her out instead. Well, today was going to be a day of action, she decided, flinging back her pretty pink-sprigged duvet cover and startling Hamish into wakefulness.

First on her agenda was, of course, breakfast. She rather fancied strawberry jam on her toast today. She was glad her daughters couldn't see her merrily opening up a fresh jar, long before the previous one was finished. There had been strict rules back when they were small, largely to prevent the entire kitchen being covered in small sticky fingerprints. Ladling the delicious concoction onto a slice, she bit into it and closed her eyes in appreciation. It scarcely seemed worthwhile making her own jam, when Hannah Betts's creations were so good. But tucking into one of the sugared strawberries suddenly reminded her of Mr Williams's ill-fated slice of cake, and those berries peeking out from the layers. She put the toast down.

Sipping at her tea, and doodling idly in her notebook, she

noticed another name on the list of art group ladies. Mavis Trussock, the ScaleScanners diva. Sarah was glad she'd never had recourse to a weight-watching group – yet – but she approved of the idea in theory and had directed patients towards such 'strength in numbers' methods in the past. Though she wasn't sure she liked the sound of the communal weigh-in. There seemed to be possibilities for bullying and humiliation there which might not prove at all helpful on a weight-loss journey.

Mavis wasn't a hugely gifted artist, but she was, of course, better than Sarah. Sarah remembered the elegant woman wiping charcoal from her hands rather fastidiously. The skin on her arms had been a little loose, she remembered. Though that could happen to anyone, she thought, pulling her own dressing gown sleeves down, it still suggested Mavis had had her own struggles with food at some point. That would be entirely logical, and was probably the reason she was at the helm of ScaleScanners. There was no one more zealous than a convert, after all.

Still, Sarah couldn't help adding a question mark after Mavis's name. She was good with computers, and she and Daphne had even seen her at the sheltered accommodation. As far as she knew, Mariella hadn't questioned her, or at least, Daphne hadn't mentioned it. Perhaps that was something worth exploring? Who else was there who stood out as a possible? Mrs Booth from the post office had been full of theories as to who might have killed Williams – but that could just be a clever way of suggesting she hadn't done it herself. On the other hand, the woman had already been questioned by Mariella. And she was a jolly sort of person who didn't seem anything like Sarah's idea of a killer. Mind you, her notions on that subject had definitely undergone a few overhauls since moving to Merstairs.

Sarah poured more tea and willed herself to concentrate. It was awful to say it, but the fact that there had now been three murders ought to mean the whole business was easier to solve. It should be like a crossword – very hard, when you'd just got one of the clues, but exponentially easier with every additional space you filled in.

Well, there were now three plots waiting to be filled at the local cemetery – but Sarah was still none the wiser. What was she missing?

Under the table, Hamish whined gently. He hadn't bargained with the breakfast phase of Sarah's day lasting so long. In his book, it was high time they were out and about on the beach. She needed a proper airing, or she'd get restive later on, he knew what she was like.

'All right, boy,' sighed Sarah. 'Not much fun watching me think, is it? Would you rather go for a walk?'

Immediately, the little Scottie was up, tail wagging faster than a metronome on prestissimo. She picked up his lead, slipped on some rather battered plimsolls and slung her bag over her shoulder, and they were off. Two minutes later, she was rather wishing she'd at least taken a cursory look in the mirror before leaving, as right outside her door at the end of the path were Charles and Daphne, involved in what looked like an earnest exchange in lowered voices.

'Well, hello you two,' Sarah said, quickly pulling her fingers through her hair. 'If you go on whispering like that, I'll get paranoid and think you're talking about me.'

She said it brightly, but when a silence fell and neither of her friends replied, Sarah really did start feeling worried. 'Oh,' she said in a crestfallen sort of way.

They both started talking at once.

'I was just saying that you—' Daphne started.

'Of course we wouldn't dream of discussing you behind your—' Charles got out.

They looked at each other, both shrugged, and Sarah

couldn't help laughing. 'Well, whatever it is, I suppose you'd better just spit it out.'

But Hamish had other ideas. All this hanging about wasn't his bag at all. Especially not when the wide expanses of Merstairs' beautiful beach were right there in front of him, looking particularly inviting on this sunny day. He pulled at his lead and the trio obligingly started walking.

'We just thought we'd better distract you from, you know, *all that*,' said Daphne, waving one arm to encompass the mess that was currently besetting the place. 'And what better way than by getting some fresh air?'

'Daphne also thought you could do with some breakfast,' Charles said, leaning towards Sarah with a twinkling smile.

'Did she, indeed?' No prizes for guessing whose stomach Daphne was really thinking about. 'Trouble is, I've already had some.'

'Oh, I dare say you could have a cup of tea while I try and nibble at something,' Daphne said. 'I can't let this terrible business affect my appetite. If I did, I wouldn't have the energy to keep up my Tarot practice and then where on earth would all my clients be?'

'Where indeed?' said Sarah, but she fell into step happily enough. She and Hamish were always up for a walk and, if the final destination was going to be the Beach Café, that would hardly be a catastrophe.

In fact they managed a much longer romp along the beach than Sarah had anticipated. Daphne, for all her other-worldly ways, was still a country girl at heart and loved the outdoors. Charles never seemed to tire of throwing sticks for Hamish, possibly enjoying the novelty of a dog that didn't expect him to fetch the stick for her and then wheedle to be picked up every two paces.

Even though the day was warm, the fresh breeze coming off the sea was a tonic, bringing with it the intoxicating scents of ozone and salt that Sarah had come to love so much. The roar of the waves, too, meant that conversation was conducted only in small snatches, their words being stolen by the wind. It was relaxing to just look at each other and smile occasionally, Charles stretching out a languid hand when either Sarah or Daphne stumbled over a bit of drift-wood or a small rock pool. Eventually, even Hamish stopped bobbing about on the shoreline and when Sarah signalled for them all to turn away and walk to the café, there was universal assent.

A few minutes later, they settled themselves at a table with a view of all they had just enjoyed. They were lucky to get it; a queue of customers was snaking right around the perimeter of the café for the second day in a row and, judging by the disgruntled looks on people's faces, it wasn't moving any too quickly.

'I'll do the honours,' said Charles gallantly, leaping to his feet again. Sarah was feeling too puffed to resist and Daphne just took it as her due.

'A full English for me,' she said, fiddling with her scarf, which had been blown this way and that.

'I'll just have that tea, please,' Sarah said, smiling up at Charles.

Once he'd gone, Daphne sniffed. 'Well, you two are getting on well now.'

'Are we?' Sarah said. 'I'm not sure. Anyway, let's not worry about all that now. I wonder why the queue is so bad today?'

'Hmm. It's not like this while Hannah's around. Betsy must be running the place again and, quite honestly, she's not up to it,' said Daphne.

'I wonder how she's doing with those anxiety issues?'

'Doesn't look like she's coping that well,' Daphne said, as someone brushed past their table. The line to get served now started almost where they were sitting. 'Mind you, she must be better than she was, to have made it in to work at all. I heard she wouldn't even leave her bed last week, let alone the house. Complete breakdown for some reason.'

'Poor girl. I wonder whether something happened? At least she's back now. I always feel sorry for people in cafés when things get too busy. It all seems to snowball quite quickly.'

Daphne shrugged. 'Well, you know what they say. If you can't stand the heat, get out of the kitchen.'

'That's not very understanding of you, Daph,' Sarah said mildly.

'I'm hungry. It's all right for you, you've had breakfast already. I've walked about ten thousand miles on an empty stomach and it's not good for my energy alignment,' Daphne said with dignity.

'I've got some good news for you, in that case,' said Sarah. 'Look what's coming our way.'

Sure enough, Charles was approaching with a heaped tray. At once, Daphne's skittishness evaporated and she was all smiles as she took possession of one of the largest cooked breakfasts Sarah had ever seen.

'I wasn't quite sure what you wanted, Daphne, so I got one of everything,' Charles said, plonking his own plate down and sliding Sarah her tea.

'Only one?' Daphne looked up briefly from sawing her toast and dipping it in bright yellow egg yolk. 'Oh well, never mind.'

Charles caught Sarah's eye and they exchanged a quick conspiratorial smile. 'What seems to be the hold-up in the kitchen? Or is it just pressure of numbers slowing everything down?' she asked.

Charles pushed his straw hat back with a finger. 'No. Looks like there might be a bit of a problem there.'

Immediately, Sarah sat a little straighter. 'Problem? What kind of problem?'

THIRTY-NINE

Daphne looked as alarmed as anyone can while chewing a large mouthful of sausage.

'Nothing terrible, dear lady, don't panic,' Charles said quickly, and Daphne munched a little less frantically. 'It's just that Hannah Betts seems to have disappeared,' he added.

'What?' said Sarah, while Daphne went puce. Sarah watched her carefully as she finished chewing and her colour returned to normal. 'Where on earth has she gone?'

'That's just the thing,' said Charles with a lift of his shoulders. 'Nobody knows. She hasn't been seen since yesterday afternoon.'

'Good grief,' Sarah said.

'Yes,' said Charles. 'She was supposed to go to a council meeting last night for businesses on the beach. Francesca was very surprised she didn't show up.'

'Really?' said Sarah thoughtfully, digesting the fact that Charles and his ex seemed to be in such constant communication. 'The last time I saw her she was fine. Well, as much as anyone can be when there's been a murder committed just round the corner.'

'Yes,' said Daphne, swallowing quickly. 'You saw her at the sheltered accommodation, didn't you? When Pat...'

'Yes. She must be taking all this worse than anyone expected,' said Sarah.

'I suppose it must have been awful just having to carry on and do the catering for that gala. The whole business is enough to give anyone the collywobbles,' said Daphne, spearing a fried mushroom with her fork.

'Is that an official term?' said Charles. 'I rather like it.'

'Did you order from Betsy, then? Is she running the café?' Sarah asked Charles, who was showing signs of wanting to turn the conversation away from murder.

'Yes. Bit out of her depth. She looks little more than a teenager,' he added.

'She must be nineteen or twenty now. Mari used to babysit for her when she was tiny. Nice girl. Not sure she's cut out to work here, though,' Daphne said.

That was becoming all too clear. The queue now snaked right past their table and onto the golden sands of Merstairs beach. They'd been very lucky to get served as quickly as they had. Sarah thought of ordering herself another cup of tea, but would that be a fool's errand? After a moment, she got up anyway.

'I'm getting a refill, do either of you need anything?' she asked. 'Hamish will be OK with you, won't he?'

Hamish opened one lazy eye and assured his mistress that all would be tickety-boo. Daphne looked as though she was considering what else she might be able to find room for, but Charles waved Sarah away. 'No, we're fine. Besides, the queue is so long, if we change our minds we'll be able to tell you as you pass.'

In the end, the line of people started moving a little more quickly and by the time Sarah got closer to the counter, she could see why. Betsy had drafted in friends again to help out, as she had yesterday. The girls probably didn't know the kitchen that well but they were perfectly capable of taking down the orders. When Sarah got to the front, she asked for a tea, but couldn't resist asking, 'Is Hannah OK? I'm surprised she's not here on such a busy day.'

Betsy gave her rather a hunted look and pushed her fine dark hair off her forehead. It seemed rather lank, maybe because of the gathering heat of the day, or possibly the girl's stress levels. She looked very flushed. 'Poor Aunty Hannah. I'm not sure where she's got to, to be honest. I had to open up on my own this morning. She didn't say a word about not coming in. Mind you, it's been tough on her, the last couple of days. Anyway, anything else I can get you?' she asked with a polite but pointed smile.

It wasn't fair to hold things up further, so Sarah just shook her head and wandered back to her seat. But she remained thoughtful as she patted Hamish.

'What's up?' asked Daphne. 'I know that look.'

'Only thinking... It's just so odd about Hannah. Oh, just behind you, Daph. Isn't that Mavis from the slimming group?'

'ScaleScanners, you mean? So it is,' Daphne said, waving her hand above her head. 'Coo-ee! Mavis.'

For a moment, it looked as though Mavis Trussock was trying to duck away from Daphne's loud greeting, but then she gave a rather grudging smile and came over. As she exchanged hellos with Charles and Daphne, Sarah studied her covertly. The woman, while enviably slim and elegant, didn't look that well. There were hollows under her expertly made-up eyes and her silk shirt, surely rather formal for a walk on the beach, was hanging off her. Perhaps she'd been following her own diet regime a little too carefully.

'We never see you at the group any more,' Mavis was saying to Daphne.

'Well of course not, I've done so well. Absolutely no need

for that now,' said Daphne, taking a large mouthful of hash browns. 'You must try this all-day breakfast, Mavis, it's delicious.'

Mavis looked at Daphne's plate, with its congealed egg yolk and few remaining baked beans, and shuddered. 'Looks lovely,' she said, turning faintly green. 'Well, I must get on.' With that, she turned away and almost ran up the beach.

'Do you know, I think Mavis might be getting a tiny bit eccentric,' said Daphne. 'Mind you, they say some of the best people are. I wouldn't know myself.'

Sarah hardly heard her. She was lost in thought. Though she'd retired as a GP, she still got medical journals delivered to the cottage. She wasn't exactly reading them cover to cover these days, but she flipped through them for old times' sake occasionally, when she wasn't tussling with a crossword or out in the garden repairing Hamish's ravages. There was something nagging at her now; something she'd read recently... No, it was gone. She looked up, to find both Charles and Daphne staring at her.

'That look again,' Daphne said accusingly.

'Does that mean...? Have you had any more thoughts about this Williams business?' Charles said, a rather worried look in his piercing eyes.

'I know you were upset about Arabella's, erm, things going missing,' Sarah said. 'But is there anything else bothering you?'

'Other than the fact that there's a triple murderer somewhere in this town?' he said with a grim smile. 'No, not a thing.'

Daphne swivelled this way and that in her seat, staring at their neighbours in the café as though willing someone to out themselves as the killer. When she'd settled herself down again, she hissed at Sarah, 'I can't believe there's no sign of Hannah. And we haven't made a breakthrough yet. Usually by this time something's clicked.'

Despite herself, Sarah couldn't help hearing the note of

accusation in her friend's tone. 'Well, I'm sorry if I'm being slow on the uptake. It's just such a strange business. Mr Williams and the pants, yes, I can definitely see motives aplenty there,' she said, glancing at Charles who was crushing his napkin at the very thought of the old man's nasty habit. 'But then Pat? She was, well, I was going to say a harmless old lady. That's not quite right; she had some funny ways of her own. Sorry to say this, Daph. I know she was a dear friend. But she was always making suggestive remarks about men, young or old. If she hadn't died by such a similar method to Mr Williams, then I'd think it was one of those men who'd turned on her, having got fed up with her.'

'Well, I must say, that's very harsh on poor Pat,' said Daphne. To Sarah's horror, she fished in her bag for a tissue to dab at suddenly damp eyes. 'She was a wonderful person, and she had that fabulous background as a performing artiste. She was really talented.'

'I'm sorry, Daph,' Sarah said, feeling instantly contrite. 'I probably spoke a little rashly. But there's definitely someone out there who didn't appreciate Pat, however great she was on stage.'

Here, Charles did an odd sort of harrumph. When Sarah turned to look at him, he was a little pink. 'Speaking as one who was, albeit briefly, on the receiving end of Pat's, aha, attentions, it was quite an uncomfortable place to be.'

'Oh, I didn't realise she'd had a thing for you,' Sarah said. Suddenly she wondered if this might be one reason for the old lady's slightly aggressive attitude towards her.

'It didn't last long – Francesca saw her off. She has her uses,' Charles said with a laugh, which he rapidly turned into a cough when he caught Sarah's eye. Though she tried to maintain a poker face, she was pretty sure her expression soured a little at the thought of this tussle.

Luckily, watching him juggle past, present and future loves

in rather inept fashion cheered Daphne up no end and her tears dried up like splashes of summer rain on the sand.

'Ha! Get out of that one, Charles,' she said, slapping his arm. 'Mind you, I can't imagine Francesca stooping to poison people, can you?' she added thoughtfully.

'Of course not,' Charles said automatically, then glanced at Sarah quickly.

'And there's the fact that whoever did the deed brought their cyanide to the sheltered accommodation,' Sarah said. 'I suppose Mariella has questioned all the catering staff, has she, Daph?'

'Oh, goodness, I expect so,' Daphne answered. 'But you can ask her yourself! Look, here she comes,' she said, waving her arm above her head, nearly taking a passing waitress's eye out in the process. 'Oops, sorry dear.'

Mariella was, indeed, stomping over the sand, and even at this distance Sarah could decode her mood with ease. The poor young woman was, in no particular order, tired, stressed, cross – and in Sarah's view, in urgent need of a sit-down. Luckily, Charles had already leapt to his feet and was bringing a spare chair over from a neighbouring table. He had such lovely manners. Mariella sank into it gratefully.

'I shouldn't be doing this, it's been a crazy morning. Well, a crazy week,' she said, directing a piercing look at Sarah.

'Oh! It's not exactly my—' Sarah began to defend herself.

'I know, I know,' Mariella broke in. 'But it's just so frustrating. Obviously, I'm not going to give anything away about the investigation, though I will say this. We don't seem to be any further forward.'

'We were just wondering about the catering staff at the sheltered accommodation,' Sarah said carefully.

Immediately Mariella's eyes flashed. 'We've talked to them all. Cross-questioned every single one. No one saw anything. I must say Hannah Betts keeps immaculate records so we had details for everyone on site at the time. But no joy. Either they were working in pairs, or they weren't in the area, or Hannah could vouch for them. It wasn't anyone on the catering team.'

'You know that Hannah seems to have disappeared?' Sarah said, watching Mariella carefully.

'We're covering everything,' said Mariella, tight-lipped.

'Do you think she could have been...' Sarah started, then grew quiet as Mariella glanced towards her mother and shook her head. 'All this, it's almost like a magic trick,' she added instead. 'Maybe something Pat could have pulled off herself, in her early days on stage. I'm sure I saw a picture of her acting as a conjuror's assistant on her wall.'

'Well, it would be some stunt, if she managed to kill herself and leave no trace,' Mariella said.

'I suppose you've ruled out...?'

'Yes,' the policewoman sighed wearily. 'We're still sure it wasn't suicide. There was nothing in Pat's flat to show that the cyanide could have been prepared there. Someone brought it in, then took all the evidence away with them, as though they'd never been there in the first place.'

Sarah was silenced. It looked as though they were up against someone truly resourceful this time. There was an element of planning and detail that there surely hadn't been in the previous cases she'd been involved with. Except when it came to Mr Ackroyd, however.

'The manager's murder. Do you think that was someone else entirely? It was just so different.'

'That's true,' said Mariella. 'I'm parched, is there any tea left in that pot?'

'I'm so sorry, we've had the last of it. I would offer to queue for more but they're so overrun,' Sarah said apologetically.

Even as she said it, though, she became aware that the queue was disappearing. At last, Betsy and her friends seemed to be getting the hang of things and the kitchen was turning out a steady stream of trays for the waitresses to distribute.

'Ah, looks like it would be a good moment for me to get us some reinforcements. Tea all round?' said Charles, standing up and adjusting his Ray-Bans.

'Sounds great to me,' Mariella said. The mere thought of tea on the horizon seemed to refresh her. Then she pleated her brow, thinking about the situation in Mr Ackroyd's office. 'Yes, Aunty Sarah, you're right. The attack on the manager seemed a lot less premeditated. Yet we've found nothing; no bloodstained items, no obvious murder weapon. Again, like magic.'

'They've had a bit too much luck for my liking,' Sarah said, pursing her lips. 'Being able to leave the cake with Mr Williams, and poison Pat's slice, then waft in and out of Mr Ackroyd's office – it's almost like they're someone no one notices in plain sight. It's really strange.'

'Agreed,' said Mariella, still a little glum. 'Though I'm not sure how far it all gets us. Oh, there's Mavis Trussock, Mum,' she said, nodding her head towards the esplanade.

Sarah craned to see. Mariella's eyes were definitely better than hers, because she was right. There was the ScaleScanners leader again, this time weaving her way through the strolling tourists.

'I wonder where she's off to now?' Sarah said. 'She was hurrying past the other way earlier, wasn't she, Daph?'

Daphne used a hand to shield her eyes, and followed Mavis Trussock's movements for a second or two. 'Yes, you're right. Maybe she's just trying to get her steps in, ScaleScanners is really big on that.'

'Is that why you stopped going, Mum?' Mariella's smile peeped out as she looked at her mother.

'Of course not, Mari. It's because I smashed my goals. I simply don't need to bother with all that. I'm blessed with a naturally fast metabolism in any case. And besides, you could hardly expect me to find the time to do all that walking around. I'm rushed off my feet as it is,' she said, snuggling comfortably into her chair.

'Forgive me, Mari, but was there anyone who, say, filed a complaint against Mr Williams? Either for the post office stuff or the pants-snatching?' Sarah couldn't stop herself from asking.

Mariella almost rolled her eyes at this. 'That's the first thing we checked, of course. No one had made an official complaint, exactly. But we did get reports of missing items from washing lines. No particular culprit was suggested, though. We just didn't have a moment to look into it, there's been so much happening here lately,' she said, looking pointedly at Sarah.

'Who complained?' Sarah persisted. 'Even that might narrow the field a little.'

Mariella shifted in her seat. 'Well, your Charles for one.'

'Charles? Charles Diggory?' Sarah was dumbfounded.

'The one and only,' Mariella said drily. 'But that was after the murder, in fact.' She gave Sarah a half-wink, perhaps to atone for the shock. 'As for those who made a fuss beforehand, well, there were only a couple. Mavis Trussock reported that quite a lot of the family's washing had been pinched, including all her silk camiknickers. And then the other one, you just will not believe.'

'Really? Who on earth was it?' Sarah leant closer.

FORTY

Mariella wasn't Daphne's daughter for nothing. Sarah could tell she was enjoying having the assembled company hanging on her every word. But her response, when it came, was definitely worth the suspense.

'It was only Pat Buchanan.'

'No!' Sarah and Daphne said simultaneously.

'It's true,' Mariella confirmed. 'She had a load of washing stolen from the sheltered accommodation washing line, including her undies. The line was behind the kitchen complex.'

'Mr Ackroyd said washing had gone missing – but he didn't say it was Pat's,' said Sarah in wonder.

So now they had found a motive for Mr Williams to murder Pat, as her complaint was bound to lead to him being outed as an underwear thief.

But, as they all knew, the only slight problem was that Mr Williams had died before Pat.

If Pat hadn't been killed next, Mariella admitted, the old lady would have been one of the few on their radar who had some sort of motive. But a slice of cake laced with cyanide had put paid to her as a possible suspect. The murderer's modus operandi in these first two deaths had been so similar that it seemed clear they were searching for the same perpetrator, thus neatly ruling Pat out for the first murder – though Pat would no doubt have preferred to prove her innocence in a less final way.

Charles, meanwhile, returned to the table with a tray bearing a large pot of tea and a fresh cup for Mariella. He was a little surprised to get a sideways glance from Sarah, who explained she'd just heard about his complaint over Mr Williams.

He raised his eyebrows and looked at Mariella. For a second he seemed to be on the verge of remonstrating with her, and then simply shrugged gracefully. 'Well, I admit, I was infuriated. And I can't stand it when men do such things to women,' he said.

Sarah, who found this rather heartening, smiled warmly at him.

'Anyway, we know you didn't kill him, as he was in the Beyond already when you moaned to Mari,' Daphne said helpfully.

'Well, phew,' said Charles sardonically. 'I'm glad my, erm, close friends don't think I'm the murderous type.'

There was a short, slightly uncomfortable silence, and then Mariella and Daphne started talking at once.

'Well, once I've had my tea—'

'After you've finished that cuppa—'

They both stopped and laughed. 'I wish I could sit with you all day and chat about the case, but that's not possible for so many reasons,' said Mariella. 'You know I have to get on.'

The little group agreed. Sarah particularly was feeling stressed as time flooded by, especially as all her suspects seemed to be falling by the wayside. Mariella drained her cup and took her leave of the group. 'Stay out of trouble, you three! I'll ring you later, Mum,' she said.

Sarah watched her go admiringly. She was doing a difficult job, with such dedication and grace. Then she saw another familiar face. It was Penny Booth from the art group. She waved at her, thinking of that list of initials. Mariella had said she was at work at the post office at the crucial time, but it might be worth chatting to her. You never knew. Mrs Booth saw her and made for their table.

'Greetings, ladies, and Charles, fancy seeing you here,' she said in a somewhat fluttery way. Sarah was beginning to wonder if there was any woman in Merstairs who was immune to Charles's charm, but the smile he gave her was friendly and no more. If Mrs Booth had a soft spot for him, it looked as though it was not reciprocated.

'Do sit down, Penny,' Sarah said. 'We've been meaning to ask you something... You know your initials might have been on a slip of paper in Mr Williams's cottage, the day he died?'

Penny looked affronted. 'Your Mariella asked me about that days ago. They might not have even been mine anyway, she said the writing was terrible. Like I told her, I had a shift at the post office just before the art group, as anyone queueing up for their pensions will tell you. I came over to tell you some news, but I'm not sure I want to now.'

'Oh go on, Penny. Don't take offence, you know what Sarah's like,' Daphne said, rolling her eyes at her friend.

Penny smirked and seemed mollified, and Sarah bit her tongue. 'Well, I was at ScaleScanners last night – just losing two or three pounds for my daughter's wedding in August, you understand – and there was a bit of a hoo-ha.'

'What happened?' Sarah asked. Once upon a time she would have considered herself above idle gossip – but that was before she'd moved to Merstairs. Besides, it might have a bearing on the case, and that made her interest legitimate.

'Well, we'd got to the weigh-in bit – you know how that goes, Daphne,' Mrs Booth said.

Daphne nodded, folding her arms almost defensively over her body at the memory. 'Yes, I was never a fan of that part. I know Mavis is strictly doing it for people's own good, she couldn't be kinder, but reading out the figures in a really loud voice can be quite upsetting. And there's that rhyme she always uses.'

'Ugh yes,' said Penny with a tiny shudder. 'If, God forbid, your weight goes up, she says, *"Up, up and away, This fatty wants to fly today,"* and if it goes down, it's *"Every loss is a huge win, You will soon be slim again,"* and then everyone cheers. If you've put even an ounce on, you're not allowed to have one of the special slimming crackers at break time and you have to stand up and march on the spot during Mavis's chat at the end, when everyone else can get comfy on the sofas.'

'Good grief!' said Charles. 'She sounds meaner than my old nanny.'

Sarah shook her head. 'And does all this actually work? The ritual humiliation? I'd almost call it hectoring.'

'Well, look at me,' said Daphne, with a glorious shrug. 'I'm one of the success stories, I suppose. I was only in ScaleScanners for a couple of months and now I just eat anything I like.'

This was unanswerable, so Sarah moved on. 'You said something strange happened last night?'

'That's right,' said Penny Booth. 'At the weigh-in. Old Mrs Herron, you know, from down near the Reculver bypass, she'd just got on the scales. It's quite a palaver, as she's in a mobility scooter and her knees aren't what they were.'

Sarah frowned at this, wondering if a weight-loss system like ScaleScanners was a good idea for someone who sounded as though they were facing serious health challenges. But no doubt their own GP was keeping an eye on matters.

'Well, a few of us had got her all ready for the weigh-in and were waiting to take our hands away, when Mavis, who'd been standing there tapping her foot like she does, well, she suddenly just took off. Without a word. And that was it, she rushed right out of the church hall – that's where we have the meetings, round the back of All Saints, you know – and then Mrs Jarvis from the sweet shop in the high street saw her legging it down the road. A few of us waited around for a bit but that was the last we saw of her.'

'Gosh!' said Daphne, her eyes alight at this scoop. 'And she hasn't let anyone know how she is this morning? No one's heard anything?'

'Not a dickybird,' Penny Booth said. 'What do you think of that?'

At this, Sarah lifted her eyes to Charles's. She could see her own awakening worries mirrored in his. This didn't sound good, not in a town where two people had recently been poisoned. But, she reasoned, Mavis Trussock couldn't have taken cyanide. She would have been killed pretty much on the spot if she had, and certainly wouldn't have had the energy reserves to go sprinting around the town. Besides, they'd seen her earlier.

'We did see her here briefly a while ago,' Sarah said. 'But she was acting a bit oddly...'

'Very strange,' Daphne agreed. 'It was almost as though she was getting a message from the Beyond. I sometimes have to drop everything when a message is really strong, you know.' Then she paused, and her eyes finally widened. 'Unless... you don't think?' she looked towards Charles and Sarah for support, or perhaps confirmation.

Sarah put out a hand to calm Daphne, and also to discourage her from voicing her sudden fears. Then she turned to Penny Booth. 'Do you know Mavis well? Would you say she's been OK recently? When we saw her she seemed agitated, walking very fast down the esplanade. Is she someone who's concerned to get her ten thousand steps a day done, for example? Daphne thought that might explain it.'

'I wouldn't say so. She used to be into yoga and what have

you, but one of her things at ScaleScanners has always been it's the calories you eat that you have to cut down on really hard, as exercise won't help on its own. *"There are no shortcuts if you want to wear short shorts,"* that's what she's always saying, isn't it, Daphne? Discipline and diet, she tells us – at least ten times a session.'

Daphne nodded. 'I have to say, I'm not sure it did me much good being with the group. I feel so much happier now I've cracked it and got myself into total equilibrium.'

'It's good for those of us who have a wobble now and again, though. I don't mind admitting I had a biscuit last night after I got home from the session,' said Penny with a hunted look on her face.

'There's no shame in the odd biscuit,' Sarah said firmly.

'Well, don't let Mavis catch you saying that. I heard her in the queue at the chemists the other day, having a right go at Mr Williams. He had a bag from the Seagull Bakery with him, one of their sausage rolls. Mmm, you could smell it all over the shop. They're just lovely, have you had one?'

Sarah shook her head. 'What did she say to Mr Williams? Did you happen to, er, overhear?'

'Well, I'd never eavesdrop. I have a sensitive job, at the post office. I know about client confidentiality.'

'Of course, we totally understand.' Sarah looked round the table at her friends, who nodded diligently. 'But just in case it solves the mystery of, er, what's up with Mavis, maybe you should tell us?'

'Well, I suppose in that case, it's not tittle-tattle, is it?'

'Definitely not,' said Sarah.

'It wasn't so terrible, really. She was just saying he was going to kill himself with all the fats and oils in his sausage roll and did he even know what a hardened artery was, and how about coronary thrombosis? Mr Williams, well, he was skin and bone, the only thing sticking out was those big ears of his. Whatever he was eating had been working for umpteen years, so you'd have thought he'd just shrug it off. And he was usually a merry kind of man, maybe because of all the stealing, you know. But this time he just gave her a look and said, "Maybe you're just grumpy because you're hungry. Or maybe it's that marathon stuff."'

'He might have had a point about the tetchiness,' Daphne said. 'People do say I get a tiny bit ratty myself if I've gone too long between meals.'

Charles snorted, then turned it into a cough. By the time Daphne turned to look at him, he was peering intently into his teacup.

'Marathon stuff? What do you think he meant by that?' Sarah said, ignoring Daphne and Charles's little pantomime going on to her left.

'Haven't a clue. She's not a runner, I know that much,' Penny Booth shrugged. 'She always says it's bad for your bust, you know, makes everything go south.'

Sarah smiled automatically, but behind the façade of polite interest, her mind was now whirring at a thousand miles an hour.

FORTY-ONE

Hannah Betts arrived at their table right at that moment, and started collecting their dirty plates. Sarah was very relieved to see her, but couldn't help noticing that instead of her usual methodical approach, today she was lumping the plates onto the tray all anyhow, and seemed completely distracted.

'Everything OK, Hannah?' Charles said as he passed her his cup. 'Only my wife, er, ex-wife, um, the mayor, said you weren't at the meeting last night?'

'Yes, Hannah, hope you're feeling all right? I was worried when I heard you'd gone missing,' Sarah said.

Hannah gave Charles and Sarah a harassed glance and then forced a smile. 'Missing? Hardly,' she said with a slightly shaky laugh. 'Something came up. I had to sort Betsy out. Please give my apologies to Francesca, Charles.'

'Betsy didn't seem to know where you were, though? Can I help you with those plates, Hannah?' Daphne said, sloshing tea everywhere in her bid to be useful.

'Betsy! She'd forget her head if it wasn't screwed on. I told her where I was but it went right out of her mind. She's still not really up to speed yet,' she added, a shadow passing over her face for a moment. 'She did good work earlier when we were really busy but I've had to send her home now. Anyway, how was everything?'

'Wonderful,' they chorused, and she gave an on-off smile and took the overladen tray away.

'Hannah didn't seem her usual self, did she?' Daphne said idly. 'Perhaps we should stay a bit longer? Just to keep an eye on the situation,' she added hopefully.

Sarah got up. 'Hamish and I have one or two things we have to sort out,' she said. 'But don't let me stop you both.'

Charles seemed a little surprised. 'Oh, are you sure?' he said, pulling down his sunglasses so she could see his blue, blue eyes.

'We can meet up later if you'd like,' Sarah said. 'Give me a ring.'

She bent down and woke a slightly reluctant Hamish. He'd been having rather a good dream about seagulls, involving eating every last feather of the largest bird Merstairs had ever seen, and it was a shame to come back to a world where this feat was extremely unlikely. But if they were going home he could snuggle down in the little basket in the kitchen. There might be more gulls awaiting him in his slumbers there, ready to be chased to their imaginary doom.

Back at the cottage, Sarah bustled straight to the kitchen, making sure Hamish's water bowl was topped up and then pouring herself a glass as well. She sat down at the table, and drew her notebook towards her, as well as the stack of medical journals she'd been leafing through the other day. She'd missed something before. Now she was determined to get to the bottom of it. Something she'd heard that afternoon had put her on the right track. She just had to find the correct article, and then everything would become clear, she knew it would.

* * *

Sarah had drained the glass of water, and got through several cups of tea as well, before she was interrupted in her research by the trill of her mobile phone. For a second, she wondered where on earth it was. She'd been using it earlier to do some googling, but somehow it had vanished. She realised this must be what it was like to live in Daphne's house. The table, so tidy earlier, was now piled with journals, some with articles ripped out, some plonked face down with pages turned back. There was even an old book on antique ceramics there that had belonged to her mother. Her notebook, similarly, was full of scribbles that only another GP would be able to decode.

Finally, she found the phone under two magazines with an empty mug on top, and answered. It was Daphne.

'Sarah, thank goodness! I thought you'd moved out or something. You usually pick up on the first ring.'

Sarah had a momentary pang at the thought she was normally so predictable, and apologised. 'I just got rather caught up in something – an idea I had about our investigation.'

'You haven't done that thing you usually do, have you? Where you pretend we're all in it together, and then you secretly work away on your own and make a massive breakthrough?'

Sarah, who realised this was a very fair representation of her afternoon's work, just said, 'Well, shall we meet up in a bit, and we can chat it all over?'

'That's not a no, is it? You see, I'm getting wise to you these days,' said Daphne triumphantly. 'You can't pull the wool over these ears.'

'I'd never do that. You're far too good at crochet anyway,' Sarah said kindly. Daphne's handicrafts were coming on, it was true, but only a really old friend, in a very expansive mood, would compliment her efforts. 'Listen, let's meet at the Jolly Roger, shall we? In half an hour?'

'OK then. Shall I call Charles and see if he can come along too?'

Sarah thought for a second. 'Yes, lovely. Let's make that three-quarters of an hour, though,' she tacked on. She wasn't a vain woman, but an afternoon of pulling her hair out over her researches meant she could do with tidying herself up a little.

* * *

Closing the door on her cottage a while later, Sarah surveyed her neat outfit of periwinkle blue linen trousers and a fresh white top with satisfaction. There was colour in her cheeks, and it wasn't all from a discreet touch of blusher in front of her bedroom mirror. She was rather looking forward to seeing Charles – and Daphne, of course – and laying all her cards on the table. Hamish, at her side, looked quite spruce for a change and was sporting a new blue collar which matched her outfit rather well.

As they walked briskly down the path, there was a commotion next door – a combined hissing and shouting that could only mean one thing. Daphne was trying to shut Mephisto in the house for some reason, and the ginger cat wasn't having it. Hamish pressed closer to Sarah's leg and she stroked his head reassuringly. Then the cat erupted out of the door and streaked down the road, followed at a more leisurely pace by Daphne in a kaftan of blues and oranges.

'Mephisto really doesn't seem to like the flea powder the new vet gave me,' Daphne said as she reached them.

'Really?' said Sarah, feeling itchy at the very thought. 'I didn't realise he had a problem.'

'Oh, just a precaution,' said Daphne airily, scratching her

neck. 'Well, you do look fancy,' she said, taking in her friend's outfit.

Sarah felt her colour rising, but she ignored the sensation. 'It's such a lovely day, I thought I'd get changed.'

'Hmm,' said Daphne. 'Charles can't make it, by the way,' she added.

'Oh. I see.' Sarah tried not to feel disappointed. 'Well, never mind.'

'He said he'd look in if he could, but he's got something on this afternoon.'

'Well, I doubt it's a stampede of customers in his shop,' Sarah said a little acidly. Then she shook herself mentally. It didn't matter if Charles was there or not, surely. Yes, he was a useful sounding board, and more practical than Daphne. But they could easily get things straightened out without him. Instead, she decided to enjoy the fresh feel of the breeze as they walked along the coast road, with Hamish trotting happily just in front, his little nose scenting an intoxicating cocktail of seaweed, salt and sea creatures.

It seemed almost a shame to go into the dimness of the pub after the bright sunshine, but Sarah was confident it was going to be easier to think in the dark, quiet interior, instead of outside where the tourists moved up and down the esplanade restlessly. They both sat automatically in their favourite booth, brushing the fake sea urchin out of the way. Jamie pottered over from behind the bar to take their orders and they were soon sipping cool drinks, while Sarah got her notebook out of her bag and clicked her pen, ready for action.

'Goodness, you do look businesslike,' Daphne said.

'Well, I feel this has all been weighing on us long enough,' Sarah said, taking a sip of her drink. 'I'd like to put it all behind us.'

'Do you really think you've got it sorted out? Shouldn't we have Mari here?'

Sarah took a breath. 'You know, I'm not a hundred per cent certain. The theory I have fits the facts, but I'm not sure... perhaps the best thing would be if I go over it with you?'

'I'm all ears,' Daphne said, waggling her head so her earrings quivered. Hamish looked up, a little alarmed. Those looked even heavier than usual. He hoped they wouldn't be falling on him.

FORTY-TWO

'Well, the thing is,' said Sarah, feeling uncertain all of a sudden. 'I first got an idea about who the culprit could be when you were talking about ScaleScanners.'

'Don't tell me it's Margery Jarvis!' Daphne all but shouted. 'I always knew she was fixing her figures somehow. Every week she lost pounds whereas for me, the dial kept going in the wrong direction – and there was absolutely no reason for it. Everyone knows how careful I am,' she said, fishing the orange slice out of her Dubonnet and chomping on it. 'There, look, my diet is just packed with healthy fruit,' she said triumphantly.

'I doubt it was Margery Jarvis. I think it was someone much more central to the operation,' Sarah said, lowering her voice. 'Think about it, Daph.'

'More central,' Daphne said with an expression of huge concentration on her face. 'Not... me?'

Sarah suppressed a sigh. 'No, not you, Daphne. Who runs the group?'

'Well, Mavis has always been in charge. She set it up, ooh, years back now. I think she first got the idea... wait a minute. Do you mean it's *Mavis*? Mavis Trussock?'

Sarah put her finger to her lips and looked around frantically. Luckily the bar wasn't busy. Jamie was polishing a glass behind the bar, Claire Scroggins was in the back, sorting out the latest delivery by the sounds of it. There were one or two elderly men over by the far side of the room but no one within eavesdropping distance. Nevertheless, Sarah didn't want her suspicions bandied about. Not at this point, anyway.

'Keep your voice down, Daph. It's only an idea at this stage.'

'But what on earth makes you think that? What could the connection be, between someone like Mavis, who's always so careful with her appearance, and an old codger like Mr Williams? He'd never go to ScaleScanners in a million years. Not that he needed to, he was as thin as a rake. Some of us are blessed,' Daphne said with a tiny shrug.

'I don't think Mr Williams was interested in slimming. But he did have Mavis's silk camiknickers in his horrible collection, remember. And there was that ScaleScanners leaflet about the new app in his house. There were connections between them... and I also think he may have overheard something crucial. It was something Penny Booth said that gave me the idea.'

'Really? Penny Booth? But she works in the post office. What's that got to do with ScaleScanners?'

'Well, very little, except she heard something the other day in the queue at the chemist's. She told us earlier, if you remember?' Daphne, however, looked blank. 'It's like this,' Sarah continued. 'What if the reason Mavis is so lovely and slender isn't because she watches her weight at all?' She looked intently at her friend, to see how she would take this.

'You mean, she's naturally thin? I mean, like I was saying, some of us just—'

'No. I don't mean she's got some sort of trick metabolism. Think about it, Daphne,' Sarah urged her.

Daphne didn't react at all for a moment. Then she slammed her Dubonnet down on the table, making Sarah's glass jump.

'You mean— No! Surely not. She can't have been *cheating*, can she? Not her as well as Margery!'

Sarah looked solemn. 'I really think she might have been. You know I have all those medical journals back at the cottage.'

'Heaps of them. All full of ghastly syndromes I've never even heard of. I don't know why you keep them around the place, now you're retired.'

'It's a good job I do,' Sarah said. 'They've been very handy today. I started to worry about Mavis when we saw her rushing along the esplanade. Added to that her clothes, while always beautiful, are really hanging off her. She's been losing quite a lot of weight. She also has deep circles round her eyes.'

'You're worrying me now,' said Daphne anxiously. 'You're not going to tell me she has some awful disease, are you?'

'No, no. Nothing like that. If I'm right, she's just taking a bit of a shortcut to maintain her nice figure. It is hard to keep in shape, once you reach a certain age,' Sarah said.

'Well, not if you're careful,' Daphne said with a harrumph. 'Anyway, what kind of shortcut? That's outrageous, while she's forcing everyone else to make really big sacrifices week after week, like saying no to biscuits.' She shuddered at the thought, leaving Sarah to wonder if this prohibition was the reason her friend was no longer an active ScaleScanners member.

'There's a new weight-loss injection, you've probably heard of it. It's got various different proprietary names. One of them is Marazan.'

'You think Mavis is taking that?' Daphne was looking more and more perplexed.

'Yes. She seems to have all the side effects associated with its use – and then there's that odd cryptic sentence Mr Williams apparently said to her. He mentioned marathons, don't you remember?'

Daphne took another sip of Dubonnet, with a rather blank look on her face, and then the memory seemed to resurface.

'Yes! And actually, didn't Pat say something weird about marathon running too, when we were talking to Mavis?'

'Yes. Yes she did,' said Sarah sadly. 'I think they were both mispronouncing the word Marazan. Plus he had Mavis's pants, as I said. Maybe he teased her about that, as well as the Marazan, or maybe she just guessed from something creepy he did at the art classes.'

There was a beat, and then Daphne piped up. 'Oh! But you don't think... you can't imagine Mavis would be capable of... No, it's too horrible. I know she can be mean, she was quite sharp with me sometimes when – I mean *if* – I'd gained the odd ounce. But killing people? Absolutely not.'

'But don't you see, Daphne, it's a little more serious for her than someone stealing her underthings or even not quite sticking to their weight-loss plan. If it came out that she was using drugs to keep herself slim, then why would anyone come to ScaleScanners any more? She'd be outed as a complete fraud.'

'Oh my goodness, yes she would! ScaleScanners? Scale*Scammers*, more like. I'm raging at the very thought, and I'm not even in the group any more. I can't imagine how angry people like Denise Winterbotham or Cheryl Pike would be. They must have spent thousands over the years, and they're still shopping in the extra-large section of Big Bertha's Outsize Outlet in the high street.'

'Well, there you have it, Daphne. Mavis's business would be destroyed overnight if Mr Williams and Pat were still around, spreading the word about what really lies behind that trim figure.'

Daphne sat for a moment, taking it all in. She shook her head. 'To think I believed all that stuff she said. Like "Eat less, move more" and "Greens are good." Honestly, I feel such a fool.' With that, she shot to her feet.

'Hang on a minute, Daph. Mavis had a point with those—'

Sarah remonstrated. But it was too late. Daphne had marched out of the pub, and the door was left swinging in the breeze.

FORTY-THREE

Sarah hurried to follow her friend, gathering up the sunglasses, tissues, hair band and single earring she had left behind and shoving them in her bag. She got Hamish's lead and waved a hasty goodbye to Jamie, then a minute later was standing outside on the esplanade again, blinking in the bright sunlight. After the quiet pub interior, the street seemed to be teeming with life and colour, as holidaymakers in cheerful T-shirts wandered past, carrying fishing rods and buckets and heading for the beach. Sarah looked this way and that, trying to spot Daphne's distinctive headscarf and her scarlet hair, but there was no sign. She crossed over the road, hoping that would give her a better view, but couldn't see a thing. Then Hamish barked and tugged at her linen trousers. She turned towards Marlene's Plaice, the fish and chip shop, and Sarah saw Daphne's head bobbing through the crowds.

'Well done, boy,' she said, giving the dog a pat and then they were off, weaving in and out of the groups of people, saying a 'Sorry' here and an 'Excuse me' there. There was such a difference between folk on holiday, who had all the time in the world, and Sarah, who was on a mission, seriously alarmed at what her friend might be up to. She was quite out of breath when she finally caught up with Daphne, who'd come to a halt outside Poseidon's Palace.

'Daphne! Couldn't you hear me calling you?' Sarah panted.

Daphne barely turned to acknowledge her. 'Sorry. I couldn't stop. I need to find Mavis, and give her a piece of my mind.'

Sarah caught her arm, aghast. 'Daph, you really mustn't do that. Think about it for a second. If we're right, Mavis has already killed three times. Both Mr Williams and Pat were poisoned, then she stabbed Mr Ackroyd. She isn't the kind of person you should be confronting. She's highly dangerous.'

Daphne looked at Sarah, and the red mist in her eyes seemed to clear. She shrugged. 'All right then. I just want her to pay for what she did to Pat. And the others, too.'

'We don't know for sure she's the one, yet.'

'Oh, come on, Sarah, who else could it be? It fits together beautifully. You've been your usual clever self and it all adds up. But if you won't let me have it out with her, what do you suggest we do?'

'Well, we're in the very useful position where your daughter is Merstairs' best and brightest police detective – let's run it all past her before we get ourselves in a pickle. The last thing we want is for Mavis to get wind of what we're thinking.'

Just then, an amused voice spoke up from the dark interior of the amusement arcade. 'Did someone mention my name?'

It was Mavis Trussock.

FORTY-FOUR

A moment later, Sarah and Daphne found themselves being surrounded by the gang of teenage ne'er-do-wells they'd encountered before at Poseidon's Palace. Unfortunately, Daphne's nephew Fabian was nowhere to be seen, and the expressions the others were wearing today were much less friendly. Before the women knew it, they'd been bundled inside the dark, noisy place. The cacophony of electronic bips and beeps caused Hamish to tuck his tail between his legs and gaze up at Sarah as if to say, 'This doesn't look like a nice walk on the beach to me.'

Mavis Trussock was leaning against a Formula One driving game, the machine making unrealistic vrooms and squeals as imaginary tyres went round tight corners. She crossed her arms over her baggy but still stylish oyster silk shirt. The boy closest to her had the same square jaw and pugnacious look in his eye.

'That's Mavis's son, Lambert,' Daphne whispered to Sarah. 'Believe it or not, he used to be as round as a football until his mother sorted him out.'

'Or didn't,' Sarah said out of the corner of her mouth. But

although she felt she'd been very discreet, Mavis immediately homed in on what she'd said.

'You're casting aspersions on my work, are you? You're the doctor, though. I'd have thought you'd appreciate a group trying to make Merstairs a bit healthier, one paunch at a time,' she said, with a sideways look at Daphne.

'I-I'm all for a sensible attitude to food intake, a balanced diet, plenty of exercise—' Sarah said quickly.

'Of course you are,' Mavis sneered. 'And by the same token, you're the type of medical dinosaur who'd be down on anyone who just needs to turbo-charge all that with a temporary solution for a month or two.'

'If you mean weight-loss injections, like Marazan, I agree they have a place in healthcare, especially for diabetics or those living with obesity or heart disease, who have tried other methods of weight loss. I'm not sure that's you, though, is it, Mavis?'

Mavis looked around at the teenagers surrounding the women, and gestured with her head for them to move away. Sarah breathed again as the boys slouched off to take their places at various consoles, and the beeping and banging ratcheted up a notch.

'Look, Dr...'

'It's just Sarah. Sarah Vane,' Sarah said. 'And you know Daphne, of course.'

Mavis gave Daphne a quick on-off smile. 'Yes. Not one of my more successful students. I notice there's been some backsliding, Daphne.'

Daphne looked over her shoulder. 'Where? I don't see anything.'

Mavis shrugged slightly. 'Shall we go to my office? It's a little quieter there.'

Sarah wasn't sure about this. Was it a brilliant idea to enter a confined space with someone who looked likely to have killed three times? But on the other hand, there were plenty of teenage witnesses out here. And she did want to have things out with the woman. She stepped forward. Hamish, at her feet, had other ideas, growling softly until she picked him up and stroked him.

'Don't worry, boy. Everything's fine,' she said, smoothing his tufty head and wondering what on earth her late husband would say if he could see her now.

'Come on then,' said Mavis, leading the way further into the dark interior of the arcade. At the back, and almost invisible in the black-painted gloom, was the office, its windows reduced to one long strip, through which Mavis could survey her domain.

'Do you know, Mavis, I had no idea you owned this place?' said Daphne conversationally, settling herself into a chair without being asked once they were all inside. Taking up most of the space on the desk was a large, elaborate old-fashioned cash register. Mavis sat behind it with a tut, and Sarah took the last seat.

'My husband owns it really, but he doesn't get out much,' Mavis said.

'That's right,' Daphne said slowly. 'I don't remember ever meeting him. Funny, isn't it, given the years I've lived here? I bump into you all the time.'

'Yes, well.' Mavis's voice was curiously flat. 'Robert's a bit of a recluse. I run it for him. As you've seen, my son loves it here, so it's a way to keep everything in the family,' said the slender woman with a shrug, looking at Sarah and Daphne with those curiously ringed eyes. 'Now then. You haven't come here to find out about our business arrangements, have you? I suppose you want to know what's been going on.'

Sarah tried not to look too eager. 'It would be great if you could just spell things out for us.'

Mavis looked at her, her dull eyes glaring. 'I don't know why you think any of this is your concern. Unless you believe working as a GP once upon a time somehow entitles you to poke around in people's lives?'

Sarah, who secretly did think this, demurred. 'Well, I only retired last year. And I'm not sure I "poke around". But I am concerned about you, Mavis. Your symptoms seem quite worrying to me.'

'Symptoms?' Mavis was suddenly bolt upright. She picked up a biro from the desk and started fiddling with it. 'What symptoms, exactly?'

'Oh, you know, the bowel troubles and the nausea – I'm guessing that from the way you have to keep rushing off – plus the sunken eyes, the restlessness? Quite common side effects, I'm told, but debilitating all the same. I think you ought to pause the treatment.'

Mavis threw the pen down. 'I can't stop, though, can I? I was gaining weight. Oh, not crazy amounts,' she said, directing a sly glance at Daphne. 'But enough to be noticeable. It's the damned perimenopause. I couldn't seem to stop a ring of flab growing round my waist, like a lifebelt. A lifebelt that was going to drown my business.'

'Yes,' said Sarah. 'I quite see. It would have been difficult to keep telling others to lose weight, while putting it on yourself. But it's not as if you had to get on the scales, though, is it?'

'Please.' Mavis sniffed. 'These women have eyes like hawks. They can spot a tight shirt button from the far end of the pier. I couldn't risk it.'

'So you killed Pat? And Mr Williams! Not to mention the sheltered accommodation manager,' Daphne almost shouted. 'It was your initials on that bit of paper in Mr Williams's place, wasn't it? What kind of a monster are you?'

'What?' Suddenly all Mavis's tiredness disappeared and she was fully in the room, and outraged. 'What on earth are you saying? Initials? Murders? I don't know what you're talking about. You've lost your mind, Daphne.'

'Well, I like that!' Daphne was shaking with indignation. 'A triple killer, saying *I'm* crazy?'

Sarah was keen to take things down a notch – even several notches. Making rash accusations in a small soundproofed booth containing a murderer didn't seem a sensible move.

'Let's talk about this calmly,' she said, making soothing motions with her hands. 'You might upset Hamish.'

'Well, I'm very sorry, Hamish, but I'm actually devastated by Pat's death, she was a good friend and she didn't deserve to be poisoned,' Daphne shouted.

'Hang on a minute,' Mavis said, her face suddenly red. 'Oh, damn these hot flushes,' she added, taking a sheaf of papers off the desktop and fanning herself with them. 'I did not poison Pat. Or Mr Williams. And I didn't kill anyone else, either. Goodness knows I've felt like it, these last few months. The mood swings have been terrible. But I've managed to keep a hold of myself.'

Sarah took in her words, and started to think rapidly. It did sound as though Mavis was suffering badly from the numerous downsides of the menopause, as well as the weight-loss injections she was having. 'Where were you on the Monday before Mr Williams was killed? And on the Saturday, when Pat and Mr Ackroyd were found? And why was there a ScaleScanners leaflet at Mr Williams's house?'

'Monday? That's easy, it was my monthly Marazan injection. I go to Whitstable for it. It's usually in the morning, but that day the time was moved to one thirty p.m. I left here at around one and was back by two thirty p.m. Well, I was in the art class, wasn't I? Even my brain fog isn't so bad that I've forgotten that,' she said triumphantly. 'I left early from that, I had to... well, let's just say I needed a bathroom break. I've no idea about the leaflet, they get sent to literally everyone in Merstairs. I don't know when exactly Pat and this Ackroyd man were killed, but I was busy here in the arcade more or less all day on Saturday. We had a power outage and had to get the electricity board involved, anyone out there will tell you.'

'A bunch of teenagers? They aren't the most reliable people in the world.' Sarah raised her eyebrows.

'Maybe not. But twenty of them all telling the same story, that they were desperate to get going on their games but couldn't because we failed to get things up and running, I think that will be proof enough,' said Mavis, sitting back. A moment later, she was up on her feet, clutching her stomach. 'I'm sorry, I must just—' and with that, she dashed out of the tiny office.

'Surely we should stop her? We can't let her off like that,' said Daphne furiously.

'Knowing the side effects of the drug she's taking, I don't think we'd really want to make her stay. Poor woman, it's obviously not agreeing with her.'

'She's very thin,' said Daphne, a mite enviously.

'She is, while she's having the injections. It's not really a drug that should be offered to people her size, though. She doesn't exactly look happy these days, does she?'

'No, but I suppose she's got a point. She'd be even sadder if her business went to the wall. I wonder what's up with her husband? It's very odd that he never goes out.'

'My suspicion is that he might be very overweight, and she doesn't want him to be seen as he's not a good advert for her brand. It's horrible, and another sign she really isn't a nice person,' said Sarah. 'But that doesn't concern us now. We might as well go home, and go right back to the drawing board now our latest prime suspect's off the hook.'

'Oh rats,' said Daphne. 'I really thought we'd found whoever did for Pat. I want to see them locked up for good.'

'Well, me too,' said Sarah. She was turning to go, when a neat stack of empty jam jars and catering-sized sacks of granulated sugar in the corner caught her eye. It must be the overflow store for the Beach Café's impressive jam production line. Interesting, she thought...

Then there was a rattle at the door.

Sarah was expecting Mavis to walk back in, that slightly hunted look on her gaunt face. But it was someone entirely different who advanced into the room, carrying a wicked-looking kitchen knife.

FORTY-FIVE

'Hannah!' said Daphne cheerily. 'Fancy seeing you here. We were just having a bit of a chat with Mavis, but she had to dash off.'

'Yes,' said Hannah Betts, a desperate look on her face, and the knife grasped tightly in her hand. 'I just came to fetch some extra napkins from the store for the café. I bumped into Mavis. She was in a tearing hurry, but she just managed to tell me you were going around making wild accusations.'

'Not wild, exactly. We found a theory that seemed to fit the facts. But it turns out we were mistaken,' Sarah said, her tone neutral but her mind processing this new development as fast as it could. There was something about that knife that she really didn't like. Well, a lot, in fact. Not least that it looked exactly the right sort of size to have stabbed Mr Ackroyd. *Oh dear*.

'The trouble with you two is that you will keep on going until you get the right answer, won't you? You just won't stop,' Hannah said. Her eyes seemed to be glittering with unshed tears.

'That's right,' said Daphne, blithely oblivious to Hannah's frantic mood. 'And Sarah's so good at solving these puzzles.

She's like a dog with a bone, you know. She'll find the killer, take my word for it. I wasn't sure we were totally on the right track with Mavis, but next time we'll have them "bang to rights", like they say in all the cop shows.' Daphne smiled and nodded to emphasise her words. Meanwhile Hannah's face took on a set expression.

Sarah leapt in. There might be time to stop the situation from getting too dicey, if she could just think of the right words... 'No, no, I really think we've drawn a blank. I don't have any other ideas. We'd better leave it to the police, like we were saying, Daphne. In fact, you've just rung Mariella, haven't you? She'll be here any minute.'

'What are you talking about?' Daphne's brow was pleated. 'I haven't phoned Mari. And are you really telling me you'd abandon ship on all this? Let Pat lie unavenged? You promised me you'd find out who did it and I'm going to hold you to that, Sarah,' she said fiercely, staring into her friend's face even as Sarah widened her eyes and tried to signal to her to stop. Each word was another nail in their coffins.

Hannah looked from one to the other and shook her head. 'Look, I don't know who's lying and who isn't. I just know I've got this far, and I've got to keep on. I've got a family to look after and customers to serve, everyone's depending on me keeping the business going, and all this nonsense is getting in my way.'

'Just satisfy my curiosity at least, Hannah,' said Sarah, trying to keep the nervous tremor out of her voice. 'All those pots in the corner over there... There's a reason you've been making all that apricot jam, isn't there?'

Hannah grimaced. 'Yes. It was the stones. I remembered my gran boiling them up back in the day, to get rid of hornets. I thought, that'll do. Williams was no better than a pest and I had to get rid of him, for Betsy's sake. You don't know what she's been like, poor girl. Seeing her suffer, when he stole all her knickers, it was just terrible. The rage boiled up in me, like apricot kernels in a pan, till I couldn't think of anything else. But Pat cottoned on to it. I think she was visiting Williams on the sly, and she saw me coming out of his house. That was a terrible shame, I had nothing against her, but she could have got me locked up, and what would happen to Betsy then? Pat never could shut up when she stumbled on a secret. And Ackroyd? He was horrible to my mother, and when he saw me leave Pat's place, well, I had no choice.'

'I suppose you felt guilty afterwards, and that's why you missed the meeting with the mayor?' said Sarah.

'You're right. I can hardly get out of bed in the mornings. I expect I'll be even worse when I've got rid of you two. But I've got no choice. I'll stash you round the back and then dump you in the sea tonight. You've always liked the beach, Sarah,' she added wistfully.

Sarah felt chilled to the marrow, and had no doubt that Hannah would go through with it – if she couldn't think of a way to stop her. She wondered what on earth all those teenagers outside were doing. If she could just get to the window, maybe she could attract their attention...

Hannah saw her movement, and waved the knife towards her. 'Stop right there. Look, I don't have anything against you ladies, though you are very nosy. But I suppose it's like everyone says, curiosity killed the cat.'

Hamish, who'd been dozing happily under the table, surprised by the arrival of the café lady but used by now to the strange ways of Merstairs, jumped up at the mention of the C-word, and let out a bloodcurdling growl. Surely that awful orange moggy hadn't crept into this place? He wouldn't put anything past his nemesis and it was now essential that he did a quick check of the perimeter.

The little dog lurched forward, aiming to inspect the door first, but unfortunately he spooked Hannah. As he dashed, she slashed at him and for a second Sarah was in terror that her scything blade had connected with his tufty black fur. She made a lunge for Hannah's arm, feeling a stinging pain and the hot splash of something across her hand, but getting a good purchase on the woman's sleeve. She started to shake it vigorously, but Hannah, used to putting in full days in the busy kitchen, lifting heavy pans and moving sacks of sugar, was strong and wiry and twisted easily out of Sarah's grasp. Sarah felt another burning pain as she lost her purchase on Hannah's top, but then the woman suddenly slumped to one side.

Daphne, behind her, smiled. She had just brought the antique cash register down right on Hannah's head.

FORTY-SIX

It wasn't until Mariella led Sarah and Daphne out of Poseidon's Palace later that Sarah truly felt the nightmare had ended. As before, the blinding sunlight outside on the esplanade came as a shock after the claustrophobic darkness of the arcade, and she blinked furiously to adjust. Daphne, at her side, looked at her in horror and Sarah noticed the blood dripping from her arm and hand for the first time. The cuts weren't deep, and as the knife had been so sharp the edges of the wounds were clean and would heal nicely. But Hannah had definitely left her mark. There would be scars from this day – and they wouldn't all be physical.

All around, holidaymakers gave them curious glances as she was helped into a waiting ambulance, Daphne and Hamish using all their powers of persuasion to come along for the ride. Hannah, handcuffed now and held between Tweedledum and Tweedledee, was shoved into a police car and taken off to be charged and questioned. Sarah winced to see the way that Tweedledum forced the woman's head down, then realised she was being a little absurd. That nice lady, who'd served her umpteen delicious lunches, teas and snacks during her months in Merstairs, was actually a brutal killer who'd premeditated the death of an old man and a frail elderly lady, not to mention stabbing Mr Ackroyd. And she had caused Sarah's own wounds, which were now smarting horribly as the shock and adrenaline wore off.

Once they were safely in the back of the ambulance, Daphne was all solicitude. 'Don't talk now, don't tire yourself out,' she said soothingly. 'But what on earth was all that about? Did you know it was Hannah all along?'

'You know I didn't,' said Sarah, feeling a little dizzy. 'I thought it was Mavis, right up until the moment I saw those bags of sugar in her office, and I suddenly thought of all that wonderful apricot jam – and the kernels full of potential cyanide. But even then I was sure I couldn't be right. Not lovely Hannah. I'm not sure we should really carry on with this investigation business, you know, Daph. It seems to go wrong quite a lot.'

'You didn't seem that surprised, when Hannah walked in with the knife.'

'It all finally made a horrible kind of sense. But ideally it would have been nice to have worked it out before we got to the slashing part,' Sarah said tiredly.

Daphne frowned. 'What on earth do you think she was up to? She's such a nice lady. And her sponge cake is second to none. But she killed all those people! And she would have killed us, too, if it hadn't been for wonderful Hamish creating all that racket.'

'You were fabulous too, hitting her with that antique till. And you're right, Hamish is a marvellous dog, isn't he? Peter knew exactly what he was doing when he gave him to me and told us to look after each other. I can never repay him.' She felt a tear threatening to fall and brushed it away quickly. It wouldn't do to go gooey now.

Hamish, lying on the floor of the ambulance and quite

enjoying the interesting smells, looked modest and gave Sarah a tiny lick on her good hand. She still needed a little work – she ought to stick to their routine, instead of going off at crazy tangents – but generally speaking she was shaping up nicely, he decided.

FORTY-SEVEN

Luckily Sarah's wounds were, as she'd diagnosed herself, largely superficial, and by that evening she was back on the sofa in the sitting room of her cottage, Hamish sitting attentively at her side and a teapot swamped by a blinding crocheted cosy at her side. Her left hand was bound up and looked cartoonishly large, and her arm was in a sling, but she knew she'd had a lucky escape. Three other people had not been so fortunate.

As the hours crept by and Daphne's head started to nod in the easy chair in front of the television, Sarah felt the horrors of the day recede and she, too, started to feel sleepy. It was very pleasant to lie here, a throw comfortably tucked around her, half-watching TV with the sound turned down low so as not to disturb her friend. The painkillers the hospital had given her seemed to be working a treat. But then her enjoyable doze was completely wrecked. There was a creaking sound, right outside the sitting room door. As she swivelled in alarm to see what it could be, she saw the door handle turning very, very slowly.

Sarah gasped, and struggled upright, jarring her arm in the process. She was just about to wake Daphne – though she wasn't entirely sure what her friend would do about the situation – when a familiar head popped round the door, holding a finger to his lips. It was Charles Diggory. She gave a sigh, though she wasn't sure if it was relief or annoyance. And that explained why Hamish hadn't reacted. She was pretty sure he'd have been on his feet if there'd been any real threat.

Charles advanced into the room, holding a bouquet of flowers almost as big as he was. Tinkerbell sidled in behind him and went to curl up next to the sofa.

'I'm so sorry, dear lady, I've just heard of all your, ah, travails today. How utterly terrifying that must have been.'

'Well yes,' said Sarah, realising her hair was sticking up in Hamish-like tufts after her brief snooze and brushing it out of her face. 'It wasn't great,' she said with a lot of self-restraint. 'But more to the point, how on earth did you get in? Don't tell me the door is unlocked?'

Immediately Charles was apologetic. 'Merstairs must be safer today than it's been in weeks, months even. But I'm sorry if I've given you a shock... I bumped into Mariella on the way and she slipped me her spare keys. She thought you could do with some support.'

'Oh, that's, um, kind of her,' Sarah said, resolving to have a few words with the detective when she next saw her. She didn't remember having given Mariella any keys but Daphne had more than one set, as she was always mislaying them in her maelstrom of a home. 'Daphne's here, though.'

'So she is. And I see she's doing sterling work,' Charles said with heavy irony, as Daphne shifted in her seat and gave out a loud snore. 'Can I get you a fresh cup of tea at least?'

Sarah put her hand to the pot, but it was stone cold, even under its layers of dayglo wool. 'That would be lovely,' she said, subsiding against the cushions again. She wasn't quite sure how she felt about Charles being here, and her first thoughts when Hannah had been slashing at her had been for Peter, and not for him. But now she could hear him pottering about in the kitchen, filling the kettle and clattering down some clean cups, she couldn't deny it was extremely soothing to have him around.

By the time he came back in with a full tray, she was sitting tidily upright, the throw folded neatly over the arm of the sofa, the telly was off and she had a book in front of her, though she couldn't honestly have guessed what the open page said. Daphne was still in the land of nod, and Hamish was panting quietly, looking from Sarah to Charles and back again, when he wasn't making goo-goo eyes at Tinkerbell.

Charles deposited his tray on the ottoman in front of the sofa and went back for the flowers, now arranged splendidly in a cut-glass vase given to Sarah by her mother long ago, which she never used because it was too precious. She bit her lip but resolved not to say a word. Charles was trying hard, and it wasn't his fault he didn't share any of her long history.

'There now,' he said, sitting down and presenting her with a cup. 'Just the way you like it, I hope?'

'Perfect,' said Sarah, taking a sip. It really wasn't too bad. 'Did you have a chance to talk to Mariella? While you were, ah, getting my keys.'

Charles gave Sarah a look, then continued thoughtfully. 'Yes. She was able to tell me a bit about what they've pieced together so far. Are you up to hearing it?'

'Fire away,' said Sarah, putting down the tea.

Charles shook his head. 'It's hard to credit it, really. Hannah has always seemed the nicest lady. But she was infuriated by Williams's obsession with her niece's, erm, undergarments.'

Sarah, seeing the fastidious look on his face, decided to help him out. 'Her knickers, you mean?'

'Well indeed,' he said. 'The terrible thing is that I know how she must have felt. When I first heard that awful blighter had been stealing my Arabella's things, I was boiling with rage.'

'I remember,' Sarah said. She had been quite taken aback at the fury in his eyes when he'd got the news. For someone who seemed so laid-back, that sort of anger was all the more chilling. Hannah, however, must have hidden her rage a lot better. There had been no sign of it, in the many interactions Sarah had had with her before Mr Williams's death, right up until the moment in Poseidon's Palace when the woman's façade had slipped. 'I can't help kicking myself about the whole thing. There she was, in plain sight, all along. And she'd mentioned how stressed Betsy was several times. I just didn't connect the stress with the knickers or Hannah with the deaths. I don't know why, but I didn't consider her at all.'

'I suppose it was because we all trusted her. There she was, feeding us tea and cake. It never crossed my mind that someone so nurturing could actually be a murderer,' Charles said.

'She did cover her steps well,' Sarah said grudgingly. 'I mean, buying the cakes she put the poison in, that put us off the scent. Maybe she couldn't face drugging her own lovely sponge. But she would have been well placed to concoct the cyanide, with twenty-four-hour access to the sort of cooking facilities you need to brew up the poison. She must have nipped out of the café on Monday for long enough to give Mr Williams the cake. Her catering outfit was like a SOCO uniform; I noticed that when she was prepping for the gala, though I didn't think anything of it at the time. That's how she left no traces behind. And once she was in the sheltered accommodation, she vouched for seeing members of her staff at the crucial time – which in turn gave her the alibi she needed.'

'It was apricot kernels she boiled to get the cyanide, Mariella said,' Charles put in.

'Yes. All she needed to do was collect the stones when she was making that delicious jam, then crack them, extract the kernels and make a paste from them. My God, we even ate her apricot jam, jars and jars of it, not realising it was the by-product of her poison factory. It tasted so wonderful. And all the time, she was planning to kill Mr Williams. She must have hated him so much.'

'I'm not sure it even worked, if the idea was to make Betsy better. She's off work from stress again now. The café was closed when I came past,' Charles said.

'Well, if she had even the slightest inkling that her aunt had killed Mr Williams, let alone Pat and Mr Ackroyd, that will have stressed her out a lot more than anyone nicking her knickers.' Sarah shook her head.

'I wonder why Hannah carried on killing, after he was dead?' Charles said.

'Oh, I think that's simple. I think Pat and Mr Williams were a lot closer than anybody thought. In fact, unless I'm much mistaken, there's a photo of the young Mr Williams on Pat's wall. I think he was the man she followed to Merstairs, all those years ago. Something kept niggling at me about those pictures of her dancehall days, and I'm pretty sure it was his ears.

'Then both Mr Williams and Pat made comments about Mavis Trussock and Marazan. They even mispronounced it the same way. It didn't really occur to me at the time but it does suggest they were in contact. When I assumed the killer was Mavis Trussock, it made sense for her to get rid of Mr Williams and Pat, as both were making digs about her drug use. But it wasn't Mavis at all who was the killer, it was our lovely Hannah.'

'So she decided to kill Pat?'

'Yes. I think Pat had her suspicions about Hannah killing Mr Williams,' Sarah said. 'And you know what she was like, she wasn't discreet. She must have said something to Hannah, as Hannah came equipped with the poison. Maybe that's even why she agreed to take on catering for the gala, when she was already so overstretched at the café with poor Betsy in such a state. Pat had shoplifted the red velvet cake herself, and Hannah put the poison in that. Pat wouldn't have had a problem about opening the door to her, she knew her well. I expect it seemed quite neat to Hannah, as it tied in with the way she'd killed Mr Williams. Disabling the CCTV would have been a cinch for her too, she's so practical and hands-on, and as we know there were hardly any staff around at the sheltered accommodation to notice.'

'But I suppose Ackroyd must have come in at just the wrong moment and seen her disposing of the cyanide paste that did for Pat, or something like that?'

'I'd guess so,' said Sarah. 'Pat kept calling out the repairman, maybe Ackroyd had come to tell her off about that. Hannah threw suspicion on him by saying he'd been outside Pat's flat. Maybe that was true, and he saw more than he should have. This time, Hannah didn't have the leisure to poison him. It was opportunistic and quick. She just followed him to his office and stabbed him there, with a catering knife. He'd have let her in, as he'd known her mother and hired her to do the gala food. He also seemed to have quite a low opinion of women. It was a misjudgement that cost him his life. He wasn't that nice, but no one deserves to die like that. Poor man.' She shuddered, feeling at once how close she'd come to sharing the same fate.

'What about those initials on the betting slip? Where on earth do they fit in?' Charles asked. 'Or didn't they mean anything in the end?'

'It must have been Pat's initials – the number Williams wrote was thirteen, which was Pat's flat at the sheltered housing, if you remember. Pat knew about the pants, and she said some pretty unpleasant things about the man she'd followed to Merstairs years ago, who I'm sure was Williams. She may even have blackmailed him, as she knew his dirty secret. We know she wasn't that bothered about staying on the right side of the law, she was a regular shoplifter after all. And she had a row of porcelain shepherdess ornaments in her bedroom. Not my sort of thing, but they're in my mother's old ceramics book. They're worth a tidy sum, much more than she could have afforded on a tiny pension. I think she bought them with the money he gave her. But in the end, she reported him to the police for stealing her underwear from the sheltered accommodation washing line. My guess is he was running short, which explains the betting, and she was getting angry that he wouldn't pay up. Though he would have lost on that last race, if Hannah hadn't killed him first.'

'Good grief, was Pat really the blackmailing type? Seemed like an inoffensive little old lady to me.' Charles shrugged.

'We might have to agree to differ on that,' Sarah said. 'As for Hannah, I have some sympathy with her protecting her family against Mr Williams, he was a louse really. But I honestly think it's for the best that she's kept off the streets of this town for as long as possible. She can't even say she wasn't of sound mind when she did it. There was plenty of premeditation with the first two deaths. It's going to be so hard for Daphne to get over Pat. She wasn't my cup of tea, but Daph was really fond of her.'

They both looked over to their friend, who was still slumbering on, her scarf flopping over one eye. At her feet, Hamish was curled up blissfully. Wonder of wonders, Tinkerbell was snuggled up between his forepaws, her tiny snout pillowed on his tufty fur. Well, if things were like *that*, maybe Sarah would have to revise her antipathy towards the Chihuahua, she thought with a smile.

Just then, Charles seemed to take a deep breath, then he reached across the sofa and took Sarah's hand. Next he leant forward and kissed her softly on the lips. For a moment, the world stood still, and the investigation, the horrors of Poseidon's Palace, and the whole of Merstairs seemed to melt away. Those butterflies were back, with a vengeance. Was it even right to be feeling such things, at such a moment, and at her time of life? She didn't know – she just knew it was happening.

When she could concentrate again, Sarah realised he was speaking.

'Listen, I know I haven't always been clear about... things. Well, I've been in a somewhat complex position with my ex, as you realise. But I really would like this to go somewhere, you know.' He looked at her earnestly, his blue eyes sincere, and Sarah felt her heart melt.

'I-I think I'd like that too,' she said quietly, smiling back at him shyly.

'Thank goodness, you've got that sorted out at last,' said Daphne loudly from the armchair, where she now had both eyes open and a very big smile on her face. 'This will-they, won't-they thing has been really getting on my nerves.'

Sarah couldn't help laughing, and Hamish gave a couple of happy barks, which she took for enthusiasm. Even Tinkerbell managed to look a little less haughty than usual.

'Well, that's wonderful,' said Charles, bashful again but seeming immensely relieved. 'You would have to promise me one thing, though,' he said, mock-seriously, to Sarah.

'Oh?' she put her head on one side, making no commitments but willing to listen.

'You'll have to give up all this sleuthing business. I know you love it, but it's just too dangerous, at our age particularly. I'm sure you understand.'

'Thank goodness,' said Daphne. 'I think we've had enough narrow escapes, now.'

Sarah said nothing, but produced her best smile. Hamish looked over at her. She nodded at him, and could have sworn he gave her a little doggy wink back. Give up something that made Merstairs a safer place, and helped them all sleep soundly in their beds at night? That wasn't quite what the doctor ordered.

A LETTER FROM ALICE

Welcome back to Merstairs!

Thank you so much for reading *Murder at the Tea Shop*, my third book featuring retired GP Sarah Vane, her Scottie dog Hamish, and her friend Daphne. I hope you've enjoyed it as much as I loved writing it. I've always felt so at home on the Kent coast and it's been a treat to set a series in this wonderful part of the country. If you'd like to find out what Sarah and the gang are up to, please sign up at the email link below. Your email address will never be shared and you can unsubscribe at any time.

www.bookouture.com/alice-castle

If you enjoyed this book, I would be very grateful if you could write a review and post it on Amazon or Goodreads, so that other people can discover Merstairs, too.

I'm also on social media, often talking about my own cats, who thank goodness are not quite as much of a handful as Mephisto! Hope you can join me there.

Happy reading, and I hope you'll join me soon for Sarah Vane's next outing.

Alice Castle

KEEP IN TOUCH WITH ALICE

alicecastleauthor.com

 facebook.com/Alicecastleauthor

x.com/AliceMCastle

ACKNOWLEDGEMENTS

A big thank you to my fantastic agent, Justin Nash of KNLA, my wonderful editor Nina Winters, and all the team at Bookouture, for making Merstairs real.

PUBLISHING TEAM

Turning a manuscript into a book requires the efforts of many people. The publishing team at Bookouture would like to acknowledge everyone who contributed to this publication.

Audio
Alba Proko
Melissa Tran
Sinead O'Connor

Commercial
Lauren Morrissette
Hannah Richmond
Imogen Allport

Cover design
Tash Webber

Data and analysis
Mark Alder
Mohamed Bussuri

Editorial
Nina Winters
Imogen Allport